ANGELA DU MAURIER
The Road to Leenane

Truran

Published by Truran 2003
Truran is an imprint of Truran Books Ltd.
Croft Prince, Mount Hawke, Truro, Cornwall TR4 8EE
www.truranbooks.co.uk

ISBN 1 85022 180 4
First published 1963 by Peter Davies Ltd

Printed and bound by Short Run Press,
Bittern Road, Sowton Industrial Estate, Exeter EX2 7LW

Part I

CHAPTER ONE

I

MICKY RENVYLE was nineteen and Paddy O'Malley two years younger when they set out on the coast road for the first picnic of the summer. It was the boy's birthday and the plan had been made weeks before. The day was full of sun, the sea shining, the islands glimmered in the distance, the hills were green, and the birds twittered from hedgerows.

'We'll have a bathe, the sand's looking gorgeous,' Paddy sang out.

'I bet the water's damn cold,' Micky replied.

They left the bicycles by the side of the road and ran across the sands. Both were good swimmers.

'Bet I'll win if we race back,' the girl called out presently. Micky turned and rather leisurely swam to the shore, allowing the girl to beat him.

'Where shall we actually *eat*? You choose, it's your birthday.'

'Where would you like?'

'I said you were to choose. You can do anything you like today.'

He seemed to be thinking a long time and Paddy said, 'Are you thinking what you'd like to do most?'

'No. I was just wondering where we'd eat our sandwiches. Let's go to our favourite place, down to Little Killary Bay. And afterwards we can walk to the old quay, and we can have another swim later on.'

When they were having lunch she stopped eating suddenly and said, 'Gosh, Mick! I've forgotten to give you your birthday present.'

She pulled a small parcel out of the pocket of her skirt and handed it to him. It contained a large silk bandanna handkerchief.

3

'Paddy! It's wizard. Thanks a lot.'

'No, don't put it in your pocket, silly. They go round your neck. Like this—' She bent towards him and swiftly tied it. 'Don't you ever look at pictures of men's fashions or notice how people dress in photographs?' she asked.

He shook his head. 'No. I don't think I do. But Paddy, it must have cost an awful lot. You shouldn't have—'

'Thirty-five shillings,' she announced proudly. 'I got it in Galway that day I went to the dentist.'

'But that was ages ago.'

'M'm I know. But I did.'

They were silent, and Micky suddenly realized she was looking at him, and he realized another thing, that he was looking at her as if for the first time.

'Penny?' she said.

He did not answer. It had come as a shock to realize that the girl he had known since childhood, who had been his constant companion ever since he could remember, was not only extremely pretty but that he wanted to kiss her. That he should have discovered this in such a flash seemed extraordinary, unreal and bewildering.

Her voice broke the silence. 'You're nineteen today, aren't you?'

'Yes.'

'Have you at last made up your mind what you're going to do?'

'I did that ages ago, as you know. I'm going to paint.'

'But will you make any money?'

'I suppose so. After all there are masses of painters and they don't all starve.'

'What does your father say? I know he was awfully pleased when you won that prize and then the man from England bought your picture of Cleggan, but doesn't he want you to be a doctor like himself?'

'He doesn't mind. He knows it's what I've always wanted and if he can afford it maybe I'll be able to study away somewhere. In Dublin, or even London or Paris.'

4

She looked at him in awe.

'Mick! How *wonderful*. Oh! I wish I could go away and learn to do something. But I never shall.'

'It's a funny thing, but that's the only part I don't fancy. I suppose I'd be a fool not to if I get the chance but I never want —really—to go away from here, you know.'

'You will. And you'll love it so much you'll never want to come back. Or if you do you'll look upon us all as deadly dull creatures. You'll be so grand you won't even remember me, I shouldn't wonder.'

She started to get together the remains of the picnic.

'You know that's not true. As a matter of fact I—' he stopped.

'What?'

'I've suddenly thought of something. You'll probably think it's mad. We've never thought about it till now.'

'About what?'

'We'll marry.'

She looked at him pityingly.

'I don't call that a very romantic way of proposing. How d'you know I'd say yes?'

'Well, no, I don't. But do think it over. I mean I think it'd be an awfully good plan. We'll have to marry someone one day, at least you will, and you know me so well.'

'That might actually make it all rather dull.' A remark which rather shocked him, and then she bettered it by saying, 'Where shall – should – we live?'

'Oh, I think somewhere here. Ardbreen I mean, what'd be the point of going somewhere we don't know? Of course I know it can't be for some time, and anyway you're only seventeen and still at school.'

She giggled. 'What would the nuns think if I went back at the beginning of next term and told them I'm engaged?'

They looked at each other and both laughed.

'Paddy,' he said, 'I only knew about it when you tied the scarf on me. It suddenly happened.'

'I know,' she answered.

'Did you? How on earth?'

5

'You suddenly looked different. But, Micky darling, I've always known we'd get married one day, just between ourselves.' She put her arm through his. 'I've known it since I was ten. I heard Auntie Cathleen saying to someone what a nice pair we'd make one day. So I just took it for granted. Of course, I knew you didn't know, but I also thought it would strike you sooner or later. I'm glad it's sooner.'

She stopped and stood still and turned towards him.

'Would you think me daft if I kissed you?' he asked.

Micky planted a very chaste kiss on her lips. She was very silent, and they walked on.

'D'you know, I somehow thought it would be much more exciting,' Paddy said, sometime later. 'Being kissed, I mean. I suppose neither of us has had any practice. *Have* you kissed any other girls, Mick?'

'Of course not.' This time she really had shocked him.

'Well, you might have. You're nineteen and you were away at college. Of course not having a local cinema doesn't help. I mean if we saw pictures more often with close-ups and what not I dare say we'd learn. I do think,' and she suddenly became animated, 'Micky, I do think it'd be frightfully exciting and thrilling if we *could* get worked up about each other, don't you? Let's try again.'

Rather diffidently and ill at ease Micky pulled her closer towards him. Suddenly he knew what it meant. It frightened and thrilled him and when he let her go Paddy was shaking.

'I think – I think we'd better not do it again,' she said. 'Not like that. I mean not till we're properly engaged. Or even married. It made me feel rather funny.'

'It did me, too,' said the boy.

'D'you think we ought to tell Father Delaney? In confession I mean?'

'But Paddy, we didn't do anything wrong. I only kissed you.'

'I know. But it wasn't like the first one.'

'You didn't like the first one either. You said it was dull.'

'I know I did. Never mind, darling. I dare say it'll grow on one, the other kind. It's just that we're both so new to anything of the sort, aren't we? You know,' she continued, 'in a way it's a jolly good thing getting engaged and married to someone you've known always because one can talk about everything, discuss things, sort of.'

They retrieved their bicycles and rode gaily back towards Ardbreen.

'Shall you tell your father?' Paddy asked.

'I don't think so, if you don't mind. I'd better have a settled job before we make it public, even in our families,' Micky replied rather sententiously.

'After all we might change our minds,' said Paddy.

'I shan't,' he answered firmly.

'It's just a lovely secret for now. Just ours. Oh, darling! I'm so glad your birthday wasn't in term time or none of it would have happened.'

II

Paddy O'Malley sat in front of the mirror at her dressing-table. Beside her, on the bed, lay the frock she would be wearing tomorrow. Her wedding-dress. Nearly three years had gone by since Micky Renvyle had proposed to her on his nineteenth birthday and now at last she was going to marry him. Everything was ready, cakes—even the wedding cake—were stacked high in the big kitchen below, and presents were laid out on the village schoolroom's trestle table, borrowed for the occasion and which took up a great deal of room in the drawing-room. With her, as she proceeded to try on for the sixth time her bridal veil, was Mary Kelly, the chief bridesmaid.

'Are you feeling nervous, Paddy?' the girl was asking.

'No, of course not,' Paddy replied in a voice which did not carry much conviction, 'but I can't help wishing my mother hadn't died when I was born.'

'Hasn't your aunt told you everything?'

'I'm sure there's no need for that, after all we're living in the middle of the twentieth century, we're supposed to know the facts of life.'

'But do we? You know jolly well how strict the nuns have always been and it isn't as if we can read the sort of books girls in England do. The way they ban stuff over here is ridiculous. But anyway, your aunt has always been like a mother to you and you love her.'

'Well, I know. But she is an old maid, and very strict. I shan't know how to look her in the face when I come back from our honeymoon. I mean I'll know more than she does. It's awful.'

She put a touch of lipstick on her lips, and, still arranging and rearranging her head-dress, asked: 'How's that? Does it make me look *glamorous*?'

Mary Kelly giggled. 'Aren't you awful! What would Father Delaney think if he heard you? Marriage is serious, not frivolous. But you look lovely. I'll bet Micky will be absolutely spellbound and tongue-tied when you get to the altar. Are you really *in love* with him?'

'Of course I am,' Paddy answered gaily. 'We've never liked anyone else except each other—either of us. I'm going to be an absolutely wonderful wife.' She started to dance round the room. 'I've even learnt to cook and that's a thing I thought I hated. And while Micky's working I'll do the house and everything and we'll have dozens of children, I suppose. It'll all be *wonderful*!'

'Do tell me just one thing. And I swear I won't tell a soul. Just where are you going for your honeymoon?'

'You must promise not to?'

'I swear.'

'Leenane.'

Mary Kelly's face fell.

'But—that's quite near. I thought at least you'd be going to London or somewhere exciting.'

'Leenane's sort of special to both of us. Actually I did rather

8

want to go to one of those grand hotels in Killarney for I've never been there. But then we haven't a car, and Micky doesn't drive so it's no use even hiring one. And we thought we'd save quite a lot this way, and get more stuff for the cottage. Micky's father has given him a handsome cheque and some of that will pay for the honeymoon. The rest is going on furniture. Guess what—I'll bet you never will—we've booked a private bathroom all for ourselves. I never knew you could unless you were in Paris, or somewhere like that, did you?'

'Gosh!'

'I thought that would surprise you. I think Micky's dad suggested it.'

'Being a doctor he'd know about such things I expect,' said Mary Kelly. 'I mean doctors are kind of sophisticated, aren't they? You'd think Micky would be more than he is, considering.'

'He knows lots really. He's going to write—as well as paint —he says, when we're married. To make more money.'

'What'll he write about? His life in London when he was studying art at that place?'

'Goodness, no!' said Paddy contemptuously. 'He'll write about Ireland. And birds. And fishing. And sailing. And probably he'll paint the illustrations. He says books like that cost quite a lot of money to buy. Listen. I can hear Aunt Cathleen.'.

There was the sound of a step outside, and the door opened and Cathleen O'Malley came in. She was a woman of fifty or more, and had lived with her brother bringing up his motherless child for over nineteen years. This and working for the parish were her sole interests and she was finding it difficult already readjusting a future in a household where her niece would no longer be there to lead.

'Child! What have you been doing to your face!' she exclaimed. And before Paddy could protest the older woman had taken a handkerchief and busily wiped the lipstick from the girl's lips.

'I thought it made me look nicer,' she said lamely.

9

'And would you be thinking of receiving the Blessed Sacrament tomorrow dolled up like a trollop instead of the pure bride that you'll be? Mother of God!' her aunt exclaimed in horror.

'But Miss O'Malley,' Mary Kelly joined in. 'Lots of girls wear lipstick.'

'Not at Holy Mass,' the woman answered quickly. 'Not here in Ardbreen, and not a niece of mine! Shame on you, Mary!' Relenting somewhat she turned to Paddy and said:

'What you do when you're married is another thing, and if you want to look like an actress and paint your face—well, that's up to you and Michael. But if you take my advice you'll leave that pretty face as the good Lord gave it to you,' and she took it between her hands and kissed the girl's forehead. 'I expect it's very old-fashioned you'll be thinking me,' she smiled at Mary Kelly, 'but I just can't get used to some of these modern goings-on, you know. Paddy's father and I are a pair! We never go farther than Galway. They tell me English girls cover their faces with all sorts of muck, and it's true I've noticed people come to the hotel here in the season who make their faces up in a shocking manner. I've never heard an Irish voice among the lot of 'em, the Lord be praised.'

Miss O'Malley wandered about the bedroom, tidying as she went, picking up a stocking here, a petticoat there.

'Your father wants to talk to you when Mary's gone,' she said. 'And Father Delaney said he was coming round—to give you a last blessing before tomorrow, I shouldn't wonder.'

'I'd better be going, darling,' Mary said. 'My own frock looks grand, I love it.' She kissed her friend. 'I'll be waiting for you in church.'

'Say a Hail Mary for me,' said Paddy.

Downstairs Mr O'Malley was entertaining the priest. He had opened a fresh bottle of whisky and the two men were happily discussing a race meeting when Paddy came into the room.

'And would you believe it, Father, the devil got passed ten yards from the post by Old Nick—the well-named creature—and down I went a whole pound on the race.'

'And here is our dear girl,' exclaimed the priest. 'I'll be drinking your health tomorrow I know, my child, but there's no reason why I shouldn't this evening as well.' He raised his glass. 'God bless you, Paddy, and may you and Micky live a blessèd life together.'

'Thank you, Father. I know we'll be happy.'

'He's a good lad. And I've known the two of you since you were children so I know what I'm talking about.'

'I could wish he had a steadier job,' Paddy's father said, a little sadly. 'If he gets on we'll all be proud of him, and the Lord knows this country has produced more than her share of writers and poets and painters, but when it's your daughter that's marrying one of 'em, well— but there, it's no use standing in their way, as I've told you before, Father. They run off and do it without your blessing these days, if thwarted.'

The priest shook his head. 'We're richly blessed with the children in this parish, John. There's not been a bad one for as long as I can remember. But I can feel for you in wishing Mick Renvyle had gone into medicine like his father.'

'I'd have helped him too if he'd had any leanings for my own profession,' John O'Malley remarked, as he refilled the priest's glass.

'But Micky wouldn't be right as a doctor or as a solicitor, or as anything that had to be shut up doing the same sort of thing every day,' Paddy cried. 'You wait, you'll see, both of you, in ten years' time he'll be famous.'

CHAPTER TWO

I

PADDY RENVYLE stood by the ironing-board. The radio was playing dance music, a stew was filling the little kitchen with a pleasant smell, in a cradle near by their four-month-old daughter slept peacefully, and when she looked up through the window she could see Micky coming from the ruins of the castle where he had been painting all the morning. She ran out and waved, and then quickly began to lay the table for lunch.

'Smells good,' he remarked, as he entered the cottage, dropping most of his gear on to the settle, and then he bent over to look at the sleeping child. 'How is she?' he asked.

'Fine. She really is the most remarkable baby, isn't she? You'd never know we had one in the house!'

Both of them bent over the cradle and Micky slipped his arm round his wife's shoulders and kissed the top of her head.

'Did you do a good morning's work, darling?' Paddy asked.

'Yes. All the birds were truly obliging today. That heron—the one we must have seen yesterday—came and perched beside a rock and obviously knew I wanted him to sit for me.'

'Let's have a look,' and she put down the food, and went over to where he propped the canvas. 'You've got the oyster-catchers beautifully!' she exclaimed. 'Oh, darling! I do hope it's going to make our fortune. The book I mean.'

'I don't expect it'll do that but I'm pleased with what I've done so far. It's going to rain, so I'll write this afternoon.'

'Will you be all right if I go over to Daddy and Auntie Cathleen? I've not seen them this week and they like to see Killary. They'd spoil her if they got the chance.'

'I'll be fine. You know I'm all right. Anything you want before I start, though?'

'You could bring a bit more peat in, perhaps. And if I'm late—but I won't be—will you feed the hens?'

'If I can remember!' he laughed. 'But by that time I hope I'll be well away.'

'We'll try not to disturb you, but I've noticed that bath-time is the only hour Killary likes to have a good old cry.'

Together, after they had finished the meal they washed up and Micky Renvyle watched later as his wife gave the baby its bottle.

'Auntie was terribly amused when I told her you could change Killary's nappies as well as I do,' she said.

'Well, you never know when I might have to, so it's just as well to learn early,' he answered. 'Wonder what her first words will be, don't you?'

'Oh, I suppose the usual Mum-mum and Dad-dad. I don't see why our child should be any brighter than anyone else's. But you are rather a heavenly little creature all the same,' she said, picking up the child and kissing it soundly. 'I do want our baby to have lots of kisses and know it's loved a lot,' she spoke seriously, 'it's something I never really had.'

Mick lit a pipe and looked at his child.

'I wonder what you're going to be like.'

'She's getting quite like you, several people think so.'

'Poor little thing, what a shame.' He wriggled a finger on the baby's cheek. 'And I suppose if we have a son he'll be divinely beautiful like you, and his wretched sister will have straight hair and wear specs like her pa.'

He caught sight of himself in the mirror that hung in the hall, as they came downstairs, and he put his hand on his chin.

'I couldn't have shaved this morning,' he murmured. 'I can't think how you came to marry such an oaf.'

'I didn't know anyone else,' she laughed.

'And that might be truer than you think,' he replied.

'Well, I love you so don't let's worry. It's not often you forget to shave, though I will say your hair needs cutting. Men's looks wouldn't mean a thing to me.' She tucked the baby into the pram. Micky longed to know what did appeal to her and asked her.

'I still don't know,' she said rather slowly. 'After all I'm only twenty, and I've not known other men to compare with you and I don't suppose now I ever will. But it's peaceful being married to you, isn't it? I mean we're happy, and we never had quarrels and still don't, and I love our cottage, and you're kind and patient. You were so sweet when I was having Killary and being so cross and sick as I was. I'm sure if I'd been you I'd have sloshed me one. I think that's why I like being married to you, darling, you're so kind.'

She released the brake of the pram, and waving to Micky went off towards the village.

He watched her thoughtfully until she was out of sight. He too was happy. Marriage seemed an eminently good state, yet something somehow seemed to be lacking. He knew what it was and was too shy even to acknowledge the fact, certainly in so many words. Passion was lacking. It was not that he felt no passion for his wife, he did. She was beautiful, she was very desirable (a condition he could not bring himself to admit) and she was innocent. They were both too innocent—and he knew it—to make of their marriage all that could make it completely real. He still felt a certain shyness towards her, and while he could say lightly 'I love you' across a table at meal-time, he could not bring himself to utter the same words in passion in their bed. He could never get over the fact that the prettiest girl for twenty miles round was his wife, his feelings for her bewildered him sometimes. She was his school-days' friend for one thing, and that easy companionship had continued into marriage. His awakened desire—awakened so suddenly that day now nearly four years past—embarrassed and slightly shocked him, there were times it almost seemed incestuous that he and Paddy should sleep together as man and wife. But these were revelations he tried to push away. He realized that for Paddy their life was normal and what she had hoped and wished for, and he tried to tell himself not to be a fool for being in love with his own wife.

That evening, at supper, Paddy said suddenly:

'What do you think I heard in the village? Some film company is coming down here. Just imagine!'

'Who? American? British? Irish?'

'No one seems to know. But quite a lot of them have booked at the hotel. Of course the Jamesons are thrilled.'

'Perhaps they're film stars having a holiday.'

'I don't think so,' Paddy said. 'I think they're on what I believe is called location. They're going to "shoot". You know . . . make bits of a film. Don't you think it's exciting?'

He nodded. 'Yes. There was that wonderful one done years ago in Aran. Perhaps it'll be another of the same sort. You'll find yourself being roped in before you know where you are!'

'What me? Don't be daft.' She was silent for a few minutes and then said, 'Wouldn't it be *thrilling*! But they won't want local people, Mick. They'll be bringing stars. And that will be even more thrilling. Wonder who.'

II

Two weeks later Paddy greeted Micky in great excitement.

'Darling. The film people are giving a show this evening at the hotel and I've scrounged an invitation for us.' She hurried to explain. 'I suppose the head one or somebody asked the Jamesons who to ask, but anyway, Daddy had one sent to him. Neither he nor Auntie Cathleen want to go, and Auntie says she'll look after Killary if we take her in the carry-cot. And what I mean is, Daddy says we can have their tickets.'

She was flushed with excitement and for a moment Micky Renvyle's conscience smote him.

'Poor Paddy! I suppose life here is rather dull for you. Of course we'll go.'

He had no wish to see a film that evening, and a chapter of which he was in the middle needed a lot of work.

'What shall I wear? I know, the frock I wore when I was married.'

'Your *wedding-dress*?' he asked in surprise.

'No, silly! Of course not. My going-away one.'

'D'you realize this is the first excitement we've had, I mean the first kind of party we've been to since we were married,' she said later, as they walked towards her old home, carrying the child between them. 'D'you suppose we shall see the actors close to? Wouldn't it be marvellous if we sat next to one?'

'We shouldn't be expected to talk to 'em even if we do,' he rejoined. 'Now don't you go getting yourself involved. If you do I shan't know you.'

'Don't you like meeting people? Fresh people, new people?'

'If I can talk their language, yes. I had quite a lot of fun when I was in London all those months. But I was on my own ground. I wouldn't know what to talk about to film actors. Unless they wanted to know about Ardbreen.'

'Well, darling, you never know. Don't go and miss the bus. After all, who knows? You might even do a bit of business with the boat. Hire it out. I hear they were shooting—or whatever it's called—up Tully Mountain last week and now they want to go to one of the islands but don't fancy the local small craft. So you see you really might try and do some business with *Deirdre*.'

'Where on earth do you get all this information from?'

'I walked back from the shop this afternoon with Katie Finn, she's one of the chambermaids at the hotel this season. She told me quite a lot about them.'

'And what's the film they're making?' inquired Micky.

'It's called "Paradise Found". And the star is Freda Drury, and I didn't dare say I'd never seen her!'

'Well, I haven't even heard of her.'

By the time the Renvyles reached the hotel people were crowding into the dining-room where the screen had been erected and Micky realized that his fears were groundless.

Familiar faces abounded and there seemed to be no sign of members of the film company, glamorous or otherwise.

'Isn't it kind of Mr Piers,' Mrs Jameson said, as she slipped into a seat near Micky and his wife, 'he thought we'd like to have a bit of fun and have a show for some of our friends and people in the village, so he left one of the men, Mr Green I think it is, to put this on for us.'

'Aren't we going to see any of them?' asked Paddy.

'I don't expect so, dear! They've all gone over to dine at Cong.'

'That's ruined her evening,' Mick laughed. 'Poor darling, what a shame.'

Mrs Jameson smiled. 'They're all very easy, not a bit stuck up or anything. And they're mad about Ardbreen.'

'Paddy says they're having a bit of difficulty about getting to one of the islands. I don't know if that's so, but,' Micky continued somewhat diffidently, 'if you hear they're wanting a boat to get them over, well, you know there's my *Deirdre,* and she has an engine so that if necessary I can always take her without sails. I mean, if you hear they want—'

'What he means, Mrs Jameson, is that he'd be willing to charter *Deirdre.*'

'My dears, that would be wonderful. I mean it. I'll speak to Mr Piers tomorrow. Or tonight if I see him.'

The lights went out suddenly and in hushed silence the film started.

After the show was over most of the audience gathered in the bar. Presently there was the sound of cars arriving, but the noise in the room was such that Mick Renvyle was unaware that fresh faces were appearing, besides which he had found an old friend whom he had not seen since his marriage. Paddy, on the other hand, watched with growing excitement and curiosity as one by one actors and actresses emerged from the darkness into the lounge of the hotel, all looking—to her disappointment—very much like anyone else.

'That's Freda Drury,' someone whispered into her ear, and Paddy saw a woman of about thirty come into the room wearing an ordinary-looking frock, with a head-scarf over her head and dark spectacles. She wore no make-up and looked what she was feeling, extremely tired.

'God! I'm dead, fetch me a drink, someone,' Paddy heard her ask.

Nobody took any notice of Paddy, and she was pathetically pleased when one of the local village girls remarked:

'That's a pretty dress you have on, Mrs Renvyle. Isn't it the one you wore on your honeymoon, when you drove off, I mean?'

'Yes, it is,' she answered. 'I put it on on purpose to look my best, but you're the only one who's noticed.'

'It's such a squash here, tonight, it wouldn't matter what you'd put on. That lot in there don't notice any of us, anyway.'

Paddy drifted to another room, ate an ice-cream, saw that Micky was in deep conversation with a stranger, and was about to interrupt when someone drew her attention to a notice that had been pinned on to a board by the reception desk. 'Extras Wanted,' she read, and it seemed that the film company were needing local men and women of any age for crowd work the following week, and applicants were to go to a Mr Hancock and sign on, and the pay would be two guineas a day.

'You ought to have a try,' she heard someone say. 'You're the prettiest girl in Ardbreen.'

'I wonder if Micky would mind,' Paddy said wistfully.

She was silent on the way home and was startled when Micky said suddenly: 'Well, I did it. Made a deal with *Deirdre*. To-morrow I'm taking Mr Piers over to Inishturk if it's a decent day. Mind you, I think the fellow's crazy, and I'll wager he'll settle for something closer. I mean to say if they start shooting on Inishturk and the weather packs up they'll have had it, and what a waste of time and money, not that that seems to bother them. Rum crowd, aren't they?'

'Well, I didn't see enough of anyone to know. Why don't you advise this Mr Piers to do it on one of the nearer islands? Even old Crump, you could always manage that.'

'He says he wants an island with a mountain. Priceless! The

audience aren't going to know anyway, are they? Well, I expect he'll alter his mind after tomorrow.'

'Was he nice?'

'Yes. Quite a decent chap.'

'They looked awfully unsmart for film stars, I thought,' Paddy said. 'Fancy going to dinner at Ashford Castle dressed like that Freda what's-her-name! Did you see her? Dark specs and a shiny nose. I can only think Aunt Cathleen must be very wrong about actresses.'

'I expect when you're sufficiently famous you can dress as you like, even at Ashford.'

When they were in bed Paddy told Micky about the notice in the hotel.

'Should you mind if I signed the thing and had a try, darling?' she asked.

'No. No, why should I? But what about Killary? I don't see how we can both leave her, and if I've got to take this Piers about I'll have to be on tap for him.'

'Well, I don't see why I shouldn't take her with me,' said Paddy. 'I mean if it's what they call crowd work, just to give local colour, a young woman with a baby would be quite useful, I should think, shouldn't you?'

'Probably,' Micky Renvyle yawned. 'You go ahead and all luck, love.' And when presently she asked him a further question Paddy realized her husband was sound asleep.

Next morning Micky Renvyle was off early to put *Deirdre* in readiness before collecting Spike Piers. He had breakfasted and gone off before Paddy was downstairs, so the moment she had bathed and fed little Killary and swallowed some coffee herself she put the baby in the pram and was soon queueing with other inhabitants of Ardbreen for crowd-work in the film. To her surprise she was signed on with practically no questions asked and Killary's presence presented no problems. Excitedly she told Micky on his return, before inquiring the result of his day's outing with Spike Piers.

'D'you suppose I'll have to really act?' she asked him excitedly.

'I shouldn't think so,' he said rather dampingly. 'If you remember the film we saw last evening there were a tremendous amount of people at one moment, and all they had to do was jostle each other and yell.'

'But that was to do with a battle, and anyway I call that acting,' she argued.

'Oh well, I dare say you'll have to jump around or dance or something that no real Irish girl would dream of doing, but I don't suppose you'll have to speak. They'd have to give you more than two quid.'

'I was rather good in the plays we did at school,' she announced. 'I was Brutus in *Julius Caesar* once.'

Renvyle laughed.

'Anyway, what was your day like?' Paddy asked.

'As we said, Inishturk's out of the question. As a matter of fact we may use one of the very little ones, even Inishbroom. I dare say they'll compromise and do some shots from one place and shoot with the actors at another.'

'What's he going to pay for *Deirdre*?'

'Twenty pounds a day.'

'Darling!' Paddy's eyes opened wide. 'I'd sail her to Scotland for that.'

'Well, I'll be on call for full days, it was the offer he made, I didn't ask for that amount. I must say, I nearly fell overboard when he made it.'

'I wonder how many days you'll be needed,' she said. 'Perhaps you and *Deirdre* will end up in the film itself. Perhaps we shall all be. What fun!'

III

Occasionally some of the company would mingle and chatter with the local men and women but Paddy soon realized they were not interested in them for potential talent, but seemed more interested in the lives the small community led. When she remarked on this one evening to Micky he answered, 'I expect it's local colour they're after. You can't blame them. They pick my brains for all they're worth, but I don't think I'm very much use to them. The trouble is they don't understand most of the folk, say they speak in Irish most of the time.'

'Which of course most of 'em do,' Paddy said. 'Sometimes even I find it difficult to understand.'

'I think they stand them plenty of drinks in the bar in the evenings hoping to draw them out,' Micky said.

One evening Father Delaney came over.

'I was just passing by, so I thought I'd drop in to see how you film stars are getting on,' he said, with a twinkle in his eye.

'She's disillusioned, Father,' Micky announced.

'Are you now? Why would that be?'

'It's just terribly boring, Father,' she said. 'One hangs about for literally hours doing nothing but gossiping with each other. I get terribly impatient. One doesn't even learn anything.'

'And what would you be wanting to learn, Mrs Michael Renvyle?'

'I think in her heart our Paddy thought she'd be ousting the leading lady,' her husband teased.

'No, you old silly. But it just does seem a waste of time.'

'Why go on with it, then?' the priest asked.

'Well, it's quite nice to have the money, you know. I'll be able to get some things for Killary. And I wouldn't like to be the only one to drop out. The others quite enjoy it. It was fun the first day, one was keyed up for something to happen. Mick has much more fun taking Mr Piers to the islands.'

Then, the day before the company was due to leave Ardbreen, Paddy heard a voice say:

'That's a pretty face. Wonder if there's talent with it.'

She was the last to leave and she knew it must be herself who was being discussed. She still had on the black shawl that she had been told to wear for the scene in which she had been photographed, and although a tremor of excited pleasure filled her she also felt frustrated that it had been left to this late hour to discover her. She turned toward the speaker, but again felt disappointment, the man was an apparent stranger, she recognized no one she had seen before. However, he stopped her and said:

'Were you roped in for this?'

She said she had been an extra for crowd work.

'And did you enjoy it?' she was asked.

'Frankly no,' she answered. 'I was mostly bored to tears. I thought it would be fun and exciting, but it wasn't.'

'D'you live here?'

'Yes. Over there.' She pointed out the cottage in the distance. 'With my husband and my baby.'

'Oh, you're married. Did your husband do a bit of work in it as well?'

'He chartered his boat to the producer,' she replied.

'Oh, I've met him, I think. Young Renvyle. You're Mrs Renvyle?'

She nodded.

'My name's Zeitlinger.'

The name conveyed nothing to her. 'Have you got something to do with the film?' she asked.

He smiled. 'I'm producing it,' he answered.

'But I thought Mr Piers was.' She looked at him distrustfully.

'He's directing it.'

'Oh. It all sounds the same thing to me. You've not been around all the time, though, have you?'

'No. But I've been here several days now. Been taking a look at your beautiful country. And it is beautiful.'

There was a hint of patronage in his voice. Paddy did not care for it.

'My husband thinks it's so beautiful he never wants to leave it,' she began.

'That fellow with the boat? Renvyle?'

'He's a writer,' she told him with pride, 'and he paints too.' Mr Zeitlinger was not impressed, she saw.

'And you, what are you going to do?'

She realized he was accompanying her on her way. 'How do you mean? I told you. I'm Micky Renvyle's wife and we have a baby.'

'That face is wasted here.'

She stood still and looked at him. There was something she did not like about the man.

'It's a pity then that some of you didn't notice it earlier,' she retorted. 'The film is finished, I understand. Now I must run. My family are waiting for me. Good morning.'

When she arrived back at the cottage Micky had the meal ready and had brought the child in.

'I'm thankful it's over,' she announced, and threw herself into a chair.

'Sweetheart, I've had to accept an invitation to dine at the hotel tonight. For both of us. Spike Piers has invited us,' Micky told her.

'Oh.'

'I thought you'd be pleased.'

'I've not met Mr Piers personally, I don't suppose he'll even recognize me,' she answered rather crossly. 'And I met a man this morning who I didn't like. He says he's met you and that he's the producer. He had a foreign name.'

'Oh, Zeitlinger. He's a bit of an oily type, I agree. I expect he'll probably be there this evening.'

'Darling, can't you go by yourself?'

'It's very unlike you, Paddy, not to want to—'

'I'm tired,' she interrupted. 'Let's make Killary an excuse.'

Micky Renvyle shook his head. 'No, we can't. I think it would be rude. If we were important we could, but the very fact we're not and that Piers has paid through the nose for *Deirdre* makes me feel a little under an obligation to him.'

'Oh, all right,' Paddy said wearily. 'I don't suppose Aunt Cathleen will mind having Killary again.'

'Of course she won't. She's always saying she's no trouble.'

To Paddy's relief Zeitlinger was not present when she and Micky arrived at the hotel and it was apparent he was not expected. Several members of the company joined the party, and the young Renvyles were thoroughly enjoying the evening until Zeitlinger suddenly appeared when they were drinking coffee in the bar.

'Hey! Spike,' he called out when he noticed Paddy, 'how came you to overlook this lovely young lady?' To her confusion he threw an arm round her shoulder. 'She tells me—or she did this morning when I met her—that she's been an extra throughout the time you've been out here, and that no one noticed how pretty she is.'

Paddy hotly denied saying any such thing.

'I never knew your wife was an extra,' Spike said to Renvyle.

'I did mention it, I'm sure I did,' Mick murmured.

'You're right, Max. She *is* lovely. Did they take any stills of you, my dear?' Spike Piers turned to Paddy who was by now thoroughly discomfited.

'No, of course not,' she said.

'Can you come over first thing tomorrow and we'll do a test before we pack up?'

'But what for?' both Renvyles spoke at once.

'We might use her. She may be really photogenic, and it's always a good thing to spot fresh talent and—as you say, Max—it's a very lovely face.'

'Stop, please, talking about me as if I were a cow at some market,' she began, which brought guffaws from the men present.

'I don't think it would interest my wife, you see,' Mick said slowly.

'No? Well, there'd be no harm done,' Spike replied. 'You needn't make a test if you don't want to, but I'd like some stills. In a shawl if you have one.'

'I wore it all the time,' Paddy said discontentedly.

'Fine!' Piers turned to someone and said, 'I guess that face in a peasant's shawl might do very well on an advert.'

Zeitlinger squeezed Paddy's hand.

'I can tell a good thing when I see one,' he whispered.

Disentangling her hand from his grasp Paddy made her escape towards the Jamesons who by now had joined the party.

'They tell me you're to have a test made. How exciting!' Mrs Jameson said.

'I'm not. Don't you believe it. They were just being stupid. As to that man,' and she looked to where Zeitlinger was now standing knocking back straight whiskies, 'I dislike him intensely. He makes me squirm.'

'He's known in the business as the star-maker, so I'm told,' said Mr Jameson.

To begin with, when they left the hotel later in the evening to collect Killary, the Renvyles walked in silence, but Paddy presently said, 'I'm jolly well not going tomorrow to have my photograph taken. I've never been made to look such a fool in my life.'

'They meant it kindly,' said Micky. 'You needn't have flown off the handle as you did. Actually I think it would be considered a compliment. And I'd like a nice photograph of you.'

'As long as that Zeitling whatever his name is doesn't hover in the background. Oily brute.'

'Freda Drury was in love with him once, they tell me,' Mick informed her, not considering that he should tell her that she had been Zeitlinger's mistress.

'She can have him! Darling, you are funny! Don't you see how nasty he is? Old—'

'I don't suppose he's much over forty,' Mick said.

'Well, I call that old. And I'm sure he's more than that, his hair is quite grey. And that awful fat stomach. Ugh!'

Next morning Paddy arrived at the hotel, hoping it was too late for Spike Piers's purpose but there were people about and the man who had been detailed to do the stills of her was ready. She was kept in the temporary studio for a good hour, and it seemed to her that they took enough photographs to fill an album. It was over at last, and she was preparing to go when Zeitlinger appeared in the doorway.

'Ah, Mr Zeitlinger,' the man who had been taking the photographs said, 'I think we've got some good ones. You and Spike will be pleased,' and to Paddy's discomfort she soon found herself in the room alone with the producer.

'Good morning,' she said politely, 'I hope they'll be of some use. I've got to dash now.'

'Oh, now, I'm sure you haven't got to do anything of the sort. It's early. Come and have a drink.'

'I don't drink,' she said quickly.

'Why don't you like me?'

'I didn't say that I didn't,' she stammered.

'Do you mean to tell me,' he started, 'that if you had the chance to go into pictures you'd refuse?'

'I told you, it bored me.'

He took her arm. 'I don't mean crowd work, darling. I mean real stuff. And I mean it. With a face like yours I could make you a star in a pretty short time.'

'I can't act.'

'You'd soon learn.'

For a moment she faltered. 'What would I have to do? Where would I have to go?'

'To England. I'd take care of it. I'd see you were all right.'

'And my husband and my baby? Could they come too?'

'Would it matter if they didn't? To begin with?'

Suddenly she was aware of the man's body pressing against hers. And then he kissed her. She pushed him from her.

'I can think of nothing I should hate more, Mr Zeitmann,' she said, purposely getting his name wrong.

'Most girls would give a hell of a lot for the chance,' he remarked.

'I've already told you, I'm married with a family.'

'Don't you have a nurse?'

'Don't be a fool,' Paddy answered. 'Would I be doing what I've been doing for the past couple of weeks if we could afford a nurse?' She had to laugh. 'We count every penny—'

'And turn down the chance of making a fortune. Well, have it your way, my dear, but I tell you you're making a mistake. You've got spirit too! Who says you can't act?'

Again he caught hold of her and before she could help it he was kissing her again, forcing her lips to open.

'How dare you!' she said, and tears came into her eyes.

'Little fool.' Zeitlinger seemed at last to realize she was in earnest, and let her go.

She walked back from the hotel, her face aflame. She felt besmirched. She would go to Confession that very afternoon. She could not even tell Micky. She must calm down before she reached home or Micky would sense something. What an odious man. The conceit of the creature! What a vile thing to happen to a girl.

The faster she walked the more upset Paddy became. She began to wonder. Perhaps, after all, she could act. If one could get so worked up over a stranger insulting one in such a horrible manner, perhaps after all one had what was known as temperament, so ran her thoughts. She longed to tell somebody about it, but there was no one to confide in except Micky. What would he really think? Perhaps she could tell him and pretend it had happened to one of the other girls? But he might ask who? She couldn't lie to him.

Micky was absorbed at his easel when she returned, and seemed to have forgotten what she had gone for. He answered any remarks she made in monosyllables and Paddy realized that his mind was totally engrossed. She took Killary for a walk in her pram, purposely avoiding the road to the village and they met no one.

'Micky,' she began, in the evening after they had finished supper, and she was mending one of his shirts.

'M'm?'

She saw that again he was busy. This time apparently reading over part of his unfinished manuscript.

'That Zeitlinger man must be really awful.'

'M'm?'

'D'you know something? He kissed one of the girls, one of the Ardbreen girls, I mean.' He still seemed unconcerned. 'I can't tell you who it was, of course. It wouldn't be right.' She felt her cheeks burn and she was glad Micky could not see her face.

'I expect she asked for it,' he answered, without looking up.

'Indeed she did nothing of the sort,' Paddy said hotly. 'She thinks he's hateful.'

'Oh well, that's what happens I dare say if you take up acting.'

'What do you think she should have done about it?'

At last he looked up.

'Darling, what a fuss to make about a kiss! Was it you he kissed by any chance?'

'Of course not.'

Now she would never be able to tell him the truth.

'She sounds to me rather a silly girl to be making such a fuss, as I've just said. I shouldn't be surprised if she had enjoyed it.' He started to read.

Paddy saw that it was useless to continue. But Micky's last words shocked her. *Had she enjoyed Zeitlinger's embrace?* Everything about the man revolted and nauseated her, but had she, had she enjoyed the sensation of something she had never known from Micky?

That night she found it difficult to sleep. She was restless in mind and body. Her husband's good-night kiss which she usually accepted as normal suddenly seemed—dull. She realized she longed for Micky to kiss her as Zeitlinger had.

'Father, I have sinned. . . .'

At home, washing up in the kitchen sink, putting Killary to bed, kneeling by the prie-dieu in their room it had not seemed so difficult. Confession came to her as normally as eating, as prayer, as living. It was part of life. But as she knelt behind the curtain which separated Father Delaney from her she knew for the first time in her life an ignominy of spirit and shame. All past sins seemed trivial in comparison. She hesitated, licking her lips.

'Continue, my child.'

Stumblingly and falteringly she whispered of the incident which had filled her mind for days with shame.

'But, my daughter,' Father Delaney spoke in his quiet, kind

voice, 'I cannot see that you committed a sin. You say this man only kissed you. Are you sure that is all that happened? You did not return his embrace?'

'No, no,' she hurriedly excused herself, and then, 'I'm frightened, Father, because I'm married and wish my husband kissed me in the same way. And I'm sure it's wicked.'

'I see.'

Perhaps not for the first time in his life as priest and confessor Father Delaney found himself smiling a little. The confessions of the simple lads and girls of Irish villages were often very pathetic, it was sometimes difficult to give them an adequate penance.

'Say ten Hail Marys, my child, and ask our Holy Mother to keep you pure and unsullied.' And when presently the soothing words of Absolution fell on her ears Paddy felt she had emerged from a prison of her own making.

CHAPTER THREE

KILLARY was four years old when John Renvyle, her grand-
father, died and left what money he had to Micky, together
with his house. Micky and Paddy discussed whether to move
from the cottage or sell the larger house. Old Mr O'Malley and
his sister had their opinions frequently asked, as did Father
Delaney, the Jamesons and other friends.

'If you can afford it, I think you should persuade Micky to
take you to his father's old house,' Miss O'Malley said. 'The
cottage is very small for children and you'll be having another
baby before long.'

It was the knowledge of this fact that became the prime factor
of Micky leaving the cottage where he had lived for nearly five
happy years. They had been fruitful years where his work had
been concerned, for not only had two books been published by
a prosperous firm of London publishers but he had just had a
picture accepted by Burlington House for the summer exhibition, and several others had been hung in exhibitions in London,
Paris and Dublin. But now that Paddy was expecting a second
child it certainly would seem providential to make the move.
One evening soon after they had gone into the new house she
was standing on a ladder, hanging a picture, when she lost her
balance and fell. That night she woke in great pain, but before
the doctor could be called they realized that she was having a
miscarriage.

For some time following this Paddy was very listless. Nothing
interested her, and many things irritated her. She tried to be
patient with Killary but with Micky she was often downright bad-tempered. Her father and aunt remonstrated with
her.

'If I were your husband I'd take a stick to you,' Miss O'Malley remarked on one occasion when Paddy had been unnecessarily unreasonable.

'I almost wish he would,' her niece answered. 'It's one of the things about Mick that gets on my nerves. I mean that nothing rattles him. I know I'm behaving abominably or have been, but I can't help it. That new doctor says it happens to people very often when they've had what I had.'

'Well, dearie, you're not the only woman who's lost a child. You must try and take a pull on yourself, if only for Killary's sake.'

'I know. I will try.'

Micky Renvyle made the best he could of the sorry business. He loved his wife, he had been looking forward to what they both hoped would be a boy. He blamed himself for Paddy's fall, saying he should never have allowed her to have climbed ladders, and where Paddy's outbursts would have driven many another man from the house he would listen silently and as likely as not admit whatever fault she accused him of. He complained to no one, and seemed to find consolation in the small Killary who often turned to him nowadays quickly realizing that her mother had become unreliable, and the two of them would go off for a sail in *Deirdre*.

One day, about five months after Paddy's miscarriage, a letter arrived for her with an English stamp and bearing a London postmark. She opened it and read it through, her eyes opening with growing surprise and excitement.

'Micky,' she exclaimed. 'You'll never guess who this is from and what it's about.'

He looked up expectantly. Glad of anything that brought any glimmer of interest to her.

'D'you remember Spike Piers?'

'You mean the fellow who produced that film?'

'Directed it,' she corrected him. 'Yes, well it's from him. And he writes to say he's going into management with someone— a theatre, with a play not a film—about Ireland, and wants an Irish girl and would I consider it!'

'But darling! You can't act, you never have, he must be mad.'

'Listen. He says it's a tiny part, no experience is necessary but it calls for someone who has an Irish inflection in her voice —have I, darling?—and can speak a few sentences in Irish. And she must be really lovely to look at—"which you are", he says!' she giggled.

It was the first time Micky had heard anything like a laugh for more weeks than he could remember.

'He says,' she continued reading from the letter, ' "On going through our files I came across some stills we must have taken of you." '

She went on reading the letter to herself, and when she had finished it she said:

'He says they hope to do the play at the Grand Theatre and would pay me fifteen pounds a week. And if I showed promise I might be given an understudy.' There was a few seconds' silence. 'Micky, what shall I do?'

'Darling, what d'you want to do?'

'I don't know. It's so completely out of the blue, isn't it?'

'Must you make up your mind in a hurry?' Micky asked.

She looked through the letter again. 'No, not really. He says to think it over and let him know within the next ten days or so.'

Renvyle spent the next few hours in a bewildered state of mind. He felt there was nothing to which he would not agree if it would help in the restoration to mental and physical health of his wife, at the same time the idea of her leaving to go to England for what might be an indefinite period was an appalling thought. And there was Killary to consider. The more he thought of the project the greater the difficulties seemed. Killary . . . surely it could not be right for a mother to leave a small child in order to act on an English stage? It was true he felt competent to look after her, had done throughout the time Paddy had been ill, and she was an easy child. Would she fret if her mother went away? After all, even when Paddy was ill she had been in the house and there had never been a day when the small child had been kept out of the sick-room.

'I've been thinking . . .'

32

'So have I . . .'

Daily their conversation was of nothing else.

'Let's consult your father and aunt,' Micky said, the third day after the letter's arrival.

'I'm sure Aunt Cathleen will be dead against the idea,' Paddy said. 'She'd think it dreadful to leave Killary.'

They went along at tea-time and found, rather to Paddy's consternation, Father Delaney taking tea.

'We've come for advice,' Mick began.

'A very tricky problem,' Paddy continued. Between them they told of the idea.

'I can see no problem,' Miss O'Malley said in a brusque voice. 'You just write to this Mr Piers and tell him the idea is out of the question.'

'I thought you'd say that,' Paddy said.

'I can't see that little Killary should be the only excuse, Paddy m'darling,' her father cut in. 'There's Mick to think of too. He'd be darn lonely all on his own.'

'And so would you, you silly girl,' her aunt said. 'Have you stopped to consider what you'd do by yourself in London?'

'I'd be acting.'

'Not all the time. There'd be the days to get through when your rehearsals were over and the play was running. Where would you live? Why, child, you've never been away in your life except to the convent, you don't know how lonely one can be in an unknown city. When I was young I was sent to Brussels as a governess-companion. I stood it for three months, the three unhappiest months of my whole life, I was that lonely.'

'Father, you've been silent. What do you think?' Micky turned to the priest, who was quietly puffing at his pipe and looking at them all in turn.

'I think it's something that only you two can work out for yourselves. But I will say just one or two things that may help you. Paddy, my child, you have not been yourself since you lost the baby. And I'm not at all sure a break for both of you wouldn't be beneficial. I've seen you pick on this poor lad'—

Micky made a sound as if to demur and Paddy blushed—'and I realized it was your poor health. But mind you, when I say a break I mean a temporary break. And I don't know that play-acting wouldn't lead to something worse. And then London is a big place and as Miss O'Malley says cities can be lonely places at that. Would it be possible for Mick and Killary to join you, do you think, if the play was to be a success? I wouldn't like to think of you becoming parted for too long.'

'Yes, why not?' She looked at Micky. 'After all you have lived there and know the ropes.'

'I was working.'

'At least your work can be done anywhere,' Mr O'Malley said. 'I mean you could write in London.'

'I can't understand why the idea interests you, child,' her aunt chipped in once more. 'It isn't as if you've ever done any acting. How do you know you can, indeed?'

'Well, I've brought Mr Piers's letter. You can all read what he says.' And the letter was passed round in silence.

'Fifteen pounds a week! H'm! That wouldn't go far in London these days from all I hear,' was Miss O'Malley's comment.

'Do you really and truly want to do this?' her father asked.

'Part of me does, and part of me doesn't,' she answered.

'And Mick, my son,' said the priest, 'what do you really feel?'

'I want her to do what she wants. I shall hate it if she goes, I admit that. On the other hand, suppose Paddy has talent that none of us know about? Nowadays one's supposed to allow women the freedom to earn their own living whether they're married or not. And who am I, who've been lucky lately both with writing, and selling my pictures, to stand in Paddy's way if she's fated to be an actress? Perhaps a very good one. She's pretty enough, bless her.'

'Takes more than a pretty face to be a good actress,' Miss O'Malley said.

'I do feel I'd like to try, having been given the chance,' Paddy said, gaining courage, and she squeezed Micky's hand with an affection she had rarely shown of late.

'You know that we'd all see that your husband and child didn't starve,' her father said with a smile.

'After all, I may be bad and sent home,' Paddy said lightly.

'I wish I could think so,' Micky remarked a little ruefully.

'Oh, darling, wouldn't you feel proud—really—if I became a famous actress?'

'Not if it were to take you away from me.'

'See here, my children,' Father Delaney started to speak again. 'I want you both to realize an important matter. You took solemn marriage vows to one another. Nothing must come between you. If you do leave Ardbreen, Paddy, then Mick and the child will have to join you sooner or later. Or alternatively you will have to come home. I know what the good Lord meant for the pair of you, and so do you, and it was not for you to go off and leave husband and child for a career on the stage. On the other hand if you make good and are wasting a talent because of living in this remote spot, then Mick must join you and realize that he will have to master his dislike for cities. Marriage is give and take, and don't you two forget it.'

On the way home Paddy said, 'They were none of them very helpful, were they?'

'Did you think they would be? It's always a forlorn hope, asking advice.'

'What a fearful responsibility making a decision is!' she sighed.

A few days later Micky said, 'Have you written to Spike Piers yet?'

She shook her head.

'You'll have to, you know. You can't keep him hanging about.'

'Whichever way I choose I shall wish I'd done the other.'

'Toss for it then.'

'That's an idea.'

She went to where her bag lay and searched for a coin.

'Now,' she said, giving him a penny, 'you do it. Heads I go, tails I stay.'

He tossed.

'It's a head,' Micky said.

'Do it again.'

'Really?'

'Yes, yes,' she said impatiently.

This time it was tails.

'Now a third and last.'

He spun the penny on the stone floor.

'Heads,' he said.

For a few seconds neither spoke.

'We needn't really go by it,' she said.

'Nonsense. It was the oracle.'

'Darling, I'll believe you want me to go,' she teased.

He put his arm round her shoulder. 'I hate the very thought of it. But I believe it's what you really want to do, and I believe it may be good for you. I dare say I'm a damn dull husband and that you lead a dull life here.'

'I've known no other.'

'All the more reason perhaps that you should try another. Who knows? You may come scurrying back before we know where we are.'

'It won't really make any difference to us,' she said, a little uncertainly.

'It can't make any difference to us.'

'Then help me write to Spike Piers,' she said.

The remaining weeks at home seemed to both Micky and Paddy Renvyle to pass in an unprecedented flash.

'I'll simply have to get some decent clothes,' she announced.

'I should wait till you get to London,' her husband replied.

'But I must have one or two things. Perhaps either you or Aunt Cathleen could come with me to Galway one day.'

The last day was very lovely. 'What shall we do?' she asked. 'I've done all my packing so that we could have a real day. And it's fine and glorious. Let's take *Deirdre* and go for a sail. Killary can come too then.'

'Wind and tide will be right for Killary Harbour,' he said.

'Oh! Lovely.'

They did not speak a great deal, and once or twice he thought he noticed tears in her eyes.

'I suppose I'm crazy,' she said.

He saw she was looking to the mainland, her eyes fixed on the mountains in the distance.

'They've never really meant to me what they do to you, you know. The Twelve Pins, I mean. I believe each separate peak is a personal friend of yours.'

'How did you know?'

'Sometimes I've watched you looking at them when you've been painting, or when we've been sailing. You look at them like a lover, you funny old thing. Sometimes I've almost felt jealous of the mountains and the islands.'

'Then you really are crazy.' This time he laughed.

'I know it is very beautiful, and I dare say I shall be home-sick and long for it. I know I shall want you and Killary, but darling, you do understand, don't you, that this is an incredible chance for me and that to have thrown it away untried would have been awfully foolish. Indeed, I think that would be really crazy.' She spoke lightly, trying to justify her decision.

'Yes, sweetheart.'

Presently they rounded the island that guarded the entrance to Killary Harbour.

'It is looking very lovely, I must say,' she said, and taking the child on her knee, she said: 'D'you remember this place, my sweetheart? D'you remember Daddy and Mummie told you what its name is?'

Killary looked at the long fjord up which they were making and her eyes lit.

'It's me,' she said with excitement. 'It's Killary.'

'Aren't you a clever brat?' Micky said. 'You're going to be a great companion.'

'I want dinner,' was the child's answer.

'I'll haul down the sail, and we'll tie up and eat. I'm ravenous too.'

They ate in rather more silence than was usual. Both felt

tension, both knew that probably nothing would be quite the same again.

'I don't believe it's ever looked quite so blue,' Paddy said. 'The water, I mean. It's awfully like pictures of Norway, isn't it?'

'It'll always be the most wonderful place in the world to me.'

'Why, Daddy?' Killary climbed on to his knee.

'Because it's got your name,' Paddy said quickly.

'Daddy, why do you love this place?'

'Because Mummie and I came here and were very happy,' he answered her, which seemed to satisfy her.

'It's all very well,' Paddy remarked later, 'but you were in love with Killary Harbour and Leenane before you were in love with me, so don't pretend.'

'You're tied up, one with the other,' he replied.

That night Paddy found herself clinging to Micky as she had never done before.

'Don't cry,' he reassured her.

'It's like going to school,' she sobbed.

'But, darling one, it's your own choice.'

'I know. And p'haps I'll love it. But you will always love me, won't you? And you won't let Killary forget me, will you?'

He comforted her and somehow the night passed from misery, and when dawn broke only Micky lay awake and knew with dull foreboding that nothing would be the same again.

CHAPTER FOUR

'DARLING MICKY,

'You never told me how beautiful London is! And I was ridiculously surprised by its size. So far I've not had time to be homesick. Of course I burst into tears after I'd waved good-bye to you from the boat and nearly jumped off it and swam ashore! But it was horribly rough and it was all I could do not to be sick. Quite different from our sailing in *Deirdre* when I've never felt a qualm. I dare say it was partly het-up-ness! My little Catholic Club is quite nice and I shall stay here for a bit, anyway. Spike Piers was awfully kind and has even given me the play to read. I'd be pretty silly if I couldn't act the tiny part they want me for. We've to meet for the first rehearsal on Monday when the whole cast will assemble. Rather alarming! I bought Killary a pretty little frock – a smock – in a shop in a street called Oxford Street, and two ties for you, which I'll post tomorrow. I went to look at Westminster Cathedral *and* Westminster Abbey, I have to admit the Abbey is much the best! But there are some good churches for me, you'll be glad to hear. I was surprised what lots of Catholic churches there are in London. And aren't the parks lovely? Specially Regent's Park. I went to the Zoo yesterday and longed for Killary. I walk a lot and the policemen are very kind and helpful about what buses to go on. I haven't tackled the tube! Luckily a bus will take me to very near the theatre and only three minutes from the club, and the whole journey won't take more than twenty minutes. Darling, don't worry if you don't hear much from me when rehearsals start, tho' I'll try and write in the evening. I wish you could come over to the First Night, but I think it would be silly to spend all that money, don't you?

'God bless you, Micky darling. Your loving wife, Paddy.'

'Darling, Am up to my eyes because what do you think, I've got to learn two parts to understudy as well as my own little one. The other two are quite big but of course not the leading one. I still think London is wonderful. A very nice girl (in the play) took me to a theatre last night. We didn't have to pay! She was given what they call house seats. I went to Mass at Brompton Oratory, it was glorious. Forgive such a short letter. X X X Paddy.'

'Micky darling, Do you mind if I call myself Paddy O'Malley? I mean for the stage. Mr Piers says it's better. Wire me if you do. I have to wear the dreariest clothes in this play, I give you my word that I've never seen an Irish girl so poorly arrayed. The English are peculiar in their ideas about the Irish, I find. Let's hope I get the chance to act one of the parts I'm understudying as they both wear gorgeous clothes. All love.'

'Darling Micky, I was *thrilled* to have your roses on the first night and telegrams too from Daddy and Auntie and one or two friends. It all went very well, and I enclose a cutting from the only paper that actually spotted *me*! I hope you'll be duly impressed to read of "the enchanting young Irish newcomer"! There was a party on the stage afterwards, with wonderful food including champagne. I didn't feel nervous, at least not very. The dress-rehearsal was much worse, specially as Cara Melton (who plays the lead) forgot a lot of her lines in the second act and I thought to myself well if *she* can go up the pole like this what chance is there for me. Darling I think I may share a tiny flat with the girl who I share a dressing-room with. Actually there are three of us in it but it's only Sue Martyn I'd share a flat with. She wants a P.G. She's rather fun.'

After Paddy started sharing a flat Micky Renvyle realized his wife's letters came less frequently. He supposed it was natural, and told himself she had things to do now in the flat as well as act at night, but he would look for the postman day after day, often with little success.

The play had been running nearly five months when Micky received a letter from his wife with the somewhat startling news that she had been promoted to one of the more important parts in the play.

'I know this will be a tremendous surprise to you, but Joan Linden has broken her leg and I'm to play her part. It was one of the two I understudy and Spike Piers was so pleased with my performance that they're going to let me continue for the rest of the run as poor Joan will be away for ages. My slight (?!) Irish voice doesn't seem to matter apparently. Oh darling *couldn't* you come over for even a week? Those cheap night flights from Dublin don't cost a lot, and you could sleep in the flat, or if you only came for a very brief stay we could perhaps afford to go to a hotel. I'm going to get twenty pounds a week, I feel a millionaire. Am sure Daddy and Auntie would have Killary.'

When Micky had read and re-read his wife's letter through half a dozen times and given it the whole day's thoughts, he asked Mr and Miss O'Malley if they would have Killary so that he could go to London. They agreed immediately and he made his plans.

The plane arrived in London too late for Micky to get to the theatre before the performance was over. Both had known this would be the case and Paddy had asked Micky to come straight to the theatre to pick her up. He arrived to see people pouring out of the building in search of taxis. He was directed to the stage door by a much bemedalled commissionaire where he asked for Mrs Renvyle.

'No such person 'ere,' he was told. He remembered then that his wife had resumed her own name.

'I mean Miss O'Malley,' he said. 'I'm her husband. I'd forgotten she was using her maiden name.'

The man looked him up and down and jerked his head in some sort of direction.

'You're expected. Up the stairs, to the left, first door on the right. You'll see their names on it, 'ers included.'

Micky walked up half a flight of stone stairs and thought the place seemed like a reformatory, collided with one or two people who rushed past him, and heard a great many voices coming from a great many rooms, and the place now seemed to him more like a school. He found the door, and rather timidly he knocked on it.

'Yes? Who's there?' He was thankful to recognize Paddy's voice.

'It's I – Mick.'

The door was flung open and Paddy threw herself into his arms.

'Darling – how marvellous! You're earlier than I'd imagined. Come on in, and meet Sue.'

He was rather startled to meet Miss Martyn wearing very few clothes. This was revealed by the dressing-gown she was wearing which was only very carelessly tied. Indeed, Paddy herself was only half clad and still had her make-up on. He felt slightly tongue-tied, the more so when the girls' dresser entered the room dangling over her arm feminine garments which she threw at Sue Martyn.

' 'ere's your girdle, dearie, and don't arsk me to wash another this week, I beg.'

She looked at Micky and turning to Paddy said: 'This 'im? We've 'eard a lot about you, Sir. Pity you didn't get 'ere in time for tonight's show, we 'ad royalty in front. 'ow long's 'e 'ere for, Miss?'

She helped Paddy out of her kimono into a frock that Renvyle did not recognize.

'Oh, I hope he'll be here for a week, Mrs Betts. Anyway, I've got him a seat for tomorrow night.'

'Darling, aren't you going to offer the poor man a drink?' Sue Martyn asked. 'Afraid it's only Scotch, and I suppose you only drink Irish. Where *is* the bloody whisky, anyway?'

She spoke in a light manner, but Renvyle could not help feeling a little disturbed by the adjective. He had heard of course that morals and language were clack on the stage, but he hoped Paddy was not picking up bad habits. It would not go down well back in Ardbreen.

Paddy poured him out a drink in a tooth mug.

'How is Killary?' she asked.

'She's fine.' He longed to get Paddy out of the room, out of the theatre, somewhere where they could be alone together.

'I'm sorry Paddy has decided to have a honeymoon at an hotel with you,' Sue Martyn said, 'but I see her point. But I hope she'll bring you along to the flat sometimes.'

'Indeed, I hope so.'

'Of course I shall,' Paddy answered. 'He'll want to see where I live and all sorts of things. And anyway don't forget we're throwing that party for him on Saturday night.'

Micky's face must have shown the consternation he felt on hearing this news, for Paddy laughed and said: 'Look at him, he's horrified by the thought. It's all right, darling, only a few people including Spike are coming back after the performance to a picnic supper. Sausages, and drinks and sandwiches. You must meet some of my friends.'

'Have another drink,' Sue proffered.

'No, thank you, I won't, Miss Martyn.'

'Sue, for Christ's sake!' the other said. Micky's inside contracted, he looked at Paddy but saw no corresponding horror in her expression.

'Well, I'm longing for something to eat; I'm taking him round the corner to the Ivy before we go back to the hotel.'

'Fortify yourselves well, my children. I don't suppose you'll be getting all that sleep. God bless.'

Paddy squeezed his arm as they went down the stone stairs, and bade good night to various people who Mick supposed were members of the company.

'What have you done with your case?' she asked.

'I dropped it near the stage door—I hope it's all right.'

He was aware that Paddy was not unknown at the restaurant and they were immediately shown to a table.

43

'I'm starving,' she said. 'And I bet you are.'

Micky kept looking at his wife. She had altered. She was even prettier than before she had left Ardbreen. Her face was slightly made-up still, a very red lipstick he noticed particularly for he knew that hitherto she never used the stuff. Her hair had been fashionably cut and set, and she wore her clothes with a chic to which he was quite unaccustomed.

'My dear, forgive me for staring, but I feel I'm out with the wrong woman.'

She giggled. 'I hope you're not regretting the pick-up.'

'You look quite lovely,' he said simply.

'Ah, that's what the stage has done for me, you see. D'you really think so, Mick?'

He swallowed. The months without his wife had been long, and looking at her across the table under the shaded lights of the restaurant he knew it was not supper he was most in need of. Various people came into the Ivy who seemed to know Paddy, but he was relieved that except for waves or nods or blown kisses no one came over to their table.

'I've got us a room at ——'s,' Paddy said, naming a small French place Micky had never heard of. 'It's not so fabulous as most of the hotels in the West End, and it's quite respectable moreover. Oh, Mick, I *am* pleased to see you,' her eyes were shining, 'have you missed me dreadfully?'

'I've tried not to think about it, but it has been pretty hellish. Is this play going to run much longer?'

'They seem to think so.'

'What are the other people in it really like?' he asked. 'Your letters don't really tell much. I mean about personalities. For instance I didn't expect Sue Martyn to be like what she is.'

'Sue's all right,' Paddy answered. 'I wish they'd buck up with our food. She drinks too much and swears like a trooper.'

'Both of which you've always hated.'

'I know, but somehow in the theatre it doesn't seem to matter. Different places, different behaviour. The French have a proverb, haven't they, about it?'

'I should hate it if you get loose-tongued, so to speak.'

44

'Oh, you needn't worry, I shan't, neither drink nor swearing appeal to me though it doesn't actually shock me as it used. And my goodness! Darling, I *was* green about a lot of things. You'd be surprised how everyone lives with everyone, in a manner of speaking. And abortions galore—well! I was really horrified to begin with, and still am if the truth be known, but it is no good being shocked if you want to get on in the theatre.'

'I hope, my darling, that you will still keep being shocked in your heart,' he said gravely.

'I expect so. Is your steak good? Mine's divine. I expect you'd like another drink while there's still time, wouldn't you?' She beckoned the waiter.

'Darling, don't you hanker after Ardbreen at all?' he asked presently.

'Hardly ever,' she admitted. 'Of course I miss you—miss you all—dreadfully. But it's still awfully exciting. I love walking down certain streets and looking into shop windows and saying to myself—this is me, Paddy O'Malley Renvyle and I'm not in Ardbreen. I'm walking down Bond Street, London, and I'm going right into Fortnum & Mason's to buy something which I could easily buy in Kensington but I choose to go to Fortnum & Mason. And I'm acting in a London production, acting, acting, me. Paddy. I'm fascinated by myself and my present life.'

He watched her as she was speaking and noticed how her eyes sparkled and how the Irish inflection had returned to her speech.

'It's the stage that has beglamoured you, I'm thinking,' he said.

After a pause she answered. 'And I'm not altogether sure it's only that. For I don't believe I'd be feeling all that excited in Dublin. But I've fallen in love with London.'

'I don't think it's London. I think it's the theatre. And you've been lucky. I wonder how it would have struck you if you were still playing your original part, and still living at the club and—'

'But I'm not. And I haven't got all that imagination. Darling, let's pay the bill and go.'

That night, as he held her close to him, Micky Renvyle thought that perhaps their enforced absence apart had after all proved a blessing, for Paddy was very sweet to him, and it seemed that their love-making was more adult than it had been in the past, that perhaps both of them had grown older, and he had a feeling that Paddy's need for him was as great as his for her, though he could not bring himself to ask this.

It was a week of great happiness to them both. He was to remember for a long time the almost shocked surprise he felt when for the first time he went to the play and watched her act. After a while he ceased to look upon the girl she was portraying as his wife, that she was an Irish girl who had never been on the stage in her life. He went into the bar during the second interval and heard someone say, 'This O'Malley girl is a find. They say it's the first time she's ever done anything!' His amazement and admiration for her grew during the third and last act and when he went to fetch her afterwards he felt hopelessly inadequate and tongue-tied.

'What did you think of it?' Paddy asked. Micky knew she meant, 'What did you think of me?'

'Go on—don't mind me,' Sue Martyn said, wiping the make-up from her face.

'I thought you were absolutely splendid, darling,' he said finally. 'Frankly I'm dumbfounded.'

Paddy made as if to kiss him. 'That's all right then,' was all she said.

He was rather silent on the way back to the hotel, and when she asked him the reason he admitted that he felt bewildered not only by her talent which had surprised him, but by what it might mean to their future.

'I'll just have to be two people,' she said gaily. 'I'll be Paddy O'Malley some of the time and Mrs Michael Renvyle when I'm with you, my darling.'

'See to it that Miss O'Malley doesn't oust Mrs Renvyle completely. That's what's worrying me, and you know it.'

She kissed him. 'I love you, you know that. I think we'll be the Renvyles while you're here, and I suggest you don't come to the theatre again. You can show me all the bits of London I haven't yet discovered and which you did when you were at the Slade.'

Micky never told her that on two different occasions he had slipped into the pit and watched the play. He knew he was falling in love more deeply with his wife than he had been when they had got married and it was a hateful thought that in a few days he would have to return to Ireland.

'Have you done anything about calling up your publisher and telling him you're in London?'

Micky admitted he had not.

'Well, I should if I were you. I must have my hair done sometime today, so try to see him.'

Although Renvyle and Geoffrey Edwards had corresponded throughout the years the firm had been publishing his books, it was the first time the two men had met. Edwards took to the younger man and invited him to dine at his house in Hampstead and to meet his wife.

'I've seen your wife's play,' he said during the course of conversation, 'and I only wish she had been able to come with you. How delightful she is in it! You must be very proud of her.'

Micky found himself telling the other man of the doubts he had for their future.

'Luckily for you, though, you have your own work to keep you fully occupied,' Edwards said.

He watched Renvyle with interest as he crossed the room. A man somewhere in the late twenties he supposed, tall, lanky, bespectacled. A sensitive mouth, clean-shaven, and behind the spectacles blue eyes that had the blind expression of the shortsighted. He stooped slightly as he walked, as if accustomed to beamed ceilings which might crack open his head. When he smiled he looked like a schoolboy, but the seriousness of his expression somehow precluded many smiles, which Edwards thought a pity.

Paddy took her husband along one morning to the flat in Kensington which she shared with Sue Martyn.

'I must get one or two things. Clothes, I mean,' she remarked one morning. 'And you can come along too and see the flat. Then you'll be able to tell them at home what it's like. Not the squalid pigsty Aunt Cathleen imagines.'

Micky was relieved to find that though very small the flat was charming. Indeed, living as he did in Ardbreen, the place seemed almost luxurious with its fridge, television and a lift; and electric fires in the two bedrooms.

'Isn't it a fascinating kitchen?' Paddy said, pointing out the various electrical equipments which were unobtainable as far as his own home was concerned.

'Sue is obviously out, so I'll show you her room.'

He looked at what was obviously the bigger of the rooms, where there was a large double bed which had been left unmade by its occupant. Clothes were littered about the place and the light which had been left on above the dressing-table revealed layers of powder, a half-smoked cigarette, and scattered sham jewellery.

'I suppose she overslept and then made a dash for it,' Paddy said. 'She's terribly untidy, but has a heart of gold.'

She peeped into the bathroom.

'Worse,' she remarked. 'But have a peep because when it's clean it's "something". Smells delicious, anyway. Mrs Simpkins —that's our daily—does what she can when she comes every morning,' Paddy told him, 'and just leaves what's beyond her. Obviously Sue had a night of it. See how nice my little room is, wee tho' it is.'

Mick peered round the door.

'Darling,' he kissed the top of her head, 'it's like a schoolgirl's. Very sweet, and I may say a darn sight tidier than yours at home ever is.'

She smiled. 'I don't have so much to do here, no husband, no child, and we share the cooking. And we have Mrs Simpkins. Go into the drawing-room and have a cigarette while I collect what I want in here. And pour yourself out a drink if you want one. There's gin I know, and probably whisky.'

He wandered about the sitting-room, admiring the few pieces of antique furniture, and bits of china, and looked at the pictures

48

hanging on the walls—Guardi and Canaletto reproductions of Venice—and on the untidy desk was the photograph of a man with a face that was somehow familiar to him.

Paddy came in, wearing a different hat and another coat. 'That's better,' she said, helping herself to a gin and tonic.

'You know who that is, don't you?' she asked, seeing him looking at the photograph, and naming a film actor. 'He's her thing at the moment.'

'Oh?'

'They're having a wild *affaire*. She says it won't last, hers never do, or so she tells me.'

'Can't she marry him?'

'He's married. I expect that's the reason for the unmade bed.'

Micky Renvyle felt at a loss. 'D'you mean he comes here? They sleep here—together?'

'Don't look so shocked! No, he has never been here for a whole session, not since I've been here, but she goes off for week-ends. Brighton and that sort of thing. And very often he comes here after the play if he's not filming and has a bit of supper. I push off to my virginal little room tactfully. I'm a good sleeper as you know, so I haven't a clue what time he departs. I dare say they don't indulge in fun and games.'

This was a completely new Paddy, and she realized by her husband's surprised look that her words had taken him aback.

'Don't worry about me, sweetie,' she said, kissing him. 'I'm old enough to take care of myself.'

'I wonder if you are,' her husband replied dryly.

'Don't be silly.'

There was a pause and he said, 'I wonder what Father Delaney would think.'

'I guess he'd know I'm not the sort to be led astray. He's been my confessor—and yours—for as long as we both remember.'

He put his arm round her. 'Sweetheart,' he said, 'I'm not afraid of you getting involved with someone else. It's not that. It's just that I find all this—' he looked about him, smelling the scent-laden air which wafted from the bathroom, indicated the man's photograph and she knew he was thinking of the unmade double bed and its implications—'isn't you. I'm surprised you fit into it and enjoy it. I couldn't.'

She looked at him.

'There's always an alternative,' she said.

'Which is?'

'That you uproot yourself, and come to London. I often wish you would. I believe you think I don't miss you, that I'm so wrapped up in my work that I don't think of you and Killary. It's not true. I'd be so happy, really so happy, if I had you both with me over here. Darling,' she went up to him and put her arms round his neck and brought his face to hers, 'will you think about it? Seriously? We could find a little house somewhere if you don't like flats. Then,' she laughed mischievously, 'I could eat my cake and have it.'

The party at the flat on the Saturday night which Renvyle was dreading turned out to be a very mild and well-behaved affair. The evening passed pleasantly and Renvyle admitted to Paddy in the taxi afterwards that at no time had there been anything said to which either Miss O'Malley or Father Delaney could have taken exception.

'After all,' said Paddy in bed later, 'just because Sue's language gets a bit lurid don't forget that there's plenty to blush at in the bars at home.'

'I know, love, but you don't happen to frequent Irish bars, not that sort anyway. But I dare say I'm a fool and merely jealous of whatever it is that takes you away.'

'Then come over and let's start a home together here,' she said sleepily.

On the Sunday she took him to Mass at the Oratory, and to Benediction at the Church of the Immaculate Conception in Farm Street. He felt very near her, and when they came out he was happy when she said:

'This is where I come to Confession always.'

'I shall tell Father Delaney. May I?'

'Of course.'

He was to fly back to Ireland after dinner which they had together at the airport.

'It's awfully like being sent back to school,' he remarked.

'Tell me you've enjoyed it though,' she said.

'You know I have. I still can't get over you—as an actress, I mean. It staggered me. I feel I don't deserve to have such a lovely wife, but you are my wife and I want you.'

She held his hand under the table.

'Then come back. And bring our Killary.'

CHAPTER FIVE

For days after Micky's return home he was in a turmoil. The relief he found in the peace and quiet of Ardbreen at first made up for the void of Paddy's absence. In the day-time he made himself go for long walks in order to satisfy and realize to the full what the country meant to him. But subconsciously the vision of Paddy kept appearing and his need for her grew and he felt his very soul being torn between desire for the normal life he knew they should be leading and the horror he had for life led in a city.

Paddy had sent toys back to Killary, including a giant panda which she refused to be parted from, and Micky was again worried by the child's sudden reawakened interest and wish for her mother.

'I want to see Mummie,' she kept reiterating after being given the panda and he was slightly nonplussed by the evening prayers in which Paddy's name kept appearing. 'God bless Daddy and Mummie and Panda—and Mummie—and Auntie Leen and Mummie and—and—Pedro and Mummie . . .'

Christmas was only three weeks away and when her father asked Killary what she wanted Father Christmas to bring her she said after a minute or two's thought, 'Mummie.'

This sudden longing for Paddy did not seem normal to Micky and he tried to disassociate the child's mind from her mother where in the past he had done his best to keep her picture fresh in the child's memory. On Christmas Day they went to the O'Malleys, and when Killary was resting Micky broached to his father-in-law the idea of uprooting himself and Killary.

'I think you should,' the older man said without hesitation. 'It looks as if this play of Paddy's will run for some time yet. And that's not all. I can see by the letters she writes home that her heart is in the theatre—'

'You don't think it's just the newness of the life which appeals and that it'll wear off?' Micky interrupted.

'That could be, of course. But I still think that you'd be wise to join her, and take Killary with you. It isn't right for man and wife to lead separate lives.'

'Indeed it isn't,' Miss O'Malley joined in, 'not that I think Paddy would ever be led astray by bad companions, but as my brother says it isn't right. Besides,' and she looked at Micky with slight disapproval, 'the girl has said several times she misses the two of you, and it's my idea she thinks it's only your own dislike for town life that's keeping you apart.'

Early in the New Year Renvyle wrote to his wife saying that if she could find a little house somewhere or a flat, he and Killary would join her in London. His letter was received with apparent pleasure and Paddy wrote that she would at once set about finding somewhere for them to settle. A few weeks later a letter came telling him that she had taken a furnished maisonnette in St John's Wood.

'Shall we go and stay with Mummie?' Micky asked his daughter, and felt his heart contract at the child's excitement which greeted his question.

He was soon aware that his decision to join Paddy met with approval on all sides. The priest came to bid him good-bye the day before he left.

'It's the right thing you're doing,' he told Micky, 'you'll not regret it.'

'I wonder how Killary will fare,' Mick replied. 'She's never known any home but Ardbreen where she's been as free as a bird. She'll be surprised when she can't wander out of a house at random.'

'She's young enough to transplant.'

'Don't use that word, Father, it sounds too final.'

Father Delaney looked at him. 'Other people have had to move from the land they love, you know.'

'Oh, I know. I dare say I've been damn self-centred. And, as Paddy frequently says in letters, I should be able to write anywhere. But that's the point, rather. Can I?'

'Why not?'

'I'm not a novelist. You know that. I write about birds; hills; Ireland; boats. And my books are illustrated with my own drawings, you remember? I'm terrified at finding myself a real fish out of water.'

'But, my dear boy, you studied in London for a time.'

'That was very different. I'm a married man now, I've got to earn enough to keep us.'

'Doesn't Paddy—'

Micky quickly interrupted the priest. 'That's a thing I can't allow. Taking her money. That was what you were going to say, wasn't it? Well, I won't. She has been keeping herself in London, that was inevitable, but I'm darned if she's going to keep me. Thank God, Edwards is pleased with my new book—short stories—and they're doing a book of water-colours I've done of birds, rather lovely though I say it myself, so with the advance for these we're all right for the time being. And if Paddy wants us to be in England with her I shall try and let the house during the summer.'

'I know she is happy to have you both joining her,' the priest said. 'At heart she's missed her family—and Ardbreen—whatever you may think.'

For the first few weeks the Renvyles' life was happy enough. The maisonnette Paddy had found was in a quiet road near enough to Regent's Park to take Killary for daily walks, and there was a little garden at the back which was full of crocuses when Micky arrived.

'I've got such a surprise for you,' Paddy said the day after their arrival. 'Do you see that little car standing outside the house?'

'M'm. I was wondering what it was doing there.'

'It's mine.' She laughed. 'I've been learning to drive since I came to England, but I didn't tell you in case I had to admit defeat. But I've passed my test, two weeks ago. And I bought that little car on the instalment system.'

'Well, I'm blowed!'

'Can we go for a drive?' Killary asked.

'Yes, darling, we'll go up to Hampstead, and you can have a lovely scamper on the heath.'

As Renvyle had expected, Paddy enjoyed entertaining and being entertained, and he soon found that the Sunday evenings which he had fondly hoped to spend alone with her were more than often spent in the company of other people. Theatrical hours too were different from those to which he was accustomed, and after a few weeks he found it easier to move into the spare room in order that Paddy should sleep late in the mornings. Except for matinée days Paddy was at home till she went to the theatre in the evenings, and she liked to have a meal before she left the house, and a rest. It was all rather different from the week which they had spent together in the autumn, but Renvyle did his best to adjust himself. He did his own work in the evenings when he was undisturbed, and this was no hardship, but he found the days frustrating and felt that he would never be able to settle in London—or in any city. He wondered if later on it would be any use suggesting to Paddy that they moved out into Surrey or Berkshire, somewhere from where she could get up easily to London in time to act and be able to return each night. The idea was doomed before he put it to her when she was discussing some people they had met out at supper, one of whom, a business-man, came up from Essex daily.

'Ghastly, I don't know how people do it,' she remarked later. 'And as to living in the country when one's playing . . . it would kill me. A week-end cottage, that I understand. But not the other.'

It was with some consternation that he learnt quite by chance that Paddy had signed a contract with the management.

'What does that mean exactly?' he asked.

'That I'm going to be in the next play at the Grand, too,' she said.

His heart sank. 'You might have warned me.'

She looked at him in surprise. 'It never struck me to. I'm jolly lucky, you should be proud of me.'

'Is the play coming off, then?'

'I shouldn't think it'd run much longer. Spike thinks the notice will go up any time. And he says there's a lovely part in the next production for me.'

She noticed his silence.

'You don't mind, do you?'

'I hoped you'd come home,' he said.

'I see.' Then, 'Of course if I get any time off we'll dash back, but I expect it'll just mean rehearsing and going straight into the new play. Still, nothing's decided yet, so I shouldn't get het up, sweetie.'

A week or two later she said to Micky, 'There's such a nice little school only two roads away from here. I've often watched the children on walks, and I believe Killary would be much happier if she went to it next term. Actually I believe she'll have to start school anyway. Shall we go and interview the people?'

'Isn't there any near-by convent?' he asked. 'I don't much care for the idea of an ordinary school.'

'I suppose you're right. But in any case we must do something about it.'

Renvyle was often surprised how quickly Killary had settled down into her new life.

'Do you like living here?' he asked her one day.

'Yes. I like it 'cos Mummie's here.'

'Which do you like best, London or Ardbreen?'

'I like London and I like Ardbreen,' was the inconclusive reply.

Sometimes Renvyle took the child down to the theatre to fetch Paddy after a matinée, where of course Killary was made a great fuss of in the dressing-room.

'Can I act?' she said when she saw some of the actors with their make-up on, and she was allowed to go on to the empty stage. 'Look, I'm acting,' she said, and began pirouetting about the place with grease-paint planted haphazard about her face.

But it was the Zoo that gave her most pleasure and Micky began to make a habit of taking her along there on his wife's matinée afternoons.

'You ought to learn to drive the car,' Paddy said one Sunday when they were coming back from a day spent with friends of hers on the river.

'What's the point? I don't feel we—I'll ever have one.'

'Don't be so glum. My goodness me! What a difference it would make at home. Think of all the places we could go to. Besides, it looks so silly for a man to be driven by a woman. A man as young as you are.'

'All right, my dear, I'll learn to drive it, if that's what you want.'

Renvyle was mapping out a chapter in his mind, and was unaware of the look Paddy bestowed upon him.

He got on quite well with Paddy's friends, some of whom considered him dull, but Spike Piers occasionally asked him to play golf—at which Micky did not shine—or to go to a football match; and sometimes he would look up people he had known in London during the days he was studying at the Slade. They were mostly young men, still unmarried, and Micky found he no longer had much in common with any of them. Paddy asked him to invite a few to drinks one Sunday, but it was not a success.

In May the notice of the play went up, but any hope Renvyle had of getting his wife back to Ardbreen was negligible.

'I'll be rehearsing all the time, darling. *Hopeless*. Do try and understand.'

Rehearsals started before the play finished, which meant Micky saw less of her than ever, and with Killary at school and his work not going as he wished, his nerves began to wear thin. London was looking lovely, the parks were in their full glory of flowering chestnuts, lilacs and pink May, and beds full of tulips, but Micky was astounded when Paddy said one day:

'Isn't it all too glorious? Have you ever seen anything more beautiful?'

'Ardbreen, Kylemore and Leenane,' he said shortly.

'How you hate it,' she said slowly.

He was silent.

'Why don't you go back?' she asked him.

'Because I love you.'

'You loved what I was. The person I used to be. I wonder if you really love the person I am, and am becoming.'

'Does all this mean so much to you, then?'

'If you mean acting, a career—yes, it does.'

'I feel I'm losing you.'

'You're not being very clever in the way you're trying to keep me.'

'I'm sorry. It's just that I don't understand your complete infatuation—for that's what it seems to me to be—for London. Frankly it stifles me. And you and I were brought up on the same bog and I'm bewildered.'

'I always said you were in love with Ardbreen. I suppose you go to sleep thinking of Altnagaighira and Garraun, and your precious Twelve Pins.'

'Sometimes they seem nearer to me than you do.'

They walked on in silence, and Killary who was riding a tricycle kept turning and re-turning and finally drove into Paddy.

'Oh, do look where you're going, Killary!' Her mother spoke sharply, and unaccustomed to the tone of voice the child's lip quivered. Micky felt his heart contract, she looked so bereft.

'It's all right, darling.'

'Mummie was cross,' she said, her lip going down farther.

'No, I wasn't. Only you must learn to drive that thing properly and not barge into people. What would happen if I did that in the car?'

Somewhat mollified, Killary returned to the tricycle.

'Don't let's drift,' Paddy said lightly, putting her arm through Renvyle's. 'It would be so easy to, and I should hate that.'

That she could so easily voice the thought that he did his best to hide, was a shock in itself.

'I wish we had dear old Father Delaney near at hand, to knock some sense into both of us,' he said.

'That shouldn't be necessary.'

And presently she spoke again. 'I suppose we're both of us being selfish. But I think I'm the less to blame.'

'That's what I meant when I said I wished the dear old Father were here. One needs a knowing friend, not just a priest to confess to.'

'I can't see that our problem is confessable—if one can coin such a word.'

'No. But selfishness is. And who's to say if we are—either of us—being selfish.'

'As I see it, Mick, we want our own careers in the place where these careers come most easy. And it may mean separation. Oh, don't look so horrified,' for she had caught a glimpse of his expression, 'I don't mean a legal one. Merely that perhaps you'd be happier and work better if you went home. You wouldn't expect me to give up a career in what I have—it seems—every chance of making a success?'

'No—I suppose not,' he sounded half-hearted, 'but suppose this new play doesn't catch on? And that you find yourself without a play to go into?'

'Let's cross our bridges when we come to them, shall we? Besides, there are films.'

'It is so utterly different from what I'd expected, our life here,' Renvyle began.

'Darling, you really can't import Ardbreen to London, you know.' She laughed impatiently. 'Sometimes you don't show the sense Killary has. Why can't you be like her? Look how well she's settled down.'

'I'm not a five-year-old child,' he said.

'Sometimes you behave like one.'

'And if I do go back to Ireland, what about her? Killary, I mean.'

'Killary can remain with me.'

'In that case you must have a nurse or someone reliable living in the house.'

'What a bore. But I dare say that Aunt Cathleen might know of someone at home who might like to come over to the bright lights of London. One of the O'Briens perhaps.'

That night he sat for a while on the side of his wife's bed, while she read through letters which had come by the evening post.

59

'One from Dad, if you'd like to read it,' she said and gave it to him. 'There's nothing much in it.'

But the local news, little enough as there was, only brought the nostalgia for Ardbreen back worse.

'Should I disturb your night if I sleep in here?' he asked.

'No, of course not. But I warn you I'm awfully sleepy,' and she yawned. She turned out the bedside light. He started to take her in his arms, but she was utterly unresponsive and after an hour or more of desire which was obviously not going to be gratified he went to his own room.

Another three weeks passed, without any decision being taken by Renvyle.

'Do I come to your opening night?' he asked diffidently one morning, as he was reading the paper.

'But of course. Would you like to bring your publisher? You can't sit all by yourself. Too dreary. Besides you owe him an outing or so, you've been up there several times and we've never had them here.'

'I'd like that,' he answered.

'Very well. I'll see about the seats.'

'Is Sue in the new play?' he asked one day.

'No, nothing for her.'

Renvyle learnt that there were only two women's parts in the new play; both very important, it seemed. One to be taken by an elderly actress, much beloved by the English public, and the other by Paddy.

'Aren't you nervous?' he asked on the evening.

'I suppose I'd be lying if I said I wasn't. But it's very exciting. Like doing a solo flight across the Atlantic for the first time.'

'You can hardly meet your death,' he teased.

'If I were rotten in the part—or the critics thought so—it could easily be the death-knell of my stage career.'

Paddy had been very non-committal and secretive about the new play and Renvyle was unprepared for the importance of her part. Geoffrey Edwards, whom he took with him, had nothing but admiration and praise for Paddy, and after the curtain fell at the end of the second act in which she had played an exacting and dramatic scene, she received an ovation. In the entr'acte that followed the two men went into the bar and Micky heard his wife's name on everyone's lips.

At the end of the play when the author came on to take a call, holding both actresses by the hand, the gallery called for 'Paddy, Paddy O'Malley'.

In the dressing-room, where Micky repaired with Edwards, he was astonished to see the amount of flowers and telegrams, and he realized his own flowers looked rather meagre beside some of the other tributes. People came crowding into the room, some of whom he knew, and plenty he did not.

'Darling, I'm afraid we can't go and have a little cosy supper such as you'd hoped. Spike expects m-us,' she quickly changed the word, 'at the Savoy.'

At the party Paddy was the star of the evening, it seemed to her husband. He longed to sit beside her, to tell her in his own words how wonderful he now thought her, but he never seemed to be able to get near her. He noticed her eyes were very bright, and he noticed too that she was drinking more champagne than was usual.

'Darling,' she said, when the party split up, 'Spike wants us to go on somewhere. But I'm thinking of Mrs Brownlow, we can't expect her to sit in for hours. It's gone midnight already. Would you mind terribly going home, and leaving me to go on? Someone will bring me back. You don't have to worry.'

He noticed the face of the woman he had been sitting next to and whose name he had not caught.

'Our small daughter,' he explained. 'We managed to find a sitter-in for the evening, but my wife thinks she'll have had enough by now.'

The woman nodded sympathetically. 'What a shame,' she said. 'And do you both have to go back at this early stage of the evening?'

'Heavens no!' Paddy smiled happily. 'I'm not. Well, good night darling, God bless. I'll try not to wake you when I get in.'

CHAPTER SIX

I

RENVYLE had been home more than a week before he saw anyone. The blind misery he had felt surge within him had abated and he tried to consider rationally the situation. He even wondered whether the impulse which had driven him to leave his wife and child was ridiculous, and whether he had in fact behaved childishly as Paddy had taunted him. It was when he was mending a fishing-net on the isolated bay that lay below the cottage in which he had begun married life and which he still owned, that he heard someone call his name and looking up saw the priest.

'Mick! God bless my soul! Or are m'eyes deceiving me? You rascal, when did you return and no one telling me?'

Renvyle put down the net, and slowly climbed up the bank to where Father Delaney was standing.

'It's good to see you.' he said. 'Forgive me, but I've been a bear with a sore head and seen nobody.'

'Are you alone? No Paddy, no Killary?' the priest asked.

'Paddy's acting, I expect you know she has made a big personal success. Killary is with her.' He took out a cigarette and lit it.

'And do you want to tell me why you have come home?'

'Come into the cottage, Father.' Noticing the priest's look of surprise he said, 'There wasn't much point going to the bigger place. It's let for two months in a few weeks' time, and anyway I was always happier in the cottage. Good thing it was empty.'

He led the way, and poured out a Guinness for each of them.

'It's been a failure,' he said in answer to the priest's questioning expression. 'I don't know whose the fault is.'

'Tell me.'

So Micky slowly described the life which he had been living for the last few months with Paddy.

'I dare say I should have tried to stick it,' he continued. 'Probably I'm wet. But something hit me between the eyes when she went off to that party after her opening night. I felt I was a complete drag on her, that I was there out of—pity—if you like.'

'Are you not dramatizing this situation, my son? Exaggerating the difficulties of what this new life meant to you?'

'I don't think so,' Micky sighed. 'Paddy has changed. I can't expect you to believe me, unless you saw her with your own eyes. Her whole life—all her interests—lie in the theatre. And in her career.'

'Yet you left the child in her care?'

Renvyle paused before replying.

'Killary is deeply attached to her mother,' he said, 'and I frankly didn't think it right to bring her away with me. Besides, Paddy loves her, and it would be wrong to give you the impression she neglects her. She doesn't, and Killary is now in a little school where she seems happy. I think a little girl should be with her mother.'

Presently the priest said: 'What are the people like with whom Paddy mixes?'

'I suppose they're not a bad lot taken as a whole. They're utterly unlike the types I'd have thought she would care for, but then, bless her, how can one judge? She married me when she was nineteen, had never been anywhere, and I suppose she finds them amusing. Some of 'em drink, but so do a lot of us round here, so we can't damn that. Their language is pretty lurid – I'm talking of the women mostly – but Paddy doesn't swear or use bad language – a lot of them lead immoral lives, and she seems to be vastly amused by the whole atmosphere. Maybe I sound the devil of a prig, but Paddy was divinely pure and innocent, and although nothing has touched her personally it's as if she'd been soiled by the dust of others. If you can understand me.'

'Did you try to help her?'

63

Micky looked surprised. 'Help her?'

'People who are being influenced in the wrong direction can often be brought back by gentleness and tact. Do you think you nagged or too openly showed disapproval? Paddy is mettlesome, headstrong, I can believe she would not react to what she might consider mere disapproval of her friends. She is still young, Mick – you both are.'

'I don't think I nagged. I felt she despised me.'

'I cannot believe that.'

'I hope I was wrong. I still love her and long for the life we used to live. But she did not seem particularly distressed when I told her I was coming back to Ardbreen. I think she was relieved.'

'Have you seen your father-in-law or Miss O'Malley?'

'No. I've not felt like seeing anyone.'

'Rather cowardly, Mick?'

'I suppose you could say that. I feel a failure. I mean it does sound—and seem—weak not to be able to do my own stuff away from here. But I couldn't, you know. It was hellishly frustrating.'

'And you were perhaps a little jealous of Paddy's success?'

'I don't think so,' Micky said slowly. 'No, I was proud of her. And she was wonderful. Gosh, Father, I wish you could see her! Ah well, you will pray for the pair of us, I know.'

He was a little surprised when he received a note from John O'Malley in which his father-in-law said he heard he had returned to work better in Ireland, and that he hoped he would go to lunch or supper so that he and his sister could have first-hand news of Paddy and the child. He went to the house two days later, feeling a trifle diffident. It was obvious Paddy had written home, and he wondered what she had said. No mention was made of any quarrel or unpleasant scenes, and Micky began to wonder if Paddy was deliberately misleading her father – and herself – as to the reason he had returned.

Ten days passed before Micky himself received a letter from his wife, and when he read it he was amazed at its calm and friendly tone. No allusion was made to the sudden outburst of his which had followed the party after the first night of the play, of which he now felt ashamed. It was a friendly letter, but the letter of a sister, he thought. She wrote of Killary, and of how the play was doing, but it was none the less extraordinarily impersonal.

Getting the letter, and those which continued to follow at intervals, gradually caused Renvyle to adopt a more settled frame of mind. He began to grow used to living alone, and he started to pursue a steady routine in his daily life. He missed Paddy still, but had to admit that it was the Paddy he had first married, rather than the new and more attractive woman she had become, that he longed for. It was true that the new Paddy was infinitely desirable, but desire must be mutual, and he now had come to the hurtful conclusion that the only thing his wife cared about was her career. He started to write again, and found to his surprise that he was working better than he had for months past, and in the long summer days that followed one upon another he sailed in *Deirdre* to the islands and painted. A new freedom seemed to inspire him, and the portraits of people on Achill and hitherto unknown parts of Sligo filled him with a fresh contentment in his own work. There were times when he worried over Killary, feeling that the child should be at home by the sea instead of spending the holidays in London, but he did not wish to upset Paddy, and her father and aunt appeared to have news of the child's steady progress and good health. Summer turned to autumn and Renvyle spent a greater part of the days now painting. He had no car, and had no particular wish for one, preferring to walk with his equipment on his back, and spending nights in village pubs and hostels in districts he had not been to since his marriage. He wrote to Paddy describing the wild and strange scenery near Mannin Bay and how he had trekked the road from Clifden to Roundstone, and he sent little water-colour sketches of the loveliness of it all, the derelict ruins, the walls of ochre-coloured seaweed, the seeming multitudes of unvisited lakes.

'It's a strange bit, Paddy, I'd forgotten how strange. You and I never came here together, and beautiful as it is, our own part is by far the loveliest. I hope if the good weather continues to do the whole round on foot, returning up the Kylemore Valley where I shall try and do some good mountain scenes. The Twelve Pins are looking their best and I may do some climbs. I've a feeling a walk up the Glencoaghan valley between Derryclare and Benbreen would be wonderful, and if I can continue over Bencollaghduff back down into the Kylemore Valley road I should achieve one of my life's ambitions. The views from the tops should be unbelievable, and if I can get even rough sketches with a quick colour wash I'll be able to do some decent pictures when I get back. If I can get enough pictures finished there's every chance of my having a show in Dublin in the spring.'

Even Paddy's lack of enthusiasm and the little interest she showed in her letters for his work no longer discouraged him. When Christmas came he wrote that he would come over to spend it with them both, he wished to see Edwards, his publisher, but that in any case it was a time for families to be together, and the fact that she would be playing only served to make him realize Killary should have her father with her.

'It sounded a bit pompous, Father,' he told the priest, 'but perhaps it would be as well if Paddy realized I feel my responsibilities as a parent. Imagine that poor little brat on an English Boxing Day with no one to take her to a pantomime or circus because her mother's playing.'

Paddy appeared to be genuinely pleased to see him when he arrived, and Killary was overjoyed.

'My goodness, my darling, what a big girl you are!' he said, and she dragged him upstairs to say her evening prayers to him.

'I want to say my prayers to Daddy, to Daddy,' she kept calling.

He asked her if she went to Mass regularly.

'We always do. In the car. And I have a new lace thing to put on my head. Like Mummie's, but mine's white. And sometimes I have a candle, and do you know who I burn it for?'

She looked at him very seriously with her eyes getting bigger. 'For YOU. And I burn it under the statue of Our Lady. She's very pretty, you know. Has a blue dress.'

On Christmas Eve Paddy told Micky she would be back in time to go to midnight Mass with him, and as they knelt together and received the Blessed Sacrament he felt nearer his wife than he had for many months. He felt a flood of protective love sweep over him, and on their way home in a taxi, holding her hand, he began to visualize once more the possibility of remaining with his family; even with the sacrifice it would mean of uprooting himself from Ardbreen. The two weeks went by peacefully; Paddy and he together took Killary to the Circus and to *Peter Pan,* and on Boxing Day when she had her own matinée Micky took the child to a pantomime. He was relieved to discover from Killary herself that she was very happy in her school, but when the child said at lunch one day: 'Why doesn't Daddy live with us in London?' and Paddy answered her with: 'Because he likes Ardbreen better than us,' he quickly denied it.

'Don't you believe that, sweetheart,' he said to Killary. 'Mummie's teasing you. And what would you say, my dear,' he turned to Paddy, 'if I fell in with her suggestion?'

She was surprised, but shrugged her shoulders. 'Would it work any better than it did last time?' she asked. 'You wrote happy letters from Ardbreen. You don't really miss us. Besides, I may be going to do a film, which means I shall hardly be at home.'

'Oh!'

He saw, regretfully, that his idea meant nothing to her. If anything it seemed to have irritated her, he saw her brow contract, which was a habit of hers if she was impatient. Yet, during the past two weeks they had lived normally as husband and wife, and he had thought his love had been reciprocated.

'I don't think our marriage is working out as your father—and others, myself included—hoped,' he said the day before he was due to leave for Ireland.

'Oh, Mick, do we have to go over all this again?' she said with a bored air.

'I do try to understand how you feel about this life of yours,' Renvyle said, 'but at the same time, when we married we took each other on in the stations of life we then were in, so to speak, and we were both happy.'

'That's a silly argument, you know. What if you'd won a sweepstake or a football pool and made thousands? I suppose you'll tell me you'd have been content to go on in just the same humdrum way,' and she shrugged her shoulders.

'Our religion—' he began.

'You can't accuse me of neglecting my faith,' Paddy cut in.

'And I'm not so sure of that,' he replied shortly.

His wife looked at him strangely and said nothing.

'If the play's still running at Easter I shall come over and collect Killary for the holidays. It's nearly a year since she was at home, and I'm not going to have her forget the place. Besides, your father and Aunt Cathleen long to see her.'

She came to the airport to see him off, bringing Killary with her.

'I'd like to go in an airplane,' the child said. 'Can I go with Daddy?' She turned to her mother.

'What! And leave me?' Paddy said, pretending to be hurt. The child looked nonplussed and bewildered.

'Next holidays I'll come and fetch you and we'll go in an airplane and if Mummie's not acting she will come too.'

This idea pleased the child, and when he had kissed them both before boarding the plane Renvyle felt more sure of the future, for Paddy had kissed him with more warmth than she had for several days and said, 'Silly old boyo, aren't you? Never mind, we love each other really.'

'Is that true? Do you still love me?'

Her eyes opened and she replied, 'But of course I do. And you know it too, and just pretend these foolish notions to suit your own convenience.'

Once again he knew the visit had unsettled him, but Geoffrey Edwards had been pleased with the new book, although admittedly his advance was small. On arrival in Dublin he went along to see the man who was arranging the show of his pictures, a two-man show it was to be, and by the time he returned to Ardbreen he began to cease worrying.

In Lent Father Delaney suggested he should go into retreat, something he had never done, and the secluded peace of the monastery restored much of Renvyle's own peace of mind. But a letter from Paddy on his return distressed him, for he realized that even where their religion was concerned they had grown apart. He was determined, however, not to be unduly depressed, and when he next wrote to his wife it was merely to tell her of the plans he was making to collect Killary for the holidays.

When he went to London in April he realized a distinct change in Paddy's attitude; she was definitely cool, and there was no question of their sleeping together.

'I can't afford to,' she said shortly when he demanded to know the reason.

'What do you mean?'

'You know our religion forbids us to take precautions. Well, last time I did, and a hell of a rocket I got when I went to confession. And I do *not* wish to be caught.'

Renvyle was shocked to the core. This was something that shook the fundamentals of marriage.

'Oh, don't look so hurt,' she cried.

'I'm not hurt. I'm confounded,' he said slowly. 'As for what you call a rocket, I should think you'll get an atom bomb if you tell your confessor that you now refuse to sleep with your husband.'

'Oh, Micky,' she said wearily, 'you really are hopeless. I don't mean that I never will, it's just at this moment I don't wish to.'

'If you asked me to come to you now I'd no longer have any wish to do so.'

'That's all right then,' she said lightly.

It was difficult during the few days he was in London for Micky to behave in his usual manner to Paddy. As a Catholic he had been more shocked than hurt by her words, but the fact that after nearly three months' absence she could so cruelly deny him the right he had not even asked for, shattered his love. He was relieved when the morning for departure came and Killary helped everything by being childishly excited.

During the child's visit Renvyle was careful not to play on her emotions, and when one day she told him she wanted to stay at Ardbreen and not go back to London, he pretended not to hear.

'Daddy, did you hear me?'

He looked at her over his spectacles.

'M'm?'

'Please let me stay with you.'

'Why? You know you love your school and being with Mummie.'

'London hasn't got any sea, or donkeys, and I'm not allowed to play by myself outside the house. There's not any sand. It's just roads.'

'Regent's Park is very pretty.'

'Please, Daddy.'

He felt inadequate and hopeless, the more so as he would dearly like to keep the child with him.

'I'll tell you what,' he answered, 'you go back this time and next holidays we'll ask Mummie to let you stay much longer.'

'Why can't Mummie come home?' she asked, and kicked his chair aimlessly several times.

'Because she has to act.'

'Nobody else's Mummie does,' she said pathetically, and Micky remembered a time when the child was a tiny baby and Paddy had reiterated her ardent wish for the child to know, to the full, parental love with plenty of kisses. She cheered up when the day came for him to take her back to England and Paddy was at the airport to meet them.

'How long are you staying this time?' she asked before going to the theatre. 'Your letters don't say.'

'That depends on you and how much I'm likely to see of you.'

'I'm fairly free this week,' she said. 'A couple of matinées, a meeting one morning. Sue asked me to lunch one day, but I suppose I can put her off.'

The week seemed interminable to him. There were no scenes, both of them appeared over-polite to each other, but Micky made no attempt to go to her room, though he would take up her breakfast to her in the mornings and they would chat in a desultory fashion over the morning papers and the post.

'I've got to take some people out to supper after the theatre,' she announced one morning. 'Are you coming along?'

'Do you want me to?'

'Yes, of course. It looks so silly if you never go about with me. People will say we don't get on or you've left me or something.'

He was tempted to ask if they wouldn't be right but held his peace.

'Anyway, it's nice to have a man to pay the bill.'

'Thank you!'

'Well, you know what I mean. What's the point of having a husband?'

'I do sometimes wonder.'

III

After he had returned once more to Ireland he realized Paddy had never inquired about the success of the Dublin show and whether he had sold many pictures. And he remembered how on the evening they had taken the people to supper, and he had been asked about his new book, she had immediately turned the subject to other channels so that his own work was dismissed. It had not penetrated his mind at the time, but on looking back now it struck him as being strange.

It was in July that he received the letter which told him she was going to America. Apparently the play was to open in the fall ('Why can't she say autumn?' Micky thought impatiently) with the London company playing their original parts, so – and the letter went on – 'Killary had better come over to you for the summer holidays and you must make arrangements to keep her and find a school near, or something. I leave it to you. I've told the agency I shan't keep this on, it was furnished as you know and I've not bought much. When I get back I'll have to look for something else. Something smaller as it's obvious you don't intend to live over here ever. I'm looking forward to being in New York tremendously.'

There was no hint of any kind that at the end of the London run Paddy should herself bring the child over and see her father and aunt, neither of whom she had seen for two years.

'I've written to Paddy and given her a piece of my mind,' Miss O'Malley told Renvyle. 'Her father never says anything, but *I* know it's hit him quite hard that she never suggests any meeting. You'd think she might ask him over.'

'Would he care about that?'

'He wouldn't go, but he'd like to be asked. And now, gallivanting off to the United States of America like this without even so much as good-bye . . . I can see it has hurt him. Why can't she fly to Dublin with Killary and we'd go over and meet them and bring her back? It wouldn't be asking much. I've told her so.'

Rather to Renvyle's surprise his wife agreed to this plan. In a letter to him she said she supposed he would accompany her father and aunt, when—she said—she could bid farewell to them all together. Old Mr O'Malley seemed pathetically pleased to think he was going to see his daughter, and wrote off at once to book rooms at the Shelbourne.

'We can bring the child back with us,' he told Renvyle, 'if

you want to go back to England for a few days with Paddy and see her off to America.'

But Micky replied that he knew his wife would be too busy to spend any time with him and he would only get in the way, and his father-in-law did not pursue the subject.

Paddy was in vivacious mood when they met her and had brought presents for her father and her aunt. Renvyle noticed that the old man could not take his eyes off her, and Miss O'Malley whispered to Micky that she was the living spit of her brother's dead wife.

'She always reminded me of her,' she said, 'but there was something lacking before. Paddy's mother had great gaiety, and what the French call "chic" which the girl has developed and now has. She was hard though, that's where Paddy has got it from—I never really cared for her, but my! she was a beauty. She was only twenty-three when she died—having Paddy.'

John O'Malley had booked the rooms at the hotel for two nights, including that preceding his daughter's arrival.

'Killary can sleep in the room Mick had last night,' he told them, 'and I've booked a double for the two of you.'

'Mummie always sleeps by herself,' the child piped up. 'And when Daddy comes to stay he has the other little one, like mine.'

Quickly Renvyle told them Paddy had to sleep on in the mornings, and he could not bear to disturb her.

That night she took them to dine at Jammets and insisted they all drink champagne.

'I'm sorry about this,' Micky said when they finally went to bed.

'Don't be an old silly,' she said. 'Anyone would think I'm an iceberg. I'm not, you know.'

Micky looked at her and wondered at the unaccountability of women.

'Well? Don't you want to come in beside me? You don't know when you'll have the chance again.'

She looked very lovely, but she had killed something in him.

'I thought you no longer loved me,' he said.

73

'Love? Who's talking about love? Come here.'

Renvyle went over to where she lay, knowing he was power-less against her beauty, and against that invitation. In the early hours of the morning as he lay awake he wondered why he despised himself. She was his wife, he had only taken what was his to take, but love had been in neither of their hearts, certainly not in Paddy's. He had used her as he would a beautiful whore, and he felt unclean and, what was infinitely worse, he felt he had wronged both Paddy and himself.

CHAPTER SEVEN

GRADUALLY as the months passed Renvyle's spirit seemed to settle into a calmer channel. This was helped by the unexpected visit to Connemara of an Englishman he had known years ago at the Slade. His name was Egbert Small and Renvyle came across him by chance when one day in October he brought a catch of fish to the hotel.

Suddenly he heard a voice say, 'Renvyle? Mick Renvyle?' and he turned to see Small. Killary was at school all day and, as Egbert Small was alone, they spent many days together.

'I envy you, old Mick,' he said one day as they looked down on the far islands from the top of the track above Kingstown Bay. 'I'd give a lot to paint all this instead of the stuffed aldermen and their rich wives whose faces it seems my fate to put on canvas.'

'At a thousand a time, I hear.'

'Well, yes, I grant you it has compensations,' he laughed. 'But to live in this country, my God! It's enough to inspire a man to paint the Almighty Himself.'

'My wife can't understand I feel that way, which I do.'

It was the first time he had mentioned Paddy.

'Your wife?'

'She's on the English stage. Paddy O'Malley she calls herself. It was her name before we were married.'

'I've seen her. Very lovely. I'd like to paint *her.*'

'She's in the States at the moment.' He started to tell the other man a little about the earlier days. 'Drop in one evening and you'll see our small daughter.'

'And your wife doesn't like this place? You astound me.'

'I used to find it incredible, but I suppose it is possible for a young and beautiful woman to find life in such surroundings

75

dull. Especially if she has made a success on the London stage, which she has.'

A couple of days later Renvyle said: 'I'd like to take you to Leenane. It's on Killary Harbour, a remarkable place I always think. I'd like to know what you think of it.'

Egbert Small picked Micky up in the village. Presently he slowed down and finally stopped the car.

'All this beauty is doing something to me. Where are we?'

'This is the road to Leenane,' Renvyle answered him. 'The mountains on our right are the Maamturks.'

'What's this water we're getting to?'

'That's Killary Harbour.'

'It's magic. What are the mountains across the water?'

'The Mweelreas. We can go through Leenane and take the road round on the other side and go through the pass, on up to Clew Bay.'

They stopped at the hotel for a drink.

'This is the most enchanting place I've ever struck,' Small said.

'I'm glad you think so. Paddy and I spent our honeymoon here.'

'Here? In this hotel?'

Micky nodded.

'And what d'you say this is called?'

'Killary Harbour. My daughter is called Killary after it.'

Small noticed that Micky Renvyle was very silent as they continued the drive. He recognized the other's need for help in some form or other, and sensed Renvyle's inhibited shyness. Somehow they got on to religion.

'I've tried 'em all,' Small said. 'My trouble is that I see the best in some and flaws in all. I suppose as an Irishman you're an old papist?'

Renvyle nodded. He was amused by his companion.

'I even tried that. But I can't conform to rules.'

'One longs to ask advice of priests as men occasionally,' Mick said. 'However, it's almost impossible to forget that they are priests. Sin is sin, and that's easy enough. The confessional

76

and all that. But to talk to a chap one's known all one's life, who is at the same time a priest and one's own confessor, I find it's impossible.'

'What's troubling you?'

'My relations with my wife.'

'You're not the only chap with that one, old boy.'

Micky began to tell Small about the night in Dublin.

'You should go to a psychiatrist,' Small said.

'I don't believe in 'em.'

'Afraid I was pulling your leg! You must be the first man that thinks he's committed mortal sin for making love to his own wife. You're all tied up. It's this blasted religion of yours. Thank God I take bed as it comes but never as sin. One of life's many pleasures. Your trouble, Mick, is that you take all life far too seriously. I can see that. But believe me, no priest can send you to Hell or refuse you absolution because you made love to your wife without love in your heart. How many husbands have, after the first year's bliss has worn off?'

'What an old cynic you are!'

'No, I'm a realist. But I see God in these mountains, in the views you've shown me, and not in priests' holes and a lot of balls talked by your church about so-called morality. My God allows happiness, but your church insists that black is black and white is white, and that's what zips you up and imprisons you. I'm right, am I not?'

'Possibly. But I can't imagine not being a Catholic. My faith is one of the biggest things in life for me. I think it is to the majority of Irishmen, but we accept it and don't talk about it.'

'I've always heard you were a priest-ridden race,' the other said.

'It isn't so. Of course there are ignorant peasants, and there are unscrupulous priests, but not more so here than in many other countries. There's a lot of ignorant tommy-rot talked about Catholicism by all you heretics, come to think of it. I've sometimes heard it discounted as a coward's religion, on the grounds that we cling to the faith as remedy against mortal sin, as a help in adversity, as the straw to which the proverbial drowner clings. I cannot see it like that. Surely the man who feels he is powerful enough to meet any contingency without calling in God is committing the worst of all sins, that of pride?'

'I admire your sincerity,' Egbert Small said, 'but I maintain that too many of you harp on sin. Everything seems a sin. As to your personal problems, my dear fellow, I think you're plumb crazy. You should get out and about more, though God knows I understand the reasons which keep you here. I'd no idea I was coming to a land of such beauty.'

When Small had left Ardbreen, Renvyle felt easier in his mind. He realized it had done him a power of good to talk to a man of the same age as himself. Perhaps, he thought, he had taken some things too seriously and was in danger of losing all sense of proportion.

CHAPTER EIGHT

I

PADDY wrote fitfully from America where she was obviously enjoying her life. Wonderful presents arrived for them all at Christmas and Micky tried not to realize his loneliness as he knelt by the altar at midnight at the little village church. Yet something was amiss. During the weeks and months that followed his work began to suffer, he found concentration difficult, and little seemed to inspire him either to write or paint. At the the end of May Paddy wrote that the play was unlikely to run through the heat of the summer in New York, and that she in any case would be returning to England. She said nothing about coming to Ireland, nor was there the suggestion that either he or Killary should meet her on her return. Micky wrote begging her to come home for even a couple of weeks, and the letter he eventually received in answer was like a death-knell to any hopes he had secretly held during her absence that they would come together again.

It came when he was expecting a visit in Ardbreen from Geoffrey Edwards and he read and re-read the letter.

'I can't possibly come over to Ireland as you suggest. Although the play's coming off, it's almost certain that I'm going to do a film. Equally hopeless for you and Killary to join me in London. The flat I may be taking is absolutely tiny, and miles from any park or anywhere for a child to play and I'd have no time for either of you. Besides it's far better for her to be at Ardbreen. And you know you loathe London. *And* the theatre. *And* my friends. I thought you were painting or writing or have you had another failure? God knows *I'd* find no inspiration to do anything creative out there but you've always said it's the only place you can live and we must go our own ways and make our own lives and see each other when we can. Give Killary my

79

love and a kiss and tell her not to forget me. Love Paddy. XXX.'

It still seemed inconceivable to him that two people who had grown up together and who had married—presumably because they loved each other—should now see this world so differently.

'Is it somebody I know who's coming tomorrow, Daddy?' Killary's question broke up his reverie.

'Mr Edwards. From London. Geoffrey Edwards. Don't think you've ever seen him. He publishes books.'

'The books you write?'

'If I'm lucky.'

Both of them were in the dinghy, and the child was baling into a small container, chucking water efficiently over the side in the manner she had seen Renvyle do all her life.

'I had a letter from Mummie, Killary. She sent you her love and says you're not to forget her.'

'Why doesn't Mummie live with us?' The child dropped the baler, and looked at her father obviously expecting an answer.

'She likes living in a big town. And she likes to act. She's bored by all this.'

He straightened himself and looked across the horizon. The sea was turquoise blue, and the islands stood out like black pearls in the midst. Although it was not yet evening, shadows had already begun to cast themselves across one or two of the Twelve Pins, and the Mweelreas looked nearer than usual.

'Hope it'll keep fine for him,' Micky said. 'He's come a long way and we want Ardbreen to look its best, don't we?'

'P'haps he'll be sea-sick if it's rough,' she said hopefully. 'Does the man know Mummie?'

'He's seen her act.'

'I don't want to be an actress. I don't want to go away from home again. Ever.'

'You mean to say the two of you live alone here? No woman to look after you? No nurse to look after her?'

Renvyle laughed. It was an amusing picture to conjure: Killary with a nanny.

'She's never had one.'

'And you? Who looks after you?'

'That nice body who you may have seen outside. She'll bring in some food presently. Oh, you needn't worry,' Renvyle continued. 'She's a good cook. And you can't go wrong with a lobster from my own pots, and strawberries from the garden and cream from the cow.'

'And suppose one of you is ill?' asked Geoffrey Edwards.

'We meet our fences when we come to them. Luckily we're both of us pretty healthy.'

'Well, I don't know, I call it a pretty lonely existence.'

Micky Renvyle was silent.

'It's beginning to be apparent in your work, Mick,' said the older man. 'You've lost that flair. The last thing we did only just paid its advance, as you know only too well. And frankly I'm worried about the new one. I know you've only sent me half of it to read, but the enthusiasm you used to show is lacking. And your illustrations aren't up to your usual standard either.'

'Does this mean you're not going to take it?' Renvyle asked.

'I'm not saying that.'

'But you're not planking down an advance right away?'

'Frankly—no.'

There was a pause, and Renvyle got up to give Edwards a drink.

'Mark you, I can't say I'm surprised,' Geoffrey Edwards continued, 'I mean, living like this . . . I should go off my rocker.'

'That's what Paddy says. I had a letter from her yesterday. She's in America, and her play is finishing and I wrote suggesting she should come home for a bit. I thought she'd like to. Apparently she's going into some film.'

'Why don't you go over to England again? Get you out of a rut.'

'Afraid that's out of the question. Or so she intimates. And you must have guessed it didn't work last time.'

Edwards was silent. He knew Renvyle fairly well, but the

younger man had always seemed quiet—almost shy—and he did not care to probe into his domestic affairs and appear tactless, but he felt something had to be said, if only to help the other, whose work indeed was showing deterioration.

'Of course, I realize this is a lovely spot. And ideal in which to work. Especially for a writer or a painter. But to live here day in, day out, with a small child as one's only companion—fling me out, Mick, if I'm talking about things which aren't any concern of mine. But as I publish your stuff, I feel in a way your life is something for me to worry about. Are you and your wife washed up?'

'No. God, no! I suppose she'll come back when she wants to.'

'Have you asked her to?'

'Indeed I have. Of course I realize Killary should have her mother about her. But it's no use letting her join Paddy in England, she'd only send her to some school or other, a boarding-school at that. At least here she has me. She's a companion, I assure you. We get on extraordinarily well together. She's a cross between one's shadow and a dog.'

'Damned bad for both of you.'

'If I'm working badly here, I'd do a damn sight worse in London. Besides, I couldn't afford the life there. I live on very little, and you know only too well what I make,' and he laughed ruefully. 'I'm not in debt. But I've grown stale, I admit it. I suppose you're right, I should travel.'

'Take my advice, Mick, go away, go anywhere, take your little girl if you must. Have an affair if you like.'

Renvyle smiled. 'That's not my line of country, you know. I expect you'll think me a dullard when I tell you I've never cared for any woman except Paddy, never slept with any other. We're different over here, you know. Some people say the Irish are the most immoral in the world; I can only assure you that from my experience that is entirely wishful thinking.'

'You're an R.C., I suppose?' the other inquired.

'I'm a Catholic, of course. So is Paddy.'

'Good night, Daddy.'

Killary had come into the room, wearing a nightgown that

trailed below a dressing-gown that she had palpably outgrown. She wore no slippers.

'Did you enjoy the day, Mr Edwards?' she asked in what her father called her hostess voice.

'I did indeed. I shall have a lot to tell my kids when I see them again. About the fish I caught and that jolly tea we had when we landed on—what was the place called?'

'Crump Island. What kind of children have you got?'

'Two. Peter and Hilary.'

'That rhymes with Killary. Is she older than me?'

'She's fifteen, I'm afraid. But Peter is much younger. Only nine. They go to school, boarding-school.'

'I shouldn't like that,' said Killary after a moment's pause.

'I think you would,' Edwards said. 'Lots of jolly young people of your own age, and jolly games.'

'Well, I can't go anyway. I've got him to look after.'

She rushed over to Renvyle and hugged him, and then sedately held her hand out to Edwards. 'Good night. I expect we shall meet again,' and she left the room, quietly shutting the door behind her. Neither man spoke, and then Geoffrey Edwards said:

'I see what you mean. But you're a pathetic pair. Give me another drink.'

The following morning as Geoffrey Edwards was paying his bill at the hotel, Renvyle walked into the hall.

'I must say it's an attractive place to come to for a holiday,' said Edwards. 'Wish I could have stayed longer. I must bring Marjorie with me some time. But this American is only at Cong for two days and I want to catch him before he flies back from Shannon.'

'He must do well if he's staying there,' Micky Renvyle remarked.

'Well, you know what Americans are. Only the most expensive hotels seem to suit 'em. We did very well with his first book, and I want to know how far he's on with his new one.'

Outside the sun was shining and the fuchsias appeared in

full glory. A small donkey lay on the side of the road idly watching the two men. The smell of peat wafted across the air strongly.

'Can I drop you anywhere? Village or anything?' asked Edwards.

'I'll drive with you to the top, I've got to call in at the shop and fetch some rope.'

They climbed into Edwards's car and drove slowly up the hill towards the few houses and one shop of which the village consisted.

'Where's young what's-her-name this morning?' the older asked, aware subconsciously as of something missing.

'Killary? I don't know. She'll be about. She's quite independent in her own way as long as she knows I'm around somewhere.'

'Queer name—Killary.'

'We called her after Killary Harbour. It's where Paddy and I used to go on high days and holidays when we were children. And where we spent our honeymoon.'

'Of course, I remember now. You did a lovely water-colour of the place in an earlier book of yours. Strange place looking like a fjord.'

'That's right. I sold a picture which I called "Sunset from Killary" at the R.A. a couple of years ago, for fifty quid.'

Presently they reached the village.

'You can go to Cong by Leenane and drive alongside Killary Harbour if it'd interest you. You'll see the hotel where Paddy and I stayed, we felt like millionaires because we were given a private bathroom. First and only time such luxury has come my way.'

'Maybe I will. Perhaps by the end of this trip I'll see why Connemara has such a hold on you!'

Renvyle shook his head.

'I doubt it,' he said.

And Edwards had been, and gone again, and Renvyle realized his publisher had lost faith in him. The future looked blank indeed. If it was not for his small Killary he would almost have been tempted to follow Geoffrey Edwards's advice and go far away, travel to lands he had never seen.

He went along to see Miss O'Malley and asked her if she would have Killary for a couple of nights or more.

'I want to go for a tramp,' he said.

'Anything the matter?'

'No, not really,' he lied. 'I have a feeling I'm rusty and the mountains may help.'

'Of course she can come to us. Send her along. We shall love to have her.'

So Renvyle set out with a pack on his back and with his sketch book, and made for Achill. The weather improved, and he began to wish he had sailed in *Deirdre* after all. He stayed three nights, and was given a lift from Westport as far as Leenane on the homeward journey. Near the cross-roads which led back by Lough Fee to Ardbreen he noticed a stationary car. There was nothing unusual in this, for it probably belonged to someone fishing the lough, but he heard himself hailed and realized a woman was waving. He walked towards the car. Her face was somehow familiar although he could not place it.

'Do you know anything about cars at all?' she asked. 'It suddenly won't go. It's not a puncture.'

Micky had to confess he did not.

'You're Mr Renvyle, aren't you?'

'Yes. But—'

'I work in the library at Ballymannin. I gave you out a book the other day.'

'Of course, I remember now. And I wondered what had become of Miss O'Connor.'

'Poor thing, she's had a stroke. I've come to replace her.'

Feeling utterly incompetent, Micky Renvyle looked in the bonnet, and pushed wires he knew nothing about and finally said:

'It's no use, Miss— er?'

'Fitzgerald. Joan Fitzgerald.'

'I have to confess I don't know a damn thing about cars. My wife has one in England, but I never even learnt to drive the darn thing.' He smiled ruefully. 'I've got a boat, so I ought to be able to do something with the engine of a car, but alas, your car's engine isn't at all like my boat's.'

'What do you think I'd better do?' she asked. 'Luckily it's my day off.'

'All we need do is to walk back to Leenane for help. It's not very far.'

'That absolutely heavenly little place? I'll come with you. That's where I drove to this afternoon. Tell me about it, please.'

The girl locked the door of the car and together they strode along the road to Leenane.

'Although I'm half Irish I've never been to this part before,' she told him. 'I've lived quite a lot in England but my mother died a couple of years ago and I've made my home with my father's people in the south. In County Cork. The job of librarian in Ballymannin isn't much but I'm awfully glad I took it. I've always longed to visit Galway, and Connemara most of all.'

'Is it your own car?' Micky inquired politely.

'Oh yes. It's pretty ancient, and it was a second-hand one but it enables me to see places, which is what I bought it for.'

'I dare say I'm a fool not to have one, but I never have had, so don't miss it. Sailing is my hobby.'

'What fun!' the girl said. 'It must be heavenly sailing among all the islands.'

'It is. If you'd like to come out one day, I should be delighted to take you. My small daughter and I spend a lot of time at sea in the holidays when she's with me.'

When they reached that part of the road from where they

could catch the first glimpse of Killary Harbour Joan Fitzgerald stopped still.

'It's unutterably beautiful, isn't it?' she said quietly. 'The mountains, the water, the stillness—everything in fact. Makes one wonder how people can lose their faith.'

'How d'you mean?'

'God. You have to be God. I mean, to create all this. How can people not believe? How could all this be if there was no God? Impossible.'

There was nothing Micky felt he could reply, the sentiments were his own. They walked on, neither of them speaking for a while.

'It looked a nice hotel in the village,' she said, 'but I didn't go into it, and there's a lovely little church and convent at the far end with the view of all time . . .'

'The Convent of Mercy,' said Micky.

'Yes, I know. I explored a bit. I left the car in the village. There's a tiny cemetery which looks right down the harbour. I'd like to be buried there, I think. But the place is like a long narrow lake really, isn't it? Completely land-locked it looked from there.'

'I gather it's the first time you've been to Leenane.'

'Yes, but not the last. I feel something very strange about it. As if I belonged to it. Who knows? Perhaps one day I'll live here.'

'Is there any reason why you should?'

She laughed. 'None that I can see at the moment.'

They walked to the garage and found a mechanic who said he would drive them back to the car and see what was wrong. It proved to be a small matter and Renvyle felt foolishly inadequate that he had been unable to cope with it.

'You must let me drive you back to where you live,' the girl said to him. 'You've wasted a good hour or more with me.'

Micky hesitated, and said it would only take her out of the way.

'Nonsense,' she said, 'I don't remember where you said you live, but the day's all mine.'

'It's extremely kind of you,' he said. 'As you can see by my pack, I've been hiking and I've been away for several days. I live at Ardbreen.'

'That's that lovely bit by the sea, I know,' she said, 'I've been to the hotel sometimes with various people.'

They got into the car, and as they drove off, Micky said, 'The quietest and loveliest way is by Lough Fee and along the coast. Take this turn on the right.'

They drove in silence for most of the way, Joan Fitzgerald at times giving gasps of pleasure. Micky could not help thinking how strange it was that he should be driving with a totally strange young woman on roads which he connected solely with Paddy. He remembered the days before their marriage when the two of them would take off on bicycles, and his heart contracted in pain at the realization that those days had gone for ever. He was aware that his companion was slowing down again, and he noticed it was by the sandy stretch where he and Paddy had bathed on the day when he had asked her to marry him.

'It's—it's all so romantic and perfect, isn't it?' the girl said.

'I thought so once,' he replied and found himself telling her of the day he and Paddy became engaged.

'As for Leenane,' he continued, 'we spent our honeymoon at the hotel there, and our daughter is called Killary. Killary Mary in case the church objected,' he smiled.

'No wonder you love it all so much. But didn't you say some way back that your wife has a car in England? What's she there for?'

'She's an actress. Actually at the moment she's in the States. But she's due back any moment. Her name is Paddy O'Malley.'

'Oh, but she's quite well known, isn't she? I think I've seen her. She's very beautiful. Dark and very Irish looking. How exciting for you!'

'Exciting?'

'Well, yes. To be married to someone as lovely and glamorous.'

It might be Paddy herself talking, Micky thought. The Paddy of several years ago.

'D'you know I've never thought of it like that,' he said seriously. 'I only know it's taken her away from Ireland.'

'I see.'

'You must direct me when we get to the village,' she said presently. 'To your house, I mean.'

'Put me down at Tully Cross,' he said. 'I'm sure you don't want to go down to Ardbreen. It was indeed kind of you to come all this way.'

'But it gives me such a good excuse to look at that wonderful view from the top of the hill. I shall never forget the first time I saw it. It was one evening after a terrific shower, and there was a rainbow which began on one island, and ended on another. Oh Mr Renvyle, I envy you! For living in this part of the world, I mean.'

'But you're here now, too,' he smiled at her enthusiasm.

'Yes, but I shan't always be.'

As they neared Ardbreen, Micky said, 'I'm back in the small cottage where we began our married life, just drive on and on, and when we get to the end of everything you'll see it. When my father died he left his house to me, and we moved into it because we thought we were going to have another child. Unfortunately poor Paddy had a miscarriage. It wasn't a lucky house one way and another, and I've let it. The cottage is big enough for Killary and me.'

'And the two of you live on your own here when your wife is acting in England or America?'

He nodded. 'I tried to work in London,' he told her, 'but I couldn't.'

'I can understand that. I suppose you could write at a pinch but it would be impossible to paint.'

He looked at her with surprise.

'Have you read anything of mine?'

'But of course. I told you I was a librarian.' They both laughed. When they reached the cottage they saw Killary swinging on the gate.

'That's my daughter,' Micky said.

Joan Fitzgerald saw a small edition of Renvyle with dark hair cut like a boy's, and large blue eyes, wearing a dark-blue mackintosh and Wellington boots.

'She looks very surprised,' Joan said.

'Come in and have a drink, or a cup of tea or something.' They got out of the car.

'This is Miss Fitzgerald, Killary.'

'Your Daddy helped me when my car broke down.'

'He doesn't know about cars,' Killary said.

'Exactly.' Micky gave Joan a smile. 'She knows. You're right, sweet, I couldn't do a thing. But I walked with Miss Fitzgerald back to a garage in Leenane and we got someone to come and mend it. And she very kindly brought me all the way home.'

'Where do you live?' asked the child.

'At the moment in Ballymannin. I'm working in the bookshop there.'

They went into the house. 'What would you like, whisky? Tea? Coffee?'

When Joan Fitzgerald had gone Killary said:

'She isn't a pretty lady, is she?'

Renvyle looked down at the child. 'Wasn't she? I never noticed.'

'Not like Mummie.'

'There aren't many people as pretty as Mummie.'

'But she was nice,' the child said in slightly patronizing tones. 'She has specs like you have and she has a kind face. Can I go and have tea with her?'

'Not unless she asks you to. And do you know it's time you were in bed?'

Killary flung her arms round her father's neck and kissed him.

'Will you come up soon, so as I can say m'prayers to you?'

'Not as pretty as Mummie,' so Killary said, thought Micky, and he tried to conjure up the face of the girl who had driven him home and with whom he must have spent anything up to three or four hours. Dark, but not the exciting darkness of Paddy, and he couldn't remember what sort of hair she had at all. Long? Short? Spectacles, Killary said. Yes, horn-rimmed ones, but surely she had not worn them all the time? Neither tall nor short. All he could remember was that she had seemed a pleasant sort of creature, and one that appreciated the scenery that meant so much to him. And yes, she had an attractive voice. And she wore the usual Aran-knitted jersey. She had a happy laugh, he remembered. What was her name? Joan. He started to pour out another drink, but Killary called to him and he went upstairs.

Part II

CHAPTER ONE

I

It was inevitable that Joan Fitzgerald would become inquisitive about the man she had driven back to Ardbreen. She had, as she told him, read his work, what she did not admit was that she had only read one of his books. She now set out to read any she could lay her hands on, and as he was the only local author of any repute she was delighted to find the library in which she worked stocked most of them.

It was some weeks before she saw the man again, and then she came face to face with him in the main street of Bally-mannin.

'Miss Fitzgerald!' he said, and smiled. 'When are you coming for a sail?'

'I'm only free on Sundays, and Wednesday afternoons,' she answered. 'But how kind of you to remember. Are you coming in to get a book?' she asked. 'I'll come right back. I only dashed out to post something important.'

They walked back together.

'Has your car been behaving properly?' he asked.

'Yes, thank goodness. I wouldn't care to be stranded on some of these roads. Last week I drove for miles and never saw a soul.'

When he had chosen a book he turned to speak to her once again.

'I'll get in touch with you about a sail. And I'll remember the correct day,' he smiled at her.

'How's your little girl?'

'Killary? She's fine. We'll make it a Sunday so that she can come too.'

So began the first of many sailing days to come.

'What's your name?' Killary asked the girl when they had got home late after the first outing.

'Don't be silly, darling,' Micky said. 'I told you, Miss Fitzgerald.'

'I mean your real name. Like I'm called Killary.'

'Joan.'

'I asked Daddy if I could come to tea with you, Joan, but he said only if you asked me.'

The girl laughed. 'I'd love you to, but how are we going to manage it? You go to school and I work in a shop. Moreover, your Daddy hasn't got a car to bring you.'

Renvyle looked amused. Killary appeared crestfallen.

'Do you live in a nice house?' she asked after a minute's pause.

'As a matter of fact, I don't live in the whole of a house at all. I'm in what people call lodgings.' She looked at Renvyle. 'I try to call it a bed-sitter, but there's not much sitter about it.'

'Don't you find that rather a trial? At week-ends and in the evenings?'

'There's a sort of sitting-room downstairs which I could use, but the Flynns are there themselves, and one wouldn't get any privacy. It's awfully difficult to find anywhere that's to let furnished and I don't know quite how long this job will last. I don't know, you see, if the library keeps open during the winter.'

Renvyle told her it did.

'In that case I shall ask my boss if I'm satisfactory and if he says yes, I'll look around for something more permanent and more comfortable. I believe it would be possible to get a flat or a cottage during the winter months. I've got an invalid sister who might care to share a cottage if I found one.'

'What's an invalid?' Killary asked.

'Someone who isn't very well,' Joan Fitzgerald told her, and then turning to Renvyle said: 'She has a heart. It just keeps her from doing anything—working I mean. She's not actually ill.'

'It would be company for you,' he said.

'Yes. I haven't thought about it much. I've been lucky in meeting quite a nice lot of people since I came to Ballymannin, but they're mostly people who are here for the summer months, or visitors at the hotels.'

'Do you know any of the people around here?' he asked.

'The Jamesons. And Father Delaney. And I've talked to Miss O'Malley frequently when she comes in to change books.'

'*She* could take me in Granpa's car,' Killary said.

'What an awful child you are!' Micky looked at his daughter. 'I've never known her like this before,' he said to Joan Fitzgerald.

'I think it's a great compliment. You see, Killary, I've not got a sitting-room where we could have our tea. Only my bed-room.'

'Where d'you have your dinner? And your breakfast?'

'With the people I'm staying with.'

'Oh. I see.' It was obviously a great disappointment.

A week later Renvyle ran into the priest.

'I hear you took Miss Fitzgerald out with you in *Deirdre,*' he said. 'She's a nice girl. It was kind of you.'

Renvyle explained how they had met the first time, and he told him how Killary had invited herself to tea.

'And what news of Paddy?'

'She should be back in England,' Renvyle answered.

The priest looked at him searchingly. 'Should be? Don't you know?'

'She's doing a film,' he said evasively. 'Part of it is being shot in Italy.'

'I see.' And after a pause, 'I don't want to pry, Mick, but have things gone wrong between the two of you?'

'They're not what you'd call right, I'm afraid. Her career is all that matters to Paddy. She won't come back here, and she doesn't seem to want us—either of us—in England.'

The priest looked troubled. 'I should never have advised her to take that first step,' he said. 'And yet I know she was head-ing for a breakdown, and a trip away from all of you seemed to me a possible cure—I'm surprised, aye, I'm surprised, it should have gone the way you tell me. Paddy was a good girl.'

'She still is,' Mick hastily assured the priest.

'I'm a little worried over her father. John O'Malley isn't too well. I think Paddy should know.'

'I saw him the other day,' Micky said. 'He looked tired, but seemed in good spirits.'

'It's his heart. It's as well you should know. I think maybe I'll write a line to Paddy myself and tell her one or two things.'

He waved good-bye to Renvyle, who walked home slowly. If anything was to happen to his father-in-law, a sudden bad illness—if in fact he was to die—surely Paddy would return?

As the summer weeks passed Micky began to look forward to the days on which he and Joan Fitzgerald met either to sail or if the seas were heavy she would pick him up with Killary and they would go for picnics in her car. Most of the meetings were engineered by Killary, who would always say 'and next time' and who so enjoyed the excursions that neither the man nor the woman realized their growing interest in each other's society. Many interests in common brought them closer together, and often Renvyle found himself asking Joan Fitzgerald's advice when the child was in need of some new garment. John O'Malley was weaker and his sister did not care to leave him in the house for long by himself, and it was she who had one day suggested that Miss Fitzgerald's help be sought in the matter of choosing underwear for the child.

'That nice Joan Fitzgerald, ask her to help,' she had said to Renvyle. 'I'm sure she'd pop into Carey's in her lunch-hour. And they'd send out some things for the child to try on. On approval, you know.'

It was Killary who said to her father one afternoon when they were picnicking on the boat in Ballynakill Harbour:

'Why don't *you* call her Joan?'

'Yes, why don't you?' Joan asked with a laugh which she hoped hid a blush.

'Can I? I do think of you as Joan.'

It was in the ensuing weeks that Micky realized the help he would be to the O'Malleys if he were able to drive a car, and he began to take lessons with anyone who would teach him, much to the amusement of Killary who was delighted to drive about in a car with the L plate and to know her father was having 'lessons'. Sometimes Father Delaney would take him to Clifden or Ballymannin in his car, and occasionally Joan fixed the plate on hers and they would drive on her half-day around the coast road from Clifden to Roundstone, and back by the wild road festooned with lakes on either side which necessitated a lot of gear-changing for the learner, and often reduced Joan to helpless laughter and Micky to swearing.

One day when they were out he asked her about the life she had led before coming to Connemara.

'I've always had to earn my own living. I suppose most girls have to,' she said. 'My father was killed in the war, he was in the Irish Guards. Mother was English, and she died only two years ago. Of cancer. I took a degree at Bristol University, and I was a librarian at the Times Book Club for a long time. Then when Mother was ill I had to leave and look after her, and Jill too, after a fashion—that's my sister with the bad heart. When Mother died I took whatever jobs I could, and we made our home with my grandmother near Cork. But I felt it was too much to burden her with two of us all the time. Jill lives with her.'

'Which d'you like best, England or Ireland?' he asked.

'Oh, Ireland,' she replied. 'Without any doubt. I adore it.'

'You don't miss London, theatres and things?'

'Not a bit. I couldn't afford to go to the theatre often in any case.'

'It's funny how my wife – Paddy – seems to love London. She confesses she's in love with it.'

'Seems extraordinary to me,' Joan agreed, 'when you think she could have all this.'

'Mummie's an actress,' Killary suddenly piped up. They had forgotten she was present. 'Daddy and I used to live with her once upon a time. But we don't now.'

Joan tried to appear unconcerned.

'Yes, we joined forces in London,' Micky explained, 'but I think I told you, I found I couldn't work.'

'Mummie's very, very pretty,' Killary said, looking at Joan. 'She's the prettiest person Daddy and me has ever seen. Isn't she, Daddy?'

'That's right,' he answered.

'I know,' Joan said. 'I've seen her act.'

She was silent for a long time and when the picnic was over Micky wondered why for the first time she said she wasn't sure she could come the following week. Few letters came from Paddy, and it was from an English *Sunday Times* that Renvyle learnt that she was to play the lead in one of Ibsen's plays in London in the late autumn. Joan Fitzgerald also had the paper and was leaning over the desk of the library reading it when she looked up, realizing someone was in need of assistance. She recognized Father Delaney.

'Good morning, Father, what can I get for you?'

'I'd like a jolly thriller,' he said.

She laughed and in a few moments brought back several books.

'I've brought you three. You'd better take the lot.'

'Is that an English paper you have?' he inquired. 'I must confess I like the *Sunday Times* and the *Observer*.'

'Yes. I was just reading about Michael's wife.'

'Who?'

'Mr Renvyle,' she answered in confusion.

'Oh, Micky. What's Paddy up to?'

Joan showed him the piece in the paper. The priest sighed. 'It's a sorry business,' he said.

'How? Why?' Joan tried not to appear too concerned.

'I married them, you know. I've known the two of them since they were children. I hate to see this separation of theirs lengthening the way it's doing.'

'I suppose it's inevitable,' Joan remarked, 'in the circumstances.'

'She was such a dear child,' the priest went on. 'I wrote and told her myself that her father's health was giving trouble, but in spite of a nice letter to me she did not say anything about coming to see the dear man.'

Joan swallowed hard and said: 'Was he very much in love with her?'

The priest looked at the girl. 'Micky Renvyle is devoted to his wife, and child.'

'I've found a tiny cottage,' Joan told Renvyle, the next time she saw him. 'Only ten minutes' drive from Ballymannin. And Jill is going to come up and spend the winter months with me. Isn't that wonderful?'

Micky said he was delighted.

'So tell Killary she can come to tea at last. If you hurry up and pass your test you'll be able to bring her.'

Jill Fitzgerald was very different from her sister. She had none of the younger girl's enthusiastic gaiety, and seemed always preoccupied by various maladies. Although, as Joan was quick to tell Renvyle, her sister was pleased to cook and share the little housework there was to do, the man quickly noticed with his own eyes how slowly the girl walked from one room to another, and how ready she was to lie with her feet up on the sofa in the tiny sitting-room and how rarely she was inclined to join in any expedition. He realized she was attractive in appearance, far prettier indeed than Joan, but he found himself heartily agreeing with Killary when she said, 'I like Joan's face much more than the other one.'

However, no one could accuse Jill Fitzgerald of being possessive or selfish where her sister was concerned and she never appeared to mind being left alone when Joan announced her intention of going out with Renvyle. Both sisters were devout Catholics and it would never have struck Jill to criticize Joan's friendship with Micky Renvyle or to consider it unwise, till one day an inhabitant from Ardbreen, a Protestant woman acquaintance, said to her:

'Don't you think your sister is seeing a little too much of Mick Renvyle?'

'What do you mean?'

'Well, you know he's married.'

'Certainly. And I hear his wife is very beautiful – a well-known actress – and that he's devoted to her.'

'That's as may be. But don't you think it is a little—unwise?'

'I'm afraid it's never struck me. And I'm sure it hasn't struck Joan. She likes his little girl, and she and Mr Renvyle are very good friends.'

'Quite.'

'It would be a shame to spoil their nice outings together. I can assure you there's no reason to have such ideas. What put them into your head?'

The woman refused to commit herself, but gave the hint that it could lead to gossip.

'Only if someone starts spreading it,' Jill Fitzgerald said hotly. 'And you'll forgive my saying so, but both Michael Renvyle and my sister – and I myself naturally – are good Catholics, and ideas like yours would never enter into any of our heads.'

'Really? Well, I must say you surprise me.'

The visit upset Jill Fitzgerald and she began to wonder if she should speak to her sister. She was sure there was no justification in the woman's attempt at mischief-making, at the same time it was a horrible thought that perhaps people were coupling Joan's name with a married man's. She tried to put from her various visions that from now on kept creeping into her thoughts, but it was not until she realized that with the little girl at school and her sister still spending her free afternoons with Michael Renvyle perhaps a hint dropped casually would not come amiss.

'Do you suppose Micky Renvyle's wife will be coming back? I mean when her play is over?' she began one day.

'I don't know, I'm sure,' Joan answered rather vaguely.

'Does he talk about her a lot?'

'No, not a great deal.' Joan looked up and saw the worried expression on her sister's face. She felt her own was growing hot. 'Father Delaney tells me how devoted he is to her.'

'My dear,' Jill began, and stopped.

'Yes?'

'Please don't misunderstand what I'm going to say.' It was a hateful task she had undertaken. 'Do you think,' she went on, 'that it's altogether wise for you to go out quite so much with him? People—even people here—have unkind minds, and they may start talking.'

'I suppose someone already has,' Joan said slowly.

Jill nodded.

'Oh, why can't people mind their own business?' Joan said wearily.

'It's horrid, I know. And I felt it would upset you. But it's not nice for you, or for him as I know there's no reason for such gossip.'

'If only there was!' Joan said without thinking.

Jill looked at her sister aghast. 'Joan!'

'Oh, don't worry. It's true, I do love him. And I've never been in love with anyone before. As for Michael, I doubt if he really realizes my existence. Jill, I *can't* give up these meetings. They're so completely innocent and they just make all the difference to my life.'

'Oh, my poor Joan,' her sister said, 'I *am* sorry. But surely you'll only get more and more wretched. There can never be any happiness in it for you.'

'I know. But just to see him and talk to him, somehow it does bring me happiness. He'll never know how I feel, I promise you that. It would embarrass him terribly.'

'Don't you honestly think it would be better to give up the job here and go away?'

She was dismayed by the look of agony that came into her sister's face.

'Oh *no*!' Joan cried. 'As long as I'm the only one that's suffering it can't matter. And it does mean everything to me just to go driving or sailing with him. I suppose,' she went on after a moment's pause, 'it's because Killary can't come so often. And I assure you his behaviour to me is no different when we're alone than when she's with us.'

'I imagine, though, that you prefer it on your own with him?'

'Oddly enough it doesn't matter to me if she's there or not.

I'm fond of the child, you know. She makes me laugh. We get on famously. I tell you Michael is absolutely indifferent to me, me as a woman I mean.'

'Which in itself must only bring you unhappiness,' her sister said.

'I don't know. For as you say, it could never lead to anything, and if we both cared it would be unbearable.'

'Have you told the priest in confession? Forgive me for asking.'

Joan shook her head. 'There's nothing to confess. I've not sinned in my thoughts about him. Truthfully, and I want you to believe me, physical love hasn't come into it. I won't let it. As long as I can just be with him from time to time. To hear him talk about his books and his painting. And his love of the mountains. And to help him in the car. I think he's a lonely sort of person, too.'

'That might be dangerous.'

'No. He's not lonely for a woman. Just for a companion sometimes.'

'I know, my dear, you'd never do anything wrong. I didn't realize you loved him or I don't think I could have spoken about the business.'

'In a way I'm glad you do know now. It's not always easy to hide one's emotions, sometimes it's an awful strain. Whether it's happiness or unhappiness.'

'Poor Joan. I shan't speak about it again. But you know you can always talk to me, for at least I could never be censorious. Knowing that neither of us could ever commit that sort of sin.'

II

Some weeks later Joan heard that John O'Malley had died in his sleep. When next she saw Renvyle she noticed at once how distrait he seemed, and she realized miserably that he did not even see her across the road. Later, however, he came into the library and found her.

'Thank you for writing when my father-in-law died last week,' he said. 'It was kind of you.'

'I was so sorry.' She thought how feeble her words sounded.

'He was a dear man. It's been a sad business. His poor sister is feeling it badly, though of course it wasn't entirely unexpected.'

'And your wife,' Joan had to say it. 'She will be very upset, won't she?'

'I had hoped Paddy could have got over for the funeral.'

'Didn't she?' Her relief was wicked, she knew.

'No. She was on tour. I hoped they would let her off so that she could have flown. But apparently it was impossible.'

'How sad for her. And for you.'

Neither of them spoke for a moment, and then Micky said, 'Well, I must be off. See you again before long.'

With his mind obviously on other matters, he left the library and for Joan the sunshine of the day departed.

Renvyle could not tell from his wife's letter how much upset she had been by her father's death, she seemed more perturbed on her aunt's behalf and suggested that once again Micky should live either in his father's house and take Miss O'Malley to live with him, or join her in John O'Malley's which had been left her for her lifetime.

'I can't make out, darling,' he wrote Paddy, 'what your aunt wants to do. I don't think she knows herself. I don't want to rush her into something she might regret. I think if she does want us it would be better to move up to her as a temporary measure. I have no desire to return to Dad's house, frankly, as you know I'm happy in the cottage. Of course I'll do my best to fall in with your aunt's wishes. By the way, I see that film of yours is to be shown in Galway next month. The one you made in America. I shall go and see it.'

To his surprise Paddy replied quite soon to his letter.

'Darling, don't for goodness' sake take Killary to see the film if you do go. It's very much "A" and I shouldn't like her to see it. It's not much of a film and I don't have a big part in it. I'm playing a glamorous tart! I'm sure not your cup of tea. I gather Auntie doesn't want to move, and she seems to want to remain alone in her glory, poor old sweet. You and Killary could come over at Xmas if you feel like it. The play will run for some time and there's not an earthly that I can come over to Ireland. I could always take a larger service-flat in the same building as this. I've almost forgotten what you both look like, it's time my memory was renewed. And I've certainly forgotten what the married state can be! However, don't rush over, just let the idea simmer.'

Far from wanting to rush, Micky felt no desire at all to go over at Christmas time. Paddy was someone now so remote that she had become a piece of blue note-paper and a corresponding envelope. He knew perfectly well that a visit at Christmas would be far from normal, that in order to give Killary any amusements, visits to pantomimes and circuses would be necessary, where the child would probably contract germs that the pure air of Connemara never saw. It would unsettle her too. He was appalled to realize that in fact he did not want to go. A couple of weeks went by and Killary said at lunch:

'Where's Joan?'

'At home, I expect. Why?'

'Why doesn't she come any more?'

He looked at his child. He had forgotten Joan.

'I'm afraid I'd forgotten about poor Joan. Granpa dying and one thing and another.'

'Can we see her next Sunday?' she asked.

'I've got to go into Ballymannin tomorrow. I'll go and look her up and tell her you want to see her. Then p'haps she'll come to lunch next week.'

When he went into the library Renvyle thought Joan looked unwell. She was thinner, and she looked pale too.

'You're overworking, looking after that sister of yours,' he told her. 'I've been put on the mat by Killary. She says we haven't seen you for a long time and will you please come to lunch next Sunday?'

'Oh yes, I'd love to,' Joan answered with enthusiasm.

'But are you all right? You don't look too fit.'

'I'm quite well.'

'Let's go for a drive,' Killary said the following week after they had finished their meal.

'I don't suppose Joan wants to,' Micky answered. 'She's driven all the way here and will have to all the way back.'

'I don't mind. I'd love to, but we'd better not go too far, it's dark by five. Where shall we go?'

'Where would you like to go?'

'Would it be very far—I suppose not—to do the road to Leenane? I'd love to see Killary Harbour again.'

'Oh yes, yes,' Killary shouted. 'That's my place and I've never been there in a car.'

So they drove along the shore, going very slowly to avoid the sheep that wandered aimlessly everywhere. The hills were covered with bracken now turned a deep brown, and Killary Harbour was the colour of aquamarine, reflecting the mountains on either side.

'There can't be anywhere lovelier,' Joan said. 'I don't think I could ever be tired of coming here. And do you realize we've not met another living soul?'

'It's Daddy's favouritest place,' Killary said.

'I'm not surprised.'

They stopped the car and wandered along a track which ran above, towards the mouth of the harbour.

'Aren't you glad we came?' Killary asked them both.

They nodded.

'D'you know,' said Killary, 'Daddy forgot you? When I asked him last week where you were he said he'd forgotten you.'

Micky looked a little uncomfortable at this remark but

bluffed: 'Aren't kids frightful, I hope you won't take that as gospel truth. What I meant of course—'

'Please—'

'No, but I must explain.'

' 'cos of poor Granpa,' Killary continued. 'He had lots of things to do. Poor Granpa is dead. Did you know?'

'Yes, my dear. It was very sad.'

'He didn't mean to forget you. And I didn't.'

Joan could not help laughing, but she knew there was more than a grain of truth in the child's information. It was not helped by Micky saying later: 'My wife wants me to take Killary over at Christmas.'

Joan felt something like a stone at her heart.

'And are you going to?'

'I don't know. I don't think so. I think it would unsettle Killary. By the way, I've not said anything to her, so don't mention it.' The child had run on and was out of earshot.

'But you must be longing to see your wife,' Joan found herself saying.

'I suppose so. I don't know. Not at Christmas when she'd be acting practically the whole time. I'd a damn sight rather see her here!' he laughed ruefully.

They did not notice Killary, who had rejoined them.

'You said *damn*,' she remarked, looking at her father.

'Shocking of me. I apologize,' Micky said.

'Who d'want to see?'

'Miss Inquisitive, that's what I shall have to call you.'

'Is it Mummie?'

In spite of the agony she was feeling Joan said, 'I expect it is.'

'I guessed. It's his favouritest place 'cos he and Mummie were very happy here—he telled me.'

'Told,' Micky said absently. 'And supposing you run on ahead. Joan and I are having a grown-up sort of talk.'

Why, she did not know, Joan found herself having to enlarge on the subject.

'If your wife wants to see you both it seems rather dreadful not to do as she asks. As she can't come to Ardbreen.'

'She's had various chances to come over and never has. And I'm not plunging Killary into a hot-bed of infection which I know London to be at Christmas time.'

There certainly was no sign of disappointment or frustration in Renvyle's voice and an extraordinary weight was lifted from the girl's heart. Perhaps he no longer loved Paddy O'Malley? She knew that she herself meant nothing to him, but it was a little comfort to feel that perhaps his thoughts were not wholly wrapped up in his beautiful absent wife. Surely, she argued within her mind, if he was really devoted—still in love with Paddy (miserable thought)—he would have taken the opportunity to go and see her. But then there were the remarks Killary had let slip—he loved Killary Harbour because of its associations with his wife, Killary's mother.

In bed that night Joan lay sleepless and in torment. She knew that at last the love she felt for Micky was getting out of hand. Fiercely she pushed all thoughts of the physical from her mind, it was the absorbing jealousy of Paddy Renvyle that troubled her. What matter if he no longer cared for her? He had once. Together they had brought Killary into the world. Once he had loved his Paddy as he would never love her . . . 'Oh God,' she prayed, 'take these hideous thoughts from my mind and heart. Show me the way to retain sanity in this. Don't let my love become a sin. Dear God, dear Jesus, dear Mother of God, help me.'

Christmas drew near and a few days beforehand as Renvyle was walking through the village he saw Father Delaney putting a notice on the church board, and went across the street to talk to him.

'A troublesome thing has arisen,' the priest told him. 'Poor Father Anselm has broken his leg and won't be able to take the midnight Mass at Ballymannin, and they cannot get anybody from anywhere at this late hour. So, as this is such a tiny parish, I've had to alter the services here and I'll be taking the midnight service for him over there. And they cannot have one here. It's just too bad. There'll be a few grumblers I'm thinking, especially from those who were looking forward to a long lie in on Christmas morning.'

'Can I come to Ballymannin with you, Father? Or will your car be full? I've not passed my driving test yet, I regret to say.'

'Of course you can. Delighted.'

The church at Ballymannin was full for the midnight Mass, and, lit only by candles, presented a scene of great serenity and holiness. The high voices of the children as they walked slowly up the aisle singing the *Adeste Fideles*, and later when in Irish they sang 'Silent Night, Holy Night' seemed very beautiful to Renvyle. The church itself was much older than the newly-built one in Ardbreen and it seemed as though the spirits of past monks and abbots were present. As he knelt to receive the Sacrament he realized Joan Fitzgerald was beside him. In the darkness of the church it had been impossible to notice anyone's identity. It was not until the Mass was over, and people were pouring out of the building that he was again aware of Joan who was standing outside the porch with her sister. She looked radiantly happy.

'I never expected you'd be here,' she said.

'I came with Father Delaney. You know perhaps that we've had to forgo our midnight Mass?'

'Such a shame, I know. But it's given me a wonderful chance to wish you a happy Christmas and to see you, which I shouldn't otherwise have done.'

Renvyle looked a little surprised. 'Yes, indeed. And thank you for a very handsome card which came this morning. I'm afraid I've been very remiss. I never bother about anyone except my family. This year we're with Aunt Cathleen, poor old dear.'

Jill Fitzgerald, who had been talking to various people, came up and joined them.

'I'm sure you should get your sister to bed, Joan,' he said. 'She looks very tired. I must find Father Delaney—' He smiled at the two women and, wishing them a happy Christmas, left them.

'Do you realize, Jill,' Joan said, as they drove back to the cottage, 'that by chance, accident, fate—call it what you will—Michael and I knelt beside each other at the altar rails tonight of all nights? I never even knew he was in church till he was beside me. That's the most wonderful thing that has ever happened.'

Her sister sighed. 'If it has made your Christmas, my dear,' she said, 'I'm glad.'

'Not only my Christmas.'

III

It was a few days after the New Year had started that Renvyle saw in the local paper that the film in which Paddy was acting was to be shown in Galway.

'Now is your chance, Aunt Cathleen, to see Paddy,' and he told her about the film.

'It's a terrible long way to go to a movie,' she said. 'We'll either have to drive back in the dark or stay the night.'

'I must pass that test. But in any case I can share the driving. We're not likely to come up against the glaring headlights one sees in England.'

'Very well, I'm game. You'd better let Killary come here and I'll get Katie to stay.' As an afterthought she said, 'I suppose that nice Joan wouldn't be able to come?'

'I don't think so. She only gets the afternoon on her half-day and we'll have to leave in the morning.'

Miss O'Malley went into Ballymannin later that day and called into the library. After telling Joan the plan she and Micky had, she said:

'I suggested we should ask you to come, but Mick said you'd not be able to get off in time.'

'No, I'm afraid I wouldn't,' Joan said slowly. 'What a pity.' And a moment later she asked, 'Is he—are you both—very excited at seeing Paddy?' Her name slipped out unconsciously on her lips.

'You never know with that boy,' Miss O'Malley said. 'He never shows his feelings or emotions. But I'm longing to see it myself.'

The film, as Paddy had warned Micky in her letter to him, had a sordid story, but as a water-front prostitute Paddy gave a surprisingly life-like performance and in the second half of the picture, where the girl had reached better days and was living in great luxury as a New York millionaire's mistress, she looked lovelier than Micky had ever seen her. Engrossed as he was by Paddy's performance, he was unaware of the sniffs and snorts of her aunt's disapproval. At the end of the evening he only knew that he must somehow get to his wife. Never had she appeared more desirable, more provoking, and in certain scenes more human and sympathetic. It was not the star part but Paddy O'Malley 'stole the picture', as the local press had reported.

'I dare say she was good, and looked very lovely, but it was a disgusting story and I really would rather I hadn't seen it,' Miss O'Malley grumbled as they made their way out. 'It's terrible to think our Paddy has to know about such things, much less portray such persons.'

Micky laughed, but as they left the cinema, Joan, who was queueing for the evening performance, heard him remark:

'But the enchanting loveliness of her!'

Unseen by him she watched him walk by her, his hands deep in the pockets of his duffle coat. As he passed she quickly looked the other way.

Joan had only once seen Paddy and in the days when she had no personal interest in her. Her hands gripped the sides of her seat as she watched the girl. She was beautiful, far more so than Joan had remembered. As a prostitute she looked pathetically young, but as the rich man's mistress she assumed a sophisticated attraction that was calculated to make any man lose his head. She was also an extremely able actress, Joan had to admit. The evening was torment to her. This was the woman who was Killary's mother. This was the woman who was Michael's wife. This was the woman who had asked him to go to London. And this was the woman of whom she had heard him say only two hours ago, 'But the enchanting loveliness of her.'

In utter desolation Joan drove the long road back from Galway to Ballymannin. She kept reminding herself that Renvyle had not gone to England, had not apparently wished to go. No sooner, however, had these comforting thoughts come to her than the refrain 'her enchanting loveliness' leapt to her ears. 'But he doesn't love her, I'm sure he doesn't really love her,' she said aloud as she drove the car onwards through the heavy rain which had been teeming down ever since Oughterard. It was well past midnight when she let herself into the cottage. Jill, she was relieved to find, was in bed and asleep. She heated herself some milk and then slowly went to her room. As she sat at her dressing-table she looked at the face which appeared in the mirror.

'What chance have you?' she said. She saw the long, rather thin face with its somewhat sallow complexion. She saw ordinary eyes hidden by glasses, she saw uninteresting lanky hair. And tears filled the eyes, and choking sobs hurt her throat.

'I'm wicked, wicked, wicked,' her thoughts ran, 'I want to be beautiful like her. I want him to love me. But I know it's all hopeless. Even if I were beautiful, even if Michael loved me, it couldn't ever be what I'd want. I could never do that . . . no, never. Oh, Mother of God, help me!'

CHAPTER TWO

'FUNNY old thing, aren't you . . . ?'

Paddy lay, looking up from the pillow at her husband. 'You don't grow up. Just the same old Mick.'

'I wish you'd come with me,' he answered.

'Darling, I'm *tired*. We had two shows yesterday and *you* didn't let me have much sleep, I'd like to remind you.' He took her hand and kissed her wrist. 'No, you go off to your precious Mass and let me have a nice long sleep. And maybe when you get back I'll have some coffee for you. And maybe not,' she ended with a long-drawn-out yawn.

He rose from the side of the bed on which he had been sitting and was about to leave her when she pulled him back.

'Say it,' she said.

'I love you. Sometimes I worship you.'

She rumpled his head, and kissing it said, 'Silly old boy. Now run off or you'll be late,' and before he had reached the door of the bedroom Paddy had turned over and appeared to be asleep.

There were mixed feelings in the man's heart as he walked to church. He was very much in love with his wife, but he fully realized she was clever enough to call him to her and get what she wanted from him. At the moment it apparently suited her to have her husband with her, and he supposed that as long as she pretended to love him—and he admitted to himself the possibility of pretence—he would willingly remain to be enslaved. She accused him of not growing up, did she? He felt he could not say the same thing of her. There were times when she seemed older and more experienced than Eve herself.

He had been in London nearly a month now, and every Sunday it was the same; always an excuse for not accompany-

114

ing him to Mass. In the old days, he remembered, it had been a source of great happiness to go together to receive the Blessed Sacrament, and it was almost a physical pain that he felt, this turning away from what to him was and always had been the greatest of all joys and the most important thing in life. It was not, he knew, that Paddy had become suddenly an unbeliever or was in any way agnostic. She was lapsing—as many others had before her, he had to confess—from sheer idleness, he believed. And this new-found pleasure that they were discovering in physical love and mutual companionship might readily become endangered if what to him was the major force in life was no longer to be shared.

He knelt in the splendour of the London church, so different from the intimacy of Ardbreen's rather ramshackle little building, and the far-away voice of the priest as he intoned made him long for the well-loved voice of Father Delaney. Could it be, he wondered, that subconsciously Paddy was lost in the vast metropolis in spite of the many places of worship from which to choose? Possibly she was one of those dear children of God—as Father Delaney would have put it—who need keeping up to the mark and no one in London had come forward for the job. Yet he remembered when he and Killary had lived in London with Paddy there had never been any sliding away on her part, and he remembered how fond she had been of the church in Farm Street. The sanctuary bell rang. Renvyle tried to collect his thoughts, and as the Host was raised he bowed low in gratitude for the renewal of his wife's love and begged forgiveness of his own many shortcomings.

Paddy was still asleep when Micky returned to the flat. He put the kettle on, got himself some breakfast and began to read the Sunday papers. Half-way through the morning she put her head round the door of the sitting-room.

'Hullo! Back? Be a sweetie and make some coffee for me while I run a bath. Any news in the papers? Give me the *Sunday Express*,' and seizing the paper from his hands she disappeared.

'Where d'you want your coffee?' he called, when he had it ready.

'Oh, in the sitting-room with you.'

A few minutes later Renvyle was tucking his wife up on the sofa, and saying, 'You look and smell bewitching.'

Paddy poured out her coffee and said, 'That's delicious,' and started to read from a page of the paper, the rest of which she discarded on to the floor.

'What shall we do?' she asked presently.

'Whatever you like.'

'It's a lovely fine day. Let's drive into the country somewhere.'

'It's on the late side.'

'We can make Great Fosters or that place—Hurley?—if I get dressed.'

On the way out of London they passed a church from which people were pouring.

'Hope you prayed for me this morning,' Paddy said lightly.

'I always do.' After a pause he said, 'Just why have you given it up?'

She was silent for a while. 'I don't really know,' she answered. 'There was a priest at Farm Street to whom I used to confess. When I returned from America I discovered he'd gone. Somehow I've just let things slide.'

'It's not like us. We Irish, I mean,' Micky said.

'At home it's very different, y'know,' Paddy replied. 'Take dear old Father Delaney. He really is the shepherd of the flock and comes and routles you out and asks what's the matter if you've not been to church. But it's so different here. And it was the same in New York. You're just one of an enormous number and unless you happen to know a certain priest it's a hundred to one—a thousand to one—that you're missed at Mass. And anyway with so many churches to choose from one might be at any dozen or more.'

'I can see that. But don't you miss it? Don't you find something in your life has gone from you? Isn't there a horrible void?' Micky asked.

116

'I'm afraid there isn't. In fact, darling, I'm jolly relieved to have a good lie in on Sunday mornings. And I expect that's why most of the Protestant churches are empty,' and she laughed. 'You look awfully shocked, Micky,' she taunted him.

'It hurts. It doesn't shock. It's as if you suddenly turned and hit Killary.'

'Oh.' She was silent, and then she said, 'Don't worry, sweetie. Think of the joy in heaven when I repent. You'll be one of the ninety-nine. A complete also-ran.'

Some days later Paddy said, 'You know, I'm neglecting a lot of my chums for you.'

'I should hate you to do that,' Micky answered. 'When I'm not here what do you do? Have people here? Go to restaurants? What?'

'Oh, I go to people's houses. Sometimes cook a little meal here. I very often have lunch out, and do a matinée with a girl friend.'

'Darling, do please do what you want to do. I should hate you not to.'

'It's just that it's a bit silly always to make you an excuse when I'm asked to do something.'

'Of course. Go ahead and make any plans you want.'

'Sure you don't mind?'

Micky said he would do a bit of writing.

'Yes, do,' she urged, and Renvyle was unaware of the very slight patronage in her tone of voice. 'I'm sure it's high time you did some work.'

At first Paddy's engagements were few. A lunch here, a film and lunch there; then it would happen that a day's golf would be sandwiched between a matinée day and an afternoon of bridge.

'When did you start all these new hobbies?' Mick asked in surprise after a week during which she had only lunched at home once.

'I learnt to play bridge in the States, and golf on tour. I'm equally bad at both, but I love bridge and golf's good exercise. You should play. You used to, after a fashion.'

Occasionally she would bring whomever she had been out with back to tea, and then as always there would be the hour's rest in her room before she departed for the theatre. Gradually and insidiously the rot set in as before and Renvyle began to find himself unwanted.

'Darling,' Paddy would say, giving him a quick peck before rushing out, 'I'm going out to supper tonight. I shan't be late. You don't mind?'

And he knew they were beginning to drift again. He realized he spoke a different language from most of her friends, to whom he was obviously a very dull dog. He finished some stories which his agent placed for him quite well but which were unsuitable to be published in book form, and as the days lengthened and the buds appeared on the trees in the parks and squares, the longing for Ardbreen came over him, a longing which could have been overcome had his wife not resorted once more to the neglect she had shown two years ago.

'I want to get home for Killary's holidays, Paddy,' he said one day.

'Well, there's nothing to stop you, my dear,' was her reply. 'Is there?'

'I'm afraid not.'

'What d'you mean exactly by that little remark?'

'Well, I mean, it doesn't really matter a row of pins to you if I'm around or not. Does it?'

'It was fun, when you arrived, darling. And I've enjoyed your visit.'

'Visit. Yes. That's exactly what it's been. Which isn't the way a life should be between husband and wife.'

Paddy gave an impatient sigh. 'It's always the same if you overstay your—'

'Welcome,' he cut in. 'I know!'

'It isn't that. But you do seem at such a loose end when you're over here. Once we've been to bed together there doesn't seem anything else for you to do.'

'I hate to hear you talk like that.'

'Well, but I mean it. I don't know why you can't manage

to do your work. But there it is, one can't make a silk purse out of a pig's ear or whatever the phrase is. And I suppose you'll be old Mick from Ardbreen, Connemara, to the end of your days. You really ought to take a shillelagh about with you.'

Renvyle had to laugh. 'In fact I'm about the most unsatisfactory husband you can imagine,' he said. 'It's a pity, because I happen to love you.'

'Do you really, Micky? Still? I don't know why.'

'Look at yourself . . .'

'Oh, I know there's that. But I'm very moody, I admit it, and quite bitchy at times, and after a while even that—bed, I mean—doesn't mean all that to me.'

'I wasn't meaning bed. You're so lovely, Paddy, just to look at you and know you're mine. It's bewildering to me to think we can't live permanently happy together nowadays. But I suppose you're right. I'm rustic and you've grown beyond me. The princess and the swineherd in fact.'

'Darling, I didn't call you that, only a pig's ear,' she giggled. 'And if you take that attitude I shall think you're developing an inferiority complex and that certainly would kill any feelings I have for you. For if there's one thing utterly despicable it's a man with an inferiority complex.'

'I'd better give in my notice,' Micky said, half smiling.

'You know you're itching to get back to your precious mountains. And Killary. She means more to you than I do these days. You have me like an occasional orgy sometimes, and get tipsy in the process—well, that's fine and I like it that way too, but let's face it, my sweet! We have grown apart.'

Renvyle remained silent for a while.

'Don't you ever want to see Killary?' he asked presently.

'Actually I should love to see her. She surely ought to make her First Communion soon, if she hasn't already?'

'I'm surprised you should think of that. No, she hasn't.'

'Well, if you can arrange for that when I'm not acting I will come over.'

Micky looked at his wife. 'I'm sure the Vatican would arrange for a change in the calendar to suit you, Paddy. It's a little late to shift Easter this year, but maybe His Holiness would stretch a point and alter the date of Corpus Christi, the festival chosen for Killary's First Communion. Really, my dear, what next!'

'You know,' Paddy said, as she lay beside her husband the night before he was to leave for Ireland, 'our trouble is that we knew each other too well to begin with. It's a bad thing to marry your childhood's sweetheart, and in our case there's nothing to be done about it.'

'There may be something in what you say,' he answered her, 'but no woman could ever beglamour me as you do.'

'Oh, darling, that's one of the nicest things you've ever said to me.'

'You know it's true, damn it!'

'But there's so much more to marriage than that, isn't there? We ought to be thrilled with each other's work and be interested in each other's friends. And we're not. And I alas— and I'll be honest and admit it—no longer have the burning love that you have for our faith and all it stands for. And that is what I think would be the biggest gap of all between us. Not for me, but for you.'

For the first time in his life as far as he could remember Renvyle felt his eyes smart. 'I don't think it would have mattered if you hadn't been born a Catholic,' he said slowly. 'But I feel in a way it's my fault.'

'How could it be?'

'When one loves someone, as I loved—love—you, one ought to be able to bring that someone back to her faith. As it is, it's like seeing you gradually disappear into a mist and I feel powerless to pull you back. It's like a kind of death. Horrible.' His voice shook slightly.

She bent over and kissed him. 'Suppose we end the visit on a brighter note?'

Micky took her in his arms.

CHAPTER THREE

I

RENVYLE's departure for England coming so close to his having seen his wife's film, left Joan with only one supposition. It was obvious that his love for Paddy which had lain dormant had been drastically reawakened. And as the weeks went by and there was no sign of his return she could only conclude that their marriage had become happy again. She knew there was no reason for him to write to her, but the absence of any news of him was hard to bear. She grew thinner and paler, until her sister at last said:

'Joan, my love, you must take a pull on yourself. You've no right to feel Micky Renvyle's absence. It's tantamount to becoming a sin.'

Joan was horrified. 'I never thought of it like that,' she said.

'Well, think it over. What I've said. Because what it amounts to is this: that you're eating your heart out for some-one else's husband.'

'Yes. Of course. It's true.'

'When did you last go to Confession?' Jill asked.

'Two weeks ago. No,' she replied in answer to the questioning look in her sister's eyes, 'I've never had wicked thoughts about Michael and myself, and I couldn't bear to confess as something horrible what I know is wonderful.'

'Now, look, my dear. You argue like a Protestant. You know perfectly well what we're taught as right and wrong, and no teaching of the Church, and I mean our Church, has ever given a blessing on an adulterous love.'

'But my love isn't that,' Joan cried. 'I admit I love Michael, but as a wonderful friend. A beloved brother.'

'And a father? And a son? Don't be silly, Joan. One doesn't

mope and look like a piece of chewed string if one's brother goes away.'

'It isn't just that he's gone away,' Joan said without thinking of what she was saying.

'No, it's because he's joined his wife. Out of your own mouth, you foolish girl. Oh Joan, I hate to have to say this sort of thing, but you must see a priest. Your mind will be sinning mortally even if your body isn't. Please, please go. That nice Father Delaney, go to him.'

'No, I couldn't. He'd guess. He knows my voice.'

'Wouldn't it help?'

The following day as Joan was leaving the library she walked into the priest.

'My child,' he began, 'ah, it's you, Joan. I was going to tell some unknown young lady to be more careful and not go knocking old priests off their legs!'

Joan laughed, but there was little mirth in the sound and Father Delaney gave her a swift look.

'You're looking poorly, Joan. Are you not well?'

'I'm well, physically, Father. Actually I'm sleeping rather badly. I expect it's that which makes me look such a sight.'

'Is there anything that's troubling you, child? Would you like to see me in church?'

Her worried sigh did not escape him. 'I would like to, yes. Either in church or at the presbytery.'

'Come and see me in church tomorrow evening. I'll be in the Confessional on the left. Father Anselm's.'

'So you see, Father, I don't know how to go on.' It was after all easier than she had imagined. 'We're bound to meet.'

'My daughter, this is something that you must have courage over. And you will pray Almighty God and Our Lady to help you. So far you have not sinned, your thoughts have remained pure. We cannot help loving certain people, and as long as your love for this man is a one-sided affair, as you tell me it is, and you keep that love unsullied, you are not harming yourself or him. But I don't have to stress, do I, that it's a love that is not without danger.'

'I will try, Father. Our blessed Lord knows I don't want wrong thoughts or a wicked love. But it's not easy.'

'I know. I know.'

'I keep having visions of his beautiful wife, and then I think of my own plain face . . .'

'It strikes me, my daughter, that your sins are mostly those of jealousy and envy. And the envy is being put in your heart by the Devil, to tempt you to thoughts that so far you have not fallen into. My child, make your confessions more regularly and for your penance . . .' The comforting words from the priest's lips fell on Joan's ears.

Kneeling in the church alone after she had left the Confessional she prayed that temptation would not come her way. She found herself praying that Renvyle would remain away, yet as she prayed she knew her heart was not in the words that fell from her lips.

'Oh Jesus, help me,' she besought Him.

II

Killary was with Micky the first time Joan saw him. They came into the library together, and it felt to the girl that the room started to spin, that her legs became cotton wool, and she held on to the edge of her desk like a drowning man clutching at a lifebelt.

'Joan, Joan,' cried Killary, rushing across the room.

'Well,' she said, acting, she hoped, as well as she was able, 'this is a surprise. And when did you get back, Michael?'

'A day or two back. I couldn't let the poor little thing be on her own, more or less, for her holidays. D'you think she's grown?'

'I'm sure she has,' Joan said gaily. 'How wonderful to see you—both.'

'We're getting *Deirdre* out this week, Joan. Are you going to come and sail with us one day?'

Joan hesitated.

'You'd better,' Micky said. 'She'll never leave me alone unless you do.'

One day they landed on Inishbofin and Micky delighted in showing the island to Joan.

'It's wonderful to be back, you know,' he said suddenly.

'But you must have enjoyed being in England, surely?'

He was silent.

'I mean you wouldn't have been all that time unless you had?'

'You know, I don't care for town life. I always feel hemmed in. Claustrophobic.'

'But I suppose it was lovely for you to be with—Paddy.'

'Yes and no.'

Joan's heart leapt.

'I wonder if I should be very disloyal if I tell you what's worrying me, Joan?'

She did not look at him.

'The fact is that Paddy is neglecting her religion. And to me that's worse than if she had run off with someone.'

'I didn't know you cared like that,' Joan said.

'One doesn't talk about it as a rule. What does our faith mean to you?' He put the question almost casually.

'A great deal,' Joan answered simply. 'Everything, I suppose. I hope I never let it down.'

'I suppose it's easy for you and me to talk,' Micky continued, 'and I feel it may have been difficult for Paddy in strange cities. She says one's so alone, so to speak, in places like London and New York.'

'How is she neglecting it?' Joan asked diffidently.

'Being damn idle, if you ask me. And flippant. Flippant I mean about it.'

'I see.'

'She's grown away from Ireland. From Catholicism. And also from me. Finds me an uncouth bore, I know.'

124

'Oh Michael, no, I'm sure not.'

'She does. She said I was a sow's ear! A pig's ear, I believe was her expression,' he laughed.

'How beastly of her!' Joan cried.

'I dare say she is right. After all she has made a name for herself; and a big success. One can't blame her, I certainly don't, for being bored with me, but I am distressed about the religious side of our marriage. It must draw us apart.'

'And you love her very much, I suppose.' Joan could hardly bear to hear the reply.

'I adore her. Sometimes. At others she seems a stranger. But I mustn't bore you with our troubles. One thing, Paddy did say she'd do her best to come over for Killary's First Communion.'

'Oh. Well, that's something,' Joan said, feeling inadequate. 'When is that to be?'

'Corpus Christi, I think.'

'How sweet she'll look,' Joan said. 'They always make me feel like crying, dressed up like tiny brides.'

'I'd like you and Paddy to know each other,' he remarked.

'I don't suppose she'll stay long enough for that,' Joan said.

'You could be right there,' he said. 'D'you realize she hasn't been home since she left three, four years ago, whatever it is.'

'I wonder if she's forgotten how beautiful it is. Perhaps when she sees it again she'll want to stay.'

'No such luck,' Micky said, 'and yet when we first married she seemed content enough, and as a child she adored Ardbreen. We used to have wonderful times together, cycling, bathing, going on picnics, and then when I got *Deirdre* of course we used to sail all over the place. Not far afield, I don't mean, but round the islands, and of course to Killary Harbour and Leenane.'

Joan watched his face as he spoke of early days spent with Paddy. It bore no sadness, but his eyes lit with memories of past happiness. She had visions of the two of them, sailing to some blissful El Dorado. In her imagination she saw Paddy looking as she had seen her in the film at Galway, exquisitely groomed and sophisticated and Michael with his arm round her shoulder. He'd look at her, and kiss her as the man in the film had kissed Paddy O'Malley. It was an unbearable picture.

At that moment Killary ran up and put her hand into Joan's.

'D'you like Inishbofin, Joan?' she cried, jumping about excitedly.

'I think it's enchanting,' she answered.

'So do I. Achanting. I'm glad you do too. It's fun today, isn't it? I wish you lived with us, Joan. Why can't you? Daddy, couldn't Joan come and live with us?'

'Who would look after my sister, Killary?' Joan said very quickly, and was relieved to notice that Renvyle looked only amused by the child's suggestion. It was obvious, thank God, that he had no inkling what her feelings for him were.

Their friendship began again where it had left off. Determined not to put any obstacles in the way which might stop their weekly meetings, Joan saw to it that she remained the gay laughing companion that Killary loved to be with, and as their days all together were spent happily there was no reason for her to be anything other than cheerful when she was with the Renvyles. Once or twice she saw an expression of disapproval on her sister's face, but by prevaricating she managed to persuade Jill into thinking her love for Renvyle was turning into a normal friendship. And indeed she was finding a lot of happiness in these early summer months.

'You're wonderful with children,' Micky said one day, when she had spent some arduous hours with Killary. 'You've missed your vocation.'

'How d'you mean?'

'You ought to look after 'em. Be a nurse or something.'

'I don't really know much about children. I happen to be fond of Killary.'

'She's devoted to you.'

She wondered how much of her affection for the child was because it was Renvyle's. A child of Micky's. A child of his . . . and hers . . . Quickly she pushed the thought from her.

Then one Sunday as her car drew up by the cottage in

Ardbreen Killary rushed out, her face aglow with excitement.

'Mummie's coming, Mummie's coming,' she shouted. 'She's coming for my First Communion. Isn't it lovely!'

Joan's heart missed a beat. 'Well, that's certainly splendid news,' she said.

'And you'll be able to see her at last,' the child sang. 'She's very very very pretty.'

'I know.'

Renvyle came out of the cottage. 'Telling you the exciting news, I see,' he said. 'I must say I'm a bit surprised.'

'Are you?'

'Well, the theatre doesn't allow one to have domestic emotions, you know. The show must go on, and all that. But I gather from Paddy she's not been very well and is out of the cast for the time being.'

'I hope nothing serious?'

'She didn't say so. Anyway I'm very relieved she'll be here.'

'When is she arriving?' Joan asked.

'Middle of this coming week.'

Joan's heart sank. She wanted to see Michael's wife but she did not want to meet her. She had always promised to go to the child's First Communion and she realized she was bound to be considered by Killary, at least, as part of the family.

III

Paddy Renvyle and Joan did not meet until the Corpus Christi procession later in the day. Headed by the small children who had made their First Communion earlier in the day, and still dressed, as Joan had once remarked, like tiny brides, the adults brought up the rear. Joan herself merged into the crowd of villagers from Ardbreen and Ballymannin, and saw Micky and his wife ahead of her. She did not look at all as she had done in the film, Joan was quick to realize. She was simply dressed, and looked pale, and Joan remembered being told she had been unwell. When the procession was over she hesitated, unsure whether to make herself known or not, but Killary's voice suddenly rang out: 'There's Joan. I want her,' and a second later she was being dragged over to where Renvyle stood with his wife.

'So you're Joan Fitzgerald,' Paddy said. 'I've heard a lot about you.'

Joan thought Micky looked a little surprised, but she imagined Killary had talked about her in letters.

'Come back and have a scratch meal, Joan,' Micky said.

'Oh do, Joan. Make one of your omelettes. Mummie, Joan makes gorgeous omelettes when she comes on Sundays.'

'I've only done it about twice, you're exaggerating,' she quickly intervened. 'But I don't think I can,' and she started to make excuses.

'Well, but you must come before I go back to England,' Paddy said with a bright smile.

'Aren't you going to have a real holiday here now that you've managed to come at last?' Joan asked somewhat tactlessly.

'I don't know. I'll see what it feels like to be back after so long. Who knows? I've actually no plans at the moment.'

'That's unusual, darling, isn't it?'

Micky's question, with its careless endearment, cut into Joan's heart. They belonged to each other, was all she could think.

'Where d'you live, Miss Fitzgerald?'

'Just outside Ballymannin.'

'Oh. Not Ardbreen?'

'Oh no!'

'What a long way to come out to see Mick and Killary every week!'

'I've my little car. It doesn't take long. I expect you've forgotten.'

'In my day none of us had a car, you see. Except my father, and I didn't drive then. I've always told Micky he should have one. Perhaps you can persuade him to get one. Even an old thing like that one there would do,' and she pointed to Joan's rather shabby Morris.

'That's mine,' she said humbly.

'Oh! Forgive me! But they're marvellous little cars, I know. I had one to begin with.' She turned to look for Killary. 'Come on, pet,' she called, 'you're beginning to look cold, we must get back. Good-bye, Miss Fitzgerald, I'm sure we'll be meeting sometime.'

Paddy took hold of Renvyle's arm and drew him towards a car, and Joan noticed Killary firmly clinging to the other hand. They looked a happy united family, Joan thought, and she could do nothing about it.

'What a bore the other house is let,' Paddy said after she had been in the cottage three days. 'This was all very well when Killary was tiny but we do seem to be all over each other now. I'd forgotten how small it is.'

'If I thought you'd honour us often I'd move back to Inish when those people leave it,' Renvyle said, 'but personally I'm devoted to this.'

'Oh, don't go moving for my sake,' Paddy said quickly. 'But as I've got this little hired car wouldn't you like for us to tour around a bit? D'you realize how little we both know our own country?'

'Don't you want to stay in Ardbreen?' he asked.

'As long as it keeps fine I don't mind a week of it. But I'd frankly like to go down to the south and explore. Wouldn't you? I don't believe you've ever been to Kerry or Cork, have you?'

'Cork is where Joan was living before she came up here, I believe.'

'Oh? Really? Well, Joan or no Joan, I'd like to go to Killarney. You wouldn't let us go there for our honeymoon. And I'd like to wander around.'

It was Miss O'Malley who told Joan that the Renvyles had gone off on a motor tour. And Joan thought of the hopeless daydreams she had secretly woven which she had always known could never materialize, in which she showed Micky her grandmother's home near Bantry Bay, and the beauty of Glengariff.

'Good morning, Miss O'Malley, and good morning, Joan.' It was Father Delaney's voice which broke into their conversation.

'Hello, Father,' said the older woman. 'I was just telling Miss Fitzgerald that Paddy and Mick have gone off on a motor tour to the south.'

'And a splendid notion. It's fine to see them both together again. Off on a second honeymoon I don't doubt. D'you remember it was where they wanted to go originally and neither of 'em could drive a car and they went to Leenane and told nobody till they were back.'

After spending a few days in Killarney which Paddy said was for tourists and not Irish and she was disappointed by its exploitation, the Renvyles moved to the mouth of the Kenmare river. The weather was good and Micky painted, and in the luxury of the hotel Paddy seemed glad to rest. One or two people recognized her and asked for her autograph, which secretly pleased her.

'Now, if we had a cottage somewhere near here, I might feel more like coming back oftener,' she said one day. 'Or better still at Glengariff. It's much more civilized, don't you agree? I suppose all this lush southern vegetation gets me. And the blueness of the water.'

'No bluer than Killary Harbour.'

'And it is fun to be near quite a lot of decent hotels and seeing all sorts of amusing people. At least I think so. You must admit we're very limited at home.'

'Frankly I hardly ever go into the one at home unless I want to see the Jamesons. It'd never strike me to go into it for a meal. Who with, anyway?'

'You might take your precious Joan. I should think an outing in a restaurant or hotel would do her a world of good.'

'Joan? What an extraordinary idea!'

'I suppose she's in love with you?'

'Paddy! What a monstrous idea! Of course she isn't.'

'Men *are* dense. I suppose it always take other women to spot that sort of thing. I bet she is. Don't tell me she comes out to Ardbreen every week to play with Killary or sail in rough seas.'

'Actually she and Killary seem devoted to each other. And poor Joan knows very few people. Her folk come from down here somewhere.'

'What d'you see in her? She's terribly—well, homely, to put it at its best.'

Micky looked at his wife with an air of perplexity. 'I don't think I've ever given it a thought. What I see in Joan, I mean. She's an awfully nice creature, and we have a lot in common one way and another.'

'I notice she hasn't been near us since I got home.'

'Well, dammit, give the poor girl a chance! She only has Sundays and Wednesday is her half-day, and we've been away. She doesn't come unless she's asked.'

'A door-mat. Poor Joan. I think it's a pity you don't do something about her hair.'

'*Her hair?*'

'It's deadly. Suggest she has a perm.'

'Paddy, you're crazy. I wouldn't dream of making any personal remarks to her, certainly not suggestions. What's the matter with her hair? Anyway, you've only seen her once.'

'Enough to see her hair was greasy and unsoigné. If I were really interested in her I could get her to make herself look much better. But I really don't see why I should bother to beautify a possible rival.' She gave a hard little laugh.

'You're joking,' Micky said.

'Not entirely.'

'Well, please get such ideas out of your mind. I don't find them amusing. To begin with I happen to love you and as for Joan she's very devout and would be affronted by such an idea.'

'All right, darling. I won't tease you any more.'

When the Renvyles had been home for a few days Paddy said to Killary, 'Wouldn't your friend Joan what's-her-name like to come over on Sunday? I've not met her properly.'

The child was enchanted by the prospect and said, 'I'll ring her up. Shall we ask Daddy first?'

'No. You ring her, and say—well, I leave it to you. You're old enough to invite her.'

Killary rushed to the telephone and Paddy, who was reading and pretending not to listen, heard her say, 'Mummie says will you come next Sunday?' and then, 'No, he's not in. No, he didn't, it was Mummie's idea . . . Oh goodee.'

Killary came back into the room. 'Yes, she said she'd like to come.'

'Tell me, sweetie,' said Paddy a little later, 'why do you and Daddy like Joan so much?'

Killary said she didn't know, 'But she's fun and plays games with me. She's ever so kind. She taught Daddy to drive the car.'

'Did she? I thought he learnt with a proper instructor.'

'Lots of people taught him but Joan took him out most times.'

'Do you think she's attractive?'

'What's attractive?'

'Well—sort of pretty.'

'Oh, no, Mummie. But she has a nice face. And a very pretty voice. I like her to read stories to me.'

'I see.'

When Micky returned Paddy said, 'Your girl friend is coming to lunch on Sunday.'

For a moment Micky's face was blank and then he frowned. 'D'you mean Joan?'

'Who else?'

'Who asked her?'

'Killary rang her.'

'What on earth did you do that for, ducky, without my telling you to?' he asked the child.

'But Mummie said so. She thought of it.'

'Oh. Well, that'll be splendid.' And Renvyle went upstairs.

Next day Micky said: 'We'll kill the fatted calf on Sunday, I think. Father Delaney is also coming to lunch. If I'm right, you've scarcely set eyes on him.'

'*Touchéé.*' Paddy bowed, and coloured slightly.

'He'll come after the late Mass, so I don't expect we'll get our meal till nearly two.'

Joan was not sure whether she was relieved or not to find the priest at the cottage when she arrived the following Sunday.

'I was beginning to wonder if I was going to see you at all, Paddy,' he said, when she gave him a drink. 'And why were you not at church this morning?'

'Father, it was dreadful of me. But I overslept, and never thought of putting my alarm clock on. And I couldn't do the later services as I had to cook the lunch.' She looked at the priest with large eyes. 'Please am I forgiven?'

'I hope you don't make a habit of it,' he said with a smile, but Paddy recognized the warning tones in his voice.

'What's a girl friend?' Killary asked Joan after lunch.

'Well, it depends. Why?'

'Are you Daddy's girl friend? Mummie said you were.'

'Not in the way your Mummie meant. But let's say I'm your girl friend and you're mine.'

'She made a mistake, I expect. Daddy looked a bit cross. Shall I tell her? And that you're my girl friend?'

'No, I don't think I'd bother if I were you. How long is your Mummie going to stay?'

There was a lull in the conversation and Paddy, who had been listening to Joan and Killary's talk, chipped in: 'I haven't yet decided. Can I call you Joan? It seems so silly to call you Miss Fitzgerald when I hear Joan continually on my husband's and daughter's lips.'

'Please do,' the girl answered.

'We had such a wonderful time, you know, in the south. I believe your home is down there?'

'My grandmother's house is near Bantry Bay.'

'Yes. Mick said it was. I wondered if he'd ever been there with you?'

'Good heavens, no!' Joan looked horrified, and the colour left her face.

'Don't look so outraged! After all, people motor about all

over the place these days with the most unlikely people. I do myself.'

'Well, I assure you we've not. I have to work, you know.'

'Of course. I'd forgotten. But I hear you like Connemara, anyway.'

This was firmer ground, Joan felt. 'I adore it. Specially all the bit near here. And I think Killary Harbour the loveliest of all.'

'Ah, yes. As I expect you know, Killary Harbour is very special for Mick and me.'

'Yes. Michael told me.'

'Oh, d'you call him Michael? I never think he looks like one. But then of course we were practically brought up together. Which has its pros and cons as I dare say you can guess.'

Joan felt they were nearing dangerous ground again. 'What a wonderful person Father Delaney is,' she said, trying to change the subject.

'M'm. I'm afraid I'm in his bad books. I'd better go and talk to him.'

She went over to where the priest was sitting, and refilled his cup with more coffee, and out of the corner of her eye she knew Micky had gone over to Joan.

'I'd like to see you in church, Paddy, before you go back. Or if you'd like to come up to the presbytery?'

Paddy frowned unconsciously. She knew the priest had meant he wished to hear her confession. 'I'm afraid I've slipped a bit. I've not been to Confession for ages. One of the reasons I've not been to Mass.'

'Then come along soon, dear child, and we'll put it right.' He patted her hand.

Oh dear, she thought, why do I feel I've outgrown Ardbreen? And how ridiculous Mick is, that girl is madly in love with him. Killary is getting more and more like him. What a pity . . . And oh heavens! How am I going to get out of Confession . . . ?

CHAPTER FOUR

'Darling, I wish you didn't have to go back to England. What are your plans? Can't you stay for the rest of the summer? I wish you had never gone on the stage. It's like old times having you back.'

Paddy and Micky were out in *Deirdre,* and were at anchor in Ballynakill Harbour. She was wearing an old pair of slacks, and had come up from the galley with freshly made tea for the two of them.

'You never used to wear trousers,' Micky continued, 'they suit you.'

'It's funny how one's habits change.'

'Anyway, sweetheart, you haven't answered my question.'

Paddy lit a cigarette, which was another new habit she had acknowledged. 'I haven't actually any concrete plans, Mick, but there are one or two things in the offing. Plays, two in fact, one of which will probably materialize. I shall know in about a week's time, I dare say. I love acting in the theatre. The money is good in films, of course, but I don't really care for it. As to staying on here—well—no, Micky darling. I'd soon be bored to tears. It's divine what we're doing today, but one can't spend one's life sailing in *Deirdre* and mooning around here doing chores. I couldn't, anyway. Not any longer.'

'Don't you think you owe some part of your life to Killary, even if you don't to me?'

She looked at him. 'M'm. Yes. I suppose so. But you know she seems much more your child than mine now.'

'And why? Because she hardly sees you. And her excitement when she knew you were coming was really pathetic.'

'It's worn off by now, I assure you. And I don't know what sort of life she'd have with me. School, and as I'm out so much it'd end up as a boarding school and I can't see she'd be any better off than she is now. No, I think we'll have to realize that you and I lead separate lives and meet when conditions let us.'

'I call it a damn unsatisfactory way of living.'

'At least I don't nag at you to make your home with me in London,' Paddy said. 'I realize all this is as necessary to you, as London—and the theatre—is to me.'

About a week later when Paddy was lying in the garden and Killary was running about playing, she said suddenly:

'Poor Killary! That awful plate in her mouth makes her look plainer than ever.'

'She never complains,' Micky answered. 'She's a patient little soul.'

'I really must send her a few decent clothes when I get home,' Paddy said.

The word 'home' hurt Renvyle.

'Who does buy her clothes? You, I suppose.'

'Aunt Cathleen or Joan as a rule,' he replied unthinkingly.

'I might have known it. Neither has a scrap of dress sense.' At that moment the child came up and sat down beside her mother. 'Shall I send you some nice clothes from London?' Paddy asked.

'What, new ones?'

'Well, of course! What would you like?'

Killary thought for a long time. 'I'd like a pink satin frock.'

'Whatever for? When would you wear it?' Paddy seemed amused.

'At Christmas parties. I'd like it all sticking out.'

'I'll see what can be done. What else?'

'I don't know. I growed out of my last year's summer frocks and anyway m'jeans are better on the beach and in boats. Aren't they, Daddy?' She looked to Micky for confirmation. Then her face lit up and she said: 'I know what I would like.'

'What?'

'A new nightie.'

136

'Not pyjamas?'

'No, nighties. Could you afford two?'

'I expect so.'

'With little things on them.'

'What does she mean?' Paddy looked at her husband. He shook his head.

'Little roses and things. And made of silky stuff.'

'Nylon?'

'Yes. Nylon. Like Joan's.'

'How d'you know what she wears?'

'I saw it hanging on a hook in her bedroom when I went to tea with her.'

'How sordid!'

'What's sordid?'

'Untidy.'

'She is untidy. Isn't she, Daddy?'

Renvyle was nonplussed. 'I don't know, is she? I've not seen where she lives.'

'You *have*, Daddy. That little house with Jill. That's her ill sister,' she told Paddy.

'Yes, of course. I meant I haven't been upstairs.'

'Poor Daddy, he's blushing,' Paddy said in provocative tones.

'What's blushing?'

'Going red in the face.'

'Why is he?'

'I think this is rather a stupid conversation,' Micky said. 'Suppose we talk about something else. Your school, for instance.'

'Yes. D'you like school, darling?'

'Yes, Mummie, I do. I like it very much. 'cos I like playing with other children.' She remained silent for a while and then said plaintively: 'I do wish I had a sister. Or even a brother. But I'd like a sister most.'

'Poor Killary. What a shame,' and without realizing it, she spoke aloud her thoughts, 'and you might have done.'

But Killary had seen her favourite trio of donkeys pass the gate and she ran out to talk to them.

'He or she would have been about four by now, I suppose. I wonder what it'd have been like,' Renvyle mused.

Paddy looked at him. 'I wasn't thinking of that.'

'What were you, then?'

'You know I left the cast a few weeks back?'

He nodded.

'That was why.'

'Darling!' Concern shook his voice. 'You mean you had another miscarriage? And you never even wrote and told me you were expecting another child—'

'Well, it wasn't exactly like that other time.'

'How d'you mean?'

'I—er—I didn't want it. And so—I took steps to get rid of it. That's all. It was a costly performance and not particularly pleasant, but that's why I went out of the bill.'

Renvyle recoiled. 'Do you mean to tell me,' he said slowly, 'that you deliberately got rid of a child?'

'I had an operation. Yes.'

'You, a Catholic?'

She nodded, but said nothing.

'You realize, quite apart from the sin of it, that abortion is illegal?'

'Well, naturally, Mick! I'm not quite such a bloody fool.'

He remained silent for a long while.

'I seem to have horrified you. I suppose I knew it would, which is why I didn't tell you.'

'And why, I presume, you've not been to Mass with me? Your confession is between you and Almighty God, but I suppose as a husband I can ask you. Have you seen a priest?'

'No,' Paddy said. 'Frankly I have been a coward.'

Renvyle put his head in his hands. 'I can't believe it,' he said. 'That you could dare do such a thing. To me. Our child—' and suddenly he looked at her. 'I suppose it was mine?'

'Oh yes, darling, it was yours all right. I've not added adultery to my long list of sins. Yet.'

'I feel absolutely sick,' he said. 'You don't know what you've done.'

'I certainly do,' she laughed grimly.

'You don't know what you've done to me. Mentally, spiritually. You murdered a child.'

'Oh, nonsense!'

'It's not nonsense,' and he shouted at his wife for the first time since their marriage. 'You know the Church condemns abortion not only as murder but as mortal sin of the worst kind. And that you could do it against our child, something precious, conceived in love—'

'Oh, don't be so melodramatic, Mick! Talking like something out of *Woman's Own*!' She spoke impatiently. 'It's just one of those things.'

Renvyle looked at her. 'Once, quite long ago, I thought you had killed something in me. But you hadn't. I'm talking of love, the love I'd had for you for many years. It was bruised badly, but it grew again. And I loved you, every bit as much as I had before. But this time you have. Slain it. My love. You're nothing but a monster, Paddy, God help you.'

'Is it your pride that's hurt, Mick? Fatherhood is something very special, I believe. A sort of power to boast about. Is it that that's got into you mostly?'

He shook his head. 'I'm sorry. No. To me it's just blasphemy. A sin against the Holy Ghost. Why, oh why did you do it?' Tears were in his eyes and in his voice.

'I told you,' Paddy replied, 'I didn't—and don't—want another child. I loved Killary when she was a baby and I was young, but that's some time ago, and I'm a bit older. And I don't mean in years. I'm sorry if I've killed a conception of yours—and I don't mean that as a pun—I mean I'm sorry if I've wounded, murdered, whatever you like to call it, your *amour propre.*'

'No, no, it isn't just that. But then, I suppose in my heart I've known for a long time that we've grown apart in our faith,' he said so quietly she could hardly hear the words.

'Poor Micky,' she said dispassionately. 'I've been a failure as a wife. Your wife, at any rate; I dare say as anyone's wife. I suppose I do know—really—how wrong it was. And how wicked. But people are doing it all the time, and somehow it was easy to fall into line.'

He looked at her, bewildered. 'If you'd been a wretched unmarried girl,' he began, 'seduced by some blighter who wouldn't marry you, I could have understood it, tho' not condoned, but—'

'But I've put myself beyond the pale, I see. I understand.' She got up. 'There's nothing much more to be said in the matter. Are you going to forgive me?'

He looked at her coldly.

'It's you that are melodramatic now,' he replied. 'It's not for me to forgive. You know that.' And he went out on to the shore, closing the gate behind him.

CHAPTER FIVE

RENVYLE did not see Joan for some weeks. After Paddy left hurriedly—presumably because of a call from London—he seemed to shun everybody. The most difficult person to face was Miss O'Malley, with whom they had all been invited to lunch two days after his scene with Paddy.

'But she told me only a few days ago that she wasn't expecting to do anything yet. And anyway I can't understand her not coming to say good-bye to me. I've seen little enough of her, as it is.' She sniffed. Micky continued to mumble excuses, he was no good as a liar. Miss O'Malley gave him a piercing look. 'It's my belief the whole thing is a jumped-up excuse. You've had a row and she's gone off.'

He was silent.

'Well, it's none of my business, and I dare say she's become difficult. In fact I could see that for myself. But I'd like to have seen her once more. It's not as if she comes home often.' After a pause she went on, 'And I don't suppose you know when she'll be over again?'

Renvyle shook his head. 'Perhaps I may as well tell you that Paddy and I are not likely to come together for a long while, if ever.' Seeing the look of distress on the woman's face he said, 'I'm very sorry,' and left the house.

Father Delaney was easier to hoodwink.

'Is it true that bad girl has gone off without coming to see me?' he said, when he ran into Micky, but he spoke with a twinkle in his eye.

'Yes. She left in rather a hurry.'

'I'm sorry, for I should have liked a real talk with Paddy. I thought she had altered, but it was natural, I suppose.'

Renvyle murmured something to the same effect and went his way.

'I do hope Mummie won't forget about the frock and the nighties,' Killary said. 'Do you think you could write and remind her, Daddy?'

Micky looked at the child, hardly aware of her question.

'You'd better,' he said presently when she had repeated it.

He spent his days sailing mostly, sometimes taking Killary with him, but more often than not alone.

'I don't know what the matter is, I'm sure,' Cathleen O'Malley said, when Killary complained of her father's sudden neglect.

'It's holidays, Auntie Leen. And Daddy nearly always takes me when it's holidays. First Mummie goes and then Daddy gets like this. I wish Joan would come and play.'

'It's not her holiday time, and when it is she's going to her grandmother, so she told me.'

And the child was left very much to her own devices and to the companionship of the children of the village.

It was by chance that Joan heard of Paddy Renvyle's departure, and although she found personal relief in the fact, there was nothing to surprise her in the news, for it was bound to happen at some time. She wondered all the same why it was that Micky kept himself hidden, and again she supposed his mind was still full of Paddy and that he had no time for her.

'You really ought to get out more, and with other people,' her sister said. 'I shall really be glad when you get your holiday and we go to Granny. The break will do you good.'

'Daddy, look! I've got a postcard from Joan,' Killary said one day. 'It says Bantry Bay. Isn't it pretty? She's having a holiday with her Granny. Did you know she had gone away?'

Renvyle shook his head.

'You can look at it,' Killary said. 'We haven't seen Joan for simply ages. Not since she came to dinner and Mummie was here. And Father Delaney too.'

She sighed.

'What *is a* girl friend, Daddy?'

'Someone very special, as a rule. Why?'

' 'cos Mummie said Joan was your girl friend, but Joan said no she wasn't but she and me are girl friends. It doesn't *seem* to be very special.'

'Well, she's sent you a pretty postcard. That's quite special.'

It was a few weeks later that Renvyle found himself having to take a ticket for the dance in aid of a local charity. It was to be held at Ballymannin and he had had no intention of going, but when the Jamesons asked him to join their party he could not think of an excuse and gave in to their persuasive tongues.

'Quite a crowd of us are all going from the hotel,' Mrs Jameson told him, 'and really, Mick, it's time you shook yourself up a bit.'

'I'm no great shakes at all these modern dances, y'know,' he began, but she would have none of it.

By the time he had eaten an extremely good dinner at the hotel, and found he was not expected to drive the car, he began to enjoy the evening. He had been at the dance nearly an hour and was giving Mrs Jameson a drink at the buffet bar when he heard her catch her breath and say, 'Well, would you believe it! Look who's here and me scarcely recognizing her! Joan Fitzgerald herself, and looking pretty as a picture! Glory be to God! What's come over her?'

Renvyle turned and saw Joan dancing past him. She did look different, Mrs Jameson was right.

'What has she done?' he found himself asking her.

'For one thing she's wearing a *very* pretty dress,' the woman replied. 'Of course, she always had a beautiful figure and lovely legs. But it's her hair. She's had it cut, and a perm or something. And she's wearing quite a bit of make-up. It suits her, don't you think?'

'It certainly makes her look a lot different,' he admitted.

When the music stopped and the dance finished Joan and her partner came over to the bar.

'I never thought I'd see you here, somehow, Michael,' she said.

'What have you done to yourself?' Mrs Jameson asked. 'You're looking radiant.'

143

'My new frock and my new hair-do. D'you approve, Michael?'

'I think you look absolutely charming,' he stammered.

'It was one of my aunts down in Cork,' she told them. 'She said I was letting myself go to pieces, so she bullied me into all this finery and nonsense. I'm glad you like it.' As Mrs Jameson had turned to talk to someone else, and Renvyle was the only recipient of her remarks, she blushed.

The band started up again and he said, 'Shall we have this?'

Joan was a beautiful dancer, and seemed like thistledown in his arms.

'Do you do a lot of this sort of thing?' he asked her.

'Not as much as I used.'

'D'you like it?'

'Dancing? I adore it.'

It was odd, he thought, how little a part it had played in his life. He had certainly danced with very few women, Paddy had been his regular partner in pre-marriage days. As for Joan, she wanted the evening to go on for ever. She hoped Micky did not feel her heart beating.

'It's nice to see you, Michael, after all this time,' she said later.

'That's a very pretty dress. Green suits you,' he answered.

'I don't suppose you'd have noticed if Mrs Jameson hadn't made remarks about it,' she laughed.

'Perhaps not. I don't know. You look different, though.'

'A change for the better?'

'I wouldn't like to say that,' and he smiled, 'I always liked you the way you looked.'

'I don't think you'd be one to notice how women look, except Paddy.'

She felt him stiffen. He made no reply but continued to dance in silence. When the band stopped he took her to the bar.

'Oughtn't you to rejoin your party?' she asked.

'Probably. But I'd rather be with you. And I nearly gave the whole show a miss! What'd you like?'

'I think I'd like an Irish coffee,' Joan rejoined.

'Fine. I'll have one too and then we'll sit it out and talk.'

'What did you do on your holiday apart from beautifying yourself?' he said when he brought over the glasses.

'I fished quite a bit. And got up late, the mornings I didn't! And went to a few dances. And cocktail do's. I was very social,' she said gaily.

'And I suppose you're bored at having to come back and work.'

'Oh no!' she exclaimed. 'I was longing to. As a matter of fact I had a very good job offered me in the south. I turned it down.'

'I'm glad,' he said.

She turned and looked at him. 'Are you? Are you really?'

And suddenly Paddy's words rang in his ears: 'I suppose she's in love with you.'

'Come over to Ardbreen on Sunday,' he said, changing the subject, 'Killary is longing to see you.'

For the first time since they had known each other Renvyle began to be aware of a difference in his relationship with Joan. He realized this the Sunday following the dance at Bally-mannin, when she came over to lunch. There seemed to be silences where none had been before, or if there had been he had not been aware of them. Women had played so small a part in his life that to find himself suddenly thinking of Joan when she was not with him, and equally to find conversation less easy when she was, perplexed him in the extreme. And Joan herself had changed, or so it seemed to him. The hearty laughing companion of Killary had turned into somebody very quiet.

Renvyle did not find this dull; on the contrary he sensed a new-found peace between them. He began to look at her as a woman, not just the girl he had known for some months, whom he had considered as much his child's friend as his own. He found he was telling her things about himself and his work which he had not done before. She knew very little about paint-ing, it was true, but he enjoyed discussing books and literature with her, and often they spoke about Killary's education together and it touched him to discover how genuinely fond

145

of the child she was. Each time he found himself looking forward to their next meeting, and it was not until Father Delaney tackled him one day that he realized that their mid-week meetings could lead to the compromising of Joan or give rise to gossip. Often in the autumn Wednesday afternoons with Killary in school, Joan and he would meet and either fish or drive, and on their return frequently would wave to the priest if they saw him.

'D'you think you're doing the right thing by taking Joan Fitzgerald out alone with you as often as you do?' he asked one day. Renvyle looked startled. 'I know there's no harm meant, Mick, but you're a married man and Joan is in a vulnerable position. You wouldn't want her to get talked about, now would you?'

'Great heavens, of course not! But surely a few drives here and there . . .'

'It looks as though they're weekly occurrences, Mick. She's a nice girl, a good girl, and I wouldn't want her to be hurt.'

'Hurt! Why should she be?'

'A girl can be misled—wrongly encouraged to think a man cares for her. I wouldn't like that to happen to her.'

Micky was silent for a few seconds and then said, 'I am very fond of Joan, Father. I don't think I'm in love with her. I find her a delightful companion, soothing and undemanding, and young Killary is devoted to her. And so, for that matter, is she to Killary. I think Joan would be more hurt if she had to give up our sailing and fishing and drives than she would be if— surely it's only an if?—idle gossip started about the two of us.'

'Maybe you're right, my son. But I thought I'd warn you.'

As Micky walked home from the village he felt a sudden anger surge within him. What right had anyone—even Father Delaney—to criticize his harmless friendship which was only bringing pleasure to two possibly lonely people? He hoped the priest would not talk to Joan as well, it would disturb and horrify her. 'She's in love with you. . . .' Paddy's light voice, tinged with patronizing scorn, re-echoed in his head. Was she?

Could she be? And supposing she was, what was he going to do about it? It was always flattering for a man to know a woman wanted him, but Micky Renvyle was not like many other men. Sex conquest would only leave him in a disturbed frame of mind unless he too felt the same compelling urge and reciprocation, and he denied this. Why then was he angered by the priest's words? Why did he fear the cessation of meetings?

He began to think of Paddy. What were his feelings for her now that his first furious horror was over? He knew his heart held no love for her; there was contempt, and there was still bitterness. He neither loved nor hated his wife, there was a void, it was almost as if she was not. He supposed he would have to confess this, and he wondered how he was going to tell the truth about his feelings without justifying himself, which could only come about by telling the whole of the sordid story which was not his alone to tell. In any case confession was not a means by which one hoped to justify oneself by laying sins and reasons on the shoulders of another.

'Molly Jameson is having a dinner-dance next Wednesday as it's her birthday,' Joan said to Renvyle one Sunday. 'Are you going?'

He was surprised. 'I suppose I shall have to. Are you?'

'I think I shall. One gets in a rut if one never goes out at night. And I do love dancing.'

Already, in her mind, Joan was in Renvyle's arms again. They were out walking with Killary and the dog on the hill road above Tully lake.

'Is Paddy coming for Christmas?' she asked tentatively.

'No,' and then after a pause he said, 'Joan, I may as well tell you Paddy and I have broken up.'

Joan felt her heart lighten and at the same time she was distressed for any grief Renvyle was feeling.

'Oh, Michael. I'm terribly sorry. D'you want to talk about it?'

'I don't know. I can't tell you the reason. At least I don't think I can.'

'I suppose she's fallen in love with someone else,' Joan said.

'No, it isn't that. I wish it were. I could understand it better.'

Joan looked at him and was alarmed by the hard look on his face.

'No. I'll tell you. She found she was going to have another child. Ours. She did not want it. So she had an operation. An abortion.'

'Oh, Mick . . .'

The pain in Joan's exclamation was not entirely for the grief she felt for Renvyle. There was pain for the horror she felt at the offence. And there was pain for the realization that even so recently Paddy had conceived a child by Renvyle.

'It's nice of you to care,' he said.

'How could she?' Joan was thinking as they continued the way down to the village.

'As she killed our child, so it has killed my love for her,' Renvyle said.

'Did you want another one badly, Mick? Another child, I mean?'

'N—no, not particularly. I never really thought about it. It would have been a good thing for Killary to have had a sister or brother. And one supposes it would have brought us—Paddy and myself—back to a normal life. But you can see, the thing was doomed. It was the appalling unnatural aspect of the business that revolted me. An animal wouldn't do such a thing.'

'Only because they wouldn't know how to! My dear, you must realize that it is for us—Catholics I mean—a much worse sin than for a great number of people. It's done, you know.'

'Surely *you* don't condone it?'

'I think it's frightful. But you want to get it in the right perspective, if it's possible.'

'It isn't,' he said harshly.

'I'm dreadfully, dreadfully sorry,' she said. 'Thank you for telling me. And try not to be lonely.'

Lonely, yes, she was right. For the rest of his life he would have to forgo woman's love, woman's companionship. Not companionship surely? But was it possible to have one without the other? Already Joan's very sympathy for him was verging dangerously near to something—'She's in love with you.'

Supposing one day he was to love another woman? Need another woman, want another woman? Supposing that woman was Joan?

'Daddy, Joan,' Killary ran limping towards them, blood streaming from her knee, tears running down her face, 'I've fallen down and cutted myself terribly,' she howled.

The child's plight drove all thoughts of themselves from Joan and Micky. 'We'll carry her to the stream,' Micky said, 'and wash it first. It'll be all right, darling, don't make such a row.'

Gradually the sobs subsided, and she even smiled as between them Renvyle and Joan searched frantically for something linen to bind round the deep cut.

'I can't walk home,' she complained.

'No, of course you can't,' Joan acknowledged. 'We'll carry you, between us.'

'You're not going to,' Micky said. 'She's far too heavy. I'll pick-a-back her.'

And slowly they made their way to the cottage, each adult trying to make feeble jokes to cheer the child.

CHAPTER SIX

Micky realized with a pang of annoyance that he was to sit nowhere near Joan at the Jamesons' party. And it was a long time before he was even able to ask her for a dance.

'At last!' he said somewhat impatiently. 'I thought I was never going to get you to myself.'

And this is very heaven, thought Joan.

'How's Killary's leg?' she asked.

'Quite all right again. But it was nasty, poor little thing.'

'I love that green thing you've got on,' he said a little later. 'You look like a hamadryad.'

She laughed delightedly. 'I wish I could think so.'

He felt suddenly younger, and had an insane longing to kiss the top of her head. The tune stopped and the man who was working the radiogram had disappeared for a drink.

'Let's see what they've got,' Joan said, and started to rummage amongst the records. 'Here's one I love,' she said, putting on 'This is my lovely day'. 'It's rather old, but I adore it.' And he noticed she sang the words softly as they danced.

'Past happy romantic memories?' he teased.

She shook her head. 'I haven't any.'

'I can't believe it. Never been in love?'

'I didn't say that.'

'I'm sorry. I didn't mean to—' he was all contrition.

'You don't have to apologize. I'm not remembering past memories happy or unhappy. And this song is called *"This* is my lovely day".'

He squeezed her hand slightly and they finished the dance without further conversation.

While they were having drinks at the bar someone came in and said, 'There's a glorious moon outside, but it's damn cold.'

'Finish up your whisky and put on a wrap,' Mick ordered her.

They went outside. Joan shivered.

'It's a perfect night.'

They wandered slowly across the lawn, and he held her hand in the pocket of his coat. Someone started the music up again. 'That's a very old one,' Micky said, as the strains of 'All the things you are' wafted across the air. Suddenly he took her in her arms and kissed her. 'I know this is wrong, Joan darling,' he whispered, 'but you see, I love you.'

She clung to him, troubled yet deliriously happy.

'Darling, darling, darling,' she said brokenly.

'Oh, damn,' and he pushed her from him.

'Must you? Must we?'

'We must try to be sensible,' he answered. 'I do love you, I didn't realize it till—well, I don't know when I knew it. But you know there's nothing we can do about it. And I mustn't hurt you.'

'Your love couldn't hurt me, and mine couldn't hurt you, my precious one,' she said.

'You do, then?'

'What, love you? I've loved you for ages, God forgive me.'

'Paddy said you did.'

'Oh, did she? Well, she was right. But don't let's let it make us miserable, darling. Let it be wonderful. Like the tune we danced to, "This is my lovely day"—remember?' and she started to hum.

He drew her towards him once more.

'I was very young when I got married,' he told her, 'and I loved Paddy in those days in a very un-adult fashion. I'm much older now. I don't think this can be a very happy thing for us.'

She brought his lips to hers.

'Darling,' she said, 'don't let's *think* just yet. Can't you let us enjoy what we have, for just a little while? I know we can't be married, and I know we can't belong to each other, but just loving isn't going to harm either of our souls.'

'Will it be enough?' he asked.

'Michael, love, please just do as I ask. Love me and let me love you. In our minds and hearts, I mean.'

He kissed the top of her head. 'We'd better go back. I hear other people coming.'

They turned and looked at the shore once more, the moon shone over the giant rocks and in the distance could be seen the bare black outline of islands.

'I love you,' they said together, and turned back to the hotel.

At first their declaration of love seemed a marvellous thing to both of them. Renvyle tried to push away from his mind the knowledge that love such as theirs could not be materialized in the eyes of the Church, and Joan was so happy in the realization of his love for her, that mind and spirit alone rejoiced in the fact. She had loved him for so long, denying, moreover, the physical aspects, that it did not at first strike her that the very fact that as her love had become mutual—'their' love—it might grow dangerously out of bounds. They met now as new people, stars danced in her eyes and for the first time for years Renvyle knew what it was to be young in heart. They would take the car and drive into the mountains and were happy walking hand in hand, or watching birds in childish excitement. In the evenings between meetings Joan would speak to him on the telephone.

'Where are you speaking from?' he asked the first time she rang.

'In a call-box. I didn't dare from the house, Jill would have heard me.'

'Doesn't she wonder what you're doing out at this time of the evening, my sweet?'

'I'll have to think of some excuse. I couldn't earlier, could I, or Killary would have been up. She's asleep, I suppose?'

'Yes. Darling. How wonderful. To hear you.'

'I know. I just wanted to know what you've been doing all day.'

'Thinking about you.'

Sundays were days of play-acting for both of them, for they could not allow their love to be realized by the child.

Christmas drew nearer, and Killary said, 'I wish Joan could stay with us, why can't she?'

'She has to stay with Jill,' Micky answered.

'I should like Jill to go back to their Granny and for Joan to live with us. Wouldn't that be nice?'

'It would indeed.'

But Joan's eyes were troubled when they met on Christmas Eve, and Renvyle saw that she had been crying.

'Darling, what's the matter?' he asked.

'Mick, I went to Confession. I had to say about—us. I mean that I loved you. I had to say I'd try and stop loving you. How can I?'

'I haven't been yet. Darling, don't make our love out as wrong, for it isn't. Yet,' he added as an afterthought.

'It's wrong even to love you. Because you're married,' she said brokenly.

'I'll bet it wasn't Father Delaney you went to,' Micky remarked.

'As a matter of fact it wasn't. He wasn't there.'

'You know, it's a difficult business. The Church is infallible, but priests aren't, and I know from experience that they don't always see eye to eye or agree as to what is sin. I knew a chap once who was in love with a married woman. He lived with her, her husband was miles away and had left her in actual fact. This chap and the woman adored each other, she wasn't a Catholic, he was. I know for a fact the man was given Absolution.'

'That's not going to help us,' said Joan.

'No, but I don't want you to grieve when you needn't. Love— true, selfless love—can't be sinful.'

'He said we mustn't kiss each other.'

'Oh. Well . . .'

A woman stopped to speak to Joan, and Micky left. On his way home he stopped at the Presbytery at Ardbreen where he was greeted by Father Delaney.

'Hullo, my son. Come in and have some Christmas cheer.'

153

'I will. And I've brought you some as a present,' Micky said, and put down two bottles.

'Father,' he began, 'I want to talk to you, before I make my Confession in church.'

And so, over a couple of drinks, Micky told the priest he had known all his life what had happened to his marriage. He spared him nothing, and at the end of the story he said, '*And* I admit I love Joan. You warned me, and I was annoyed at the time because then I was unaware of what she meant to me. But there it is.'

'It's a pitiful business. Poor, poor Paddy,' Father Delaney spoke slowly. 'If only she had come to see me before she went back.'

'You wouldn't have been able to have moved her, Father. She's become stone.'

'Don't allow hardness to enter your heart against her, my son.'

'Not after what she has done? To me and to our child?' he cried.

'That's her sin, not yours. Remember that. I can understand how you feel, but it isn't for you—even as her husband—to judge. Only God can judge.'

'And surely you, as His priest, must condemn—'

'Micky, son, you are not making Paddy's Confession. Please remember that.'

'I'm sorry, Father.'

'I was saying, I am truly sorry for you. Sorry that your marriage has gone on the rocks. But by prayer it may right itself.'

'Never. I could never get to love her again.'

'And what of the sin of pride, Micky?'

Renvyle was silent.

'As to your love for Joan, poor girl. You know in your heart, and in your conscience you will know, if that love is pure or whether it is an impure love, I'm not going to call it by an uglier name for I know you, Mick, know you well enough to trust your thoughts and what you make of them. You're treading on very dangerous ground, but you're two adult people, hitherto two good children of the Church, and I believe you will keep to what you know to be right. But please, boyo, come and see me in church later today, so that you can make your Confession before the Mass tonight. You'll be coming at midnight? You know we're having it back here this year.'

'Yes. I—' he hesitated. 'Joan and I wanted to be together. Will that be in order?'

The priest smiled. 'But of course. It will help both of you. God bless you, my son. And I'll be in church in two hours' time, hearing Confessions.'

For a few weeks, a few months, the love of Renvyle for Joan and Joan's for Renvyle continued smoothly, peacefully. No word at all came from Paddy beyond presents for Killary at Christmas.

'Did you know my niece is going on tour to Australia?' Miss O'Malley asked Micky one day in the following March.

He shook his head.

'I had a letter today. She sent me a *cheque*,' she sounded quite affronted, 'for my birthday. Yes, she's off quite soon. Never mentioned either you or the child.'

'We're not the only Catholics whose marriage has come unstuck,' Micky said. 'But I'm sorry and disappointed.'

'We should never have allowed her to go to England in the first place. We're all to blame.'

'You're probably right.'

'I know we are,' she snorted, and then a little less harshly she went on, 'and I'm sorry for you, Mick. It's no life for a man. And you needn't think I don't know how things are between you and Joan.'

This startled Renvyle, who began to stammer.

'I'm not blaming you. She's a nice girl, a good girl. It's unfortunate for the two of you. I sometimes think it would be wiser, though, if she left the district.'

Although the same idea had also struck Mick, he was not going to allow the interference of an outsider to accomplish such a plan.

'I don't think so,' he said stiffly.

'It's nothing to do with me, in any case,' Miss O'Malley said, to his relief.

With the coming of spring and the lengthening of days and daylight Renvyle took *Deirdre* round to Ballynakill.

'I'm going to anchor her off,' he told Joan. 'The reason being that we aren't so easily seen. It's quicker for you to get here of an evening, and I can slip over quite easily. If you come to Ardbreen every evening people are bound to talk, and I can't exist on one half-day a week of you. I don't count Sundays, Killary's there.'

'But isn't she going to think it strange, your suddenly taking every evening off?'

'Fishing? I do, frequently.'

'But keeping *Deirdre* over at Ballynakill?'

'Oh, I'll think up something. A better anchorage, which is true. Children are easily fobbed off.'

Finding themselves alone, often at sea, away from all contact with people, looking at the beauty of their surroundings—mountains, islands, sunsets—it was not so easy to keep emotion at bay, or to refrain from ardent love-making once a few kisses had been exchanged. Joan loved to sit beside Renvyle, her head leaning against his shoulder, her hand in his, and watch the beauty of the land as they sailed in silence. But the man began to find her very acceptance of their situation frustrating, and the realization that Joan was herself a far more passionate lover than Paddy had ever been only helped to irritate his nerves.

'I don't know what's going to be the outcome of it all,' he said in despair one evening, thrusting her from him, and lighting a cigarette, 'I want you, Joan.'

'If we were other people, I suppose we'd become lovers,' she said quietly, 'but darling, we can't, we mustn't.'

'Are you afraid?'

She looked at him in surprise. 'Afraid? Of course not. Not in the way you mean. But I am afraid of myself, sometimes. And my love. Darling, can't you understand what death it would be to know this love of ours would be wicked and wrong? Heaven knows I used to be wretched when I nursed what I thought was an unrequited love for you—'

'Did you? How sweet!' He kissed her again.

'But knowing we love each other has altered that. It's funny, too, because I remember telling Jill that I'd be unhappier still if you were suffering as well.'

'My God! Does she know?'

'She did. But she doesn't. I mean, she knew I was in love with you. She thinks I've got over it. Anyway she doesn't know you love me.'

'What does she think you're up to every evening?'

'I go for walks! I always was a walker on summer evenings, luckily. And she goes to bed early anyway. If she suspects anything I think she'd keep it to herself. She's very much an ostrich. Her initial warning made, I don't think she'd repeat it.'

Another evening as she lay in his arms he said:

'You don't know much about men, do you?'

'Nothing. Why?'

'Kiss me.'

A little later she looked up at him and said:

'I suppose it's because I am a virgin that it isn't quite so awful for me. I mean, I don't know what I'm missing.'

He laughed. 'You do say some gloriously naïve things occasionally, bless you. But maybe you've hit the nail on the head!'

'All the same, it's pretty ghastly for me not to be able to give you all you want, and me wanting to anyway. All because of my wretched conscience. Sometimes I wish to goodness I wasn't the good Catholic I am, and then I say to myself, Joan, that's blasphemy and worse than the venal desire you have.'

Micky stopped her mouth with a kiss.

'It's gratifying to hear you have the "venal" desire at any rate——*and* you mean "carnal", darling!'

'Oh, I have, I have.' She sat up, and started to put her hair tidy. 'Mother of God! D'you think I don't yearn to be your wife and the mother of your children? And to be with you always, looking after you, cooking for you, looking after Killary?'

'I wonder,' he said slowly, 'if I could get a divorce.'

He felt her shrink from him and saw by the look on her face that he had shocked her.

'And what would be the use of that?' she cried. 'You don't think I'd marry you like that? That would not be a Christian marriage. No marriage at all. You know it wouldn't even be legal here.'

'Catholics—some Catholics—have been able to get annulments.'

'I don't see how you could, with Killary.'

'If I could bring proof that Paddy refused to sleep with me.'

'But did she?'

'Not then. And I think she'd fight it all, anyway.'

'And think, my darling, of all the sordid details. Oh, horrible! No—we must become like great lovers in history. Tristan and Isolde, Paolo and Francesca, Abélard and Héloïse—'

'You needn't sound so pleased with the idea.'

'I'm not, I'm trying to be sane.' Later she said: 'It would kill me, but would you rather we stopped it? Now?'

'Would you?'

She shook her head. 'No. I'd rather have half a loaf. But if it would help you—as a man—for us to stop these evenings and just meet when Killary is with us, I'll do what you wish. If you feel it's easier for you not to kiss me, I'll try to understand.'

'I have every intention, my blessèd, of continuing to see you and making love to you, or as much as you allow me to.'

She sighed.

'Dear Lord, keep me strong enough to withstand the temptations—' she was whispering.

'—of the devil? Don't make me out your Mephistopheles!'

'It was Faust who got the poor girl into trouble, not the old devil,' she laughed, 'but how like a man to put it all on the girl.

I shall need all the prayers and help of the Blessed Virgin if I'm to withstand your wiles. So please, dear love, try and help me. For if I did become your—love—I should end by hating myself and you might, too, and that would be death itself. As it is, I'm wicked to be living for your kisses, you married man!'

CHAPTER SEVEN

I

On Killary's birthday, which was a Sunday, she had a picnic at little Killary Harbour. They went in Joan's car after lunching at Miss O'Malley's. Joan brought her a new Aran-knitted pullover and she had presents from Micky and her aunt, but nothing had come from Paddy.

'She's completely forgottened me. I wish you were my Mummie,' she said to Joan.

'I wish I was,' was the reply, as there was nobody in the room to hear her but the child.

'You haven't got any children, have you? Why haven't you?'

'Because I'm not married.'

'Oh. I see. You mean you haven't got a man? I mean like Daddy in the house with you?'

'That's what I mean, yes,' said Joan, trying not to laugh.

'What a pity.'

When Micky came into the room Killary showed him the pullover with great excitement.

'But isn't it a pity Joan hasn't a man and can't have any little children?'

'A husband, she means,' said Joan, stifling her laughter at Renvyle's face.

'Is Daddy a husband?'

'Yes, of course I am, silly. I'm Mummie's husband.'

'But as Mummie has gone away ages ago and has forgottened my birthday couldn't you be Joan's husband and then she could come and live with us?' And she turned joyfully to Joan and said, 'And then you could have some children after all. You'd like that, wouldn't you?'

'Go and get your things ready and stop talking nonsense,' Micky said gruffly.

'Darling, don't be cross with her,' Joan went up to him and put her arm through his. 'I think her ideas are perfectly angelic and it makes me want to cry.'

'Trouble with children is that one never knows what on earth they'll say next.'

'It's pathetic to think all three of us want the same thing,' Joan said, as they went out to the car.

'I'm to have my holiday in September this year,' she told Micky while they were sitting on the slopes above Killary Harbour, watching the child at play below. 'I shall have to go to my grandmother again. What a waste of precious days.'

'Must you?'

'I can't get out of it. Not without causing her sorrow, and she's a dear old lady. Besides Jill is longing to go. She'll probably start off before me.'

'Let me come and see you in the cottage when she has gone.'

She shook her head. 'It wouldn't be safe.'

'Darling, there aren't any near-by houses. No one would know.'

'I don't mean that. If you wanted—to love me properly—I think I should capitulate. I don't trust myself, it's not my neighbours I'm afraid of.'

'Oh darling—darling—'

'That's why these days out of doors, with Killary near us, are safest. We can talk of all we long for and get no farther. It's better that way.'

'It's torture. Don't you realize what it does to me?'

She was silent for a little while and then said, 'I do wonder, don't you, how much is counted as sin in one's mind and one's heart?'

'How d'you mean?'

'Do you suppose if every night I slept with you in my heart, thought myself in your arms, I'd be committing a sin?'

'I expect so,' Micky spoke bitterly. 'You'd better ask a priest. For my part I'd rather not have the temptation.'

'Why not?'

'You wouldn't understand. Darling, Killary's waving to us, we'd better go and see what she wants.'

It wasn't always with a sense of frustration that their meetings ended. There were days when Renvyle took his painting materials with him and was quite happy and at peace with Joan beside him either reading or knitting.

'D'you make much money?' she asked one day.

'Damn little! A few hundred a year. I have my father's little bit. But all in all I don't have much more than seven hundred. It's a poor man that you love, I fear, my Joan.' He threw down his brush and looked across at her. 'Isn't it funny, I've never been ambitious from a money-making point of view. As long as I'm not in debt and have enough for our wants—Killary's and mine—it's all I've wanted. And now I long to give you things, things that I shall never be able to afford.'

'Such as?'

'Mink coats. Diamonds. A nice car.'

Joan burst out laughing. 'Silly old darling! I hate fur coats. And what on earth would I do with diamonds? And I'm really rather fond of the little old car. But oh! I do love you for wanting to give them to me. I wouldn't love you nearly so much if you were rich, I may as well tell you.'

'Wouldn't you?'

'No. I don't think it'd suit you. I can't imagine you in smart tweeds, which I suppose you'd wear. Or puffing cigars—'

'I shouldn't, I hate 'em.'

'And imagine us—you and I—seriously going somewhere smart and grand like Ashford Castle to eat a meal. No. I want you as you are, in your shabby old duffle, and your hair blowing in the wind, and both of us excited over stale ham sandwiches. And that view.'

They were picnicking by the shore of Lough Inagh and Renvyle was sketching the Maamturks.

'Many's the night I've camped out on these peaks,' he said, 'though not since I married. Shall we do it one day? Climb and become lost and sleep in one another's arms?'

'You are hopeless.' She sighed a little as she smiled at his

162

question. 'How often do I have to tell you I'm not spending any nights with you, on mountains or anywhere else?'

'I guess I'm in danger of lapsing. Becoming a bad Catholic.'

'Oh don't, my darling. That would hurt me so terribly. It's partly because I'm so afraid for you that I have to be so strict with myself. It seems I have to protect us both.'

'From merely doing what nature intended a man and woman to do.'

'Not when one of them already has a wife, I'm afraid.'

'Thousands of Catholics have already committed adultery and thousands more will,' he said angrily.

'And I don't intend to be one of them,' she said coolly.

'Sometimes I do wonder if you care as much as you say you do,' he went on.

'What a cruel thing to say to me.' Her eyes filled.

'I suppose women do get scared the first time. When they're no longer particularly young—'

'I'm not thirty yet—'

'Not many virgins left over twenty, or so I'm told.'

'Micky, this isn't a very pretty conversation.'

'I'm not feeling in a particularly pretty mood.'

'So I see. You'd better get on with your picture, and I shall go for a walk.'

Joan got up and left him and wandered along the road by the water's edge. Micky was becoming unreasonable, she told herself. It was frightening her that a Catholic—devout as she knew him to be—should be going to pieces morally, with herself as the cause. Had she got to make the extreme sacrifice? Must she write from Cork when she reached her grandmother's and tell him she would not return? She knew she could not do this. If a break was ever to come, then it must come from him. There were plenty of people—non-Catholics—she knew well enough, who would take his side and say that a woman worth her salt should give the man she loved what he wanted in the circumstances. There were people who would say let him get a divorce in England, where Paddy was domiciled, and leave him free to legalize a marriage by registrar. How could she, how could she, Joan asked herself in torture, deny her whole faith by acceding to Mick's physical need of her? And if she gave into him once it would not stop there. She would become his mistress . . . Oh, it was unthinkable. How could he be so selfish? Did the teaching of the Church mean nothing to him any longer? And did he really mean to torment and torture her by disbelieving in her love for him?

She was away about an hour and when she returned he looked at her shamefacedly.

'Forgive me, Joan,' he said humbly, 'I talked like a swine to you. You're a saint and I'm a brute, and I'm not worthy of your love.'

'We'll forget it, my darling. It's difficult for both of us.' She started to pack up their picnic.

'Come and look at this,' he said, and she went over to the easel.

'It's lovely,' she said, putting her arm through his.

II

A few days before Joan was due to depart on her holiday she was surprised to see Renvyle come into the library.

'It's Killary,' he said. 'She's ill. The doctor doesn't seem to know what the matter is.'

'What sort of thing?'

'She has a temperature and a frightful head, and doesn't seem to want to move.'

'Could it be measles?'

'He says there aren't any cases at all anywhere. Joan, I'm desperate. Could it be polio?'

'Oh, God—' She looked into the eyes which held so much agony. 'Who's looking after her?'

'Well, I am. Aunt Cathleen is away. The doctor won't move her.'

'Darling, I shall come and nurse her if she's really going to be ill. It may turn out to be nothing at all, children sometimes run the most incredibly high temperatures and—'

'But you're off to Cork.'

'I shall wire that I can't go. A friend's very ill child. I can't let the two of you be alone here, without a woman to cope. Now, darling, please don't argue. And I shall either ring or come right out this evening.'

Killary's illness was meningitis.

'Doctor Malone says she mustn't be moved,' Renvyle told Joan when she rang. 'He's sending a nurse, but of course she can't do it day and night.'

'That's all right, my dear. I'll take on the extra and do anything—absolutely anything—I can. Doctor Malone is my own doctor and I'll go along and see him about it.'

For several weeks Killary's life seemed to hang in the balance. She was in constant pain and cried out if she was moved, yet withal very rarely lost consciousness. She lay in a darkened room and seemed happiest when Joan was with her holding her hot little hand. Various drugs were administered until at last one seemed to alleviate the pain, and very gradually the use of her limbs began to return.

'Did you ever let Paddy know?' Joan said suddenly one day. 'I forgot all about her.'

'I don't know where she is. She has an agent but God knows what his name is. She's in the Antipodes or somewhere, anyway.'

In their worry about the child neither Micky nor Joan gave thought to themselves. All Renvyle knew was that he seemed entirely dependent on her, and for the time being all sense of desire for her had abated. Father Delaney came in several times a week to inquire after Killary, and although he knew gossiping tongues were rife now in the village, he made no attempt to tell either Micky or Joan.

It was through Miss O'Malley, on her return, that Joan first heard of the wagging tongues in Ardbreen.

'You've been a godsend, my dear,' the older woman said,

when she first went along to the cottage. 'It must have been a desperately anxious time for poor Mick. And my heart bleeds for that poor little thing upstairs. She looks all eyes.'

'She's much better now, I assure you, but it was heartrending at times. A child in pain is.'

'I could slay all the owners of vile tongues. In fact I could almost say I'd like to commit murder. Indeed the sooner I go to Confession the better.'

'But what are you talking about?' inquired Joan.

'Oh, my dear, don't you both realize what you were laying yourselves open to? People in the village are talking. Shame on them!'

'Because I'm here? But then so is Sister.'

'You're doing night duty,' Miss O'Malley said dryly. 'I suppose all over the world there are some people who have dirty minds.'

'If only they could see us,' Joan said slowly. 'I in Killary's room behind a screen, and every night at eleven sharp I send Mick off to his room, and there I imagine he goes to sleep. Really, I wouldn't have believed it of the people in Ardbreen.'

'I'm afraid it's not been unnoticed that the two of you have been seeing a good deal of each other, Joan. And there are those who wonder why Paddy wasn't sent for.'

'Mick doesn't know where she is. Don't they know she's miles away?'

'I don't know, I'm sure. But rest assured, Joan, that if anything is said to me I'll speak my mind.'

'Then no one has? Gossiped unkindly, I mean?'

'No. I heard from another source.'

Joan guessed it was probably through the priest but said nothing. 'Miss O'Malley,' she said, 'you would like me to go on, wouldn't you?'

'Indeed, my child, yes. I think you have all our prayers. But I'm afraid the people at the library must be upset, aren't they?'

'They've been extraordinarily kind and understanding.'

'I'll look in tomorrow, I expect, just to see how things are going. I know I'm old, but if there's anything I can do, make that boy tell me. And don't worry. I dare say it was downright foolish of me to let it out.'

'I ought to have realized it could happen,' Joan said, 'but it doesn't make any difference. I love Killary.'

Killary's illness and gradual convalescence brought Micky and Joan even closer together. For some weeks it seemed their physical need for each other had abated, and conversation generally centred round the child's daily health. As far as their own meetings were concerned they saw less of each other than normally, for Joan would come about seven in the evening, and have very little time with Renvyle before going to the sick-room and taking what orders there might be from the nurse, and during the night-time she never saw him. They breakfasted together and occasionally Joan remained till about ten o'clock, but she was often tired and talk was often desultory and impersonal.

'When Killary is really better I shall have to go to my grandmother, Mick,' she said one day.

'Darling, you're looking worn to a shred as it is. Of course you must go. What are the library people going to do? They're very decent allowing you to do this for me.'

'I'm on indefinite leave. They have a very good substitute in Mary Keeley, the hotel proprietor's daughter, y'know? You look very worried, darling, what's the matter?'

'I must be mad or something, but it's only just struck me you've been getting no money . . .'

'That's all right,' she laughed.

'It isn't. What do they pay you?'

'Listen, darling—if you think that for one single moment I'd take a penny from you for looking after a child I wish was mine, you're wrong. In fact I'd be hurt and insulted.'

'I'll never be able to make it up to you,' he said wretchedly.

'Tell me you love me still. You've not told me for a long time and I'd like to hear it again.'

He came over to where she was sitting, and kissed her head.

'You're the sunshine in my life, you know that I love you.'

167

'That's all I ask. And when one comes to think about it, it's a big enough "all".'

'I feel I should take Killary away when she's well enough. That old-fashioned idea of a change of air is probably a sound one,' Renvyle said to Joan and Miss O'Malley one day as they were all sitting together downstairs.

'Take her somewhere on the Wicklow coast,' said Miss O'Malley. 'Bray—or even up to Dalkey. If you like I'll come too and lend a hand.'

'That would be a splendid idea,' Joan agreed.

'Dalkey I think,' Renvyle said. 'And if you really mean you'd come, Aunt Cathleen, it would be wonderful as I'd be able to make a few belated contacts in Dublin.'

'She's a dear little soul,' the nurse said to Miss O'Malley one afternoon. 'I shall be really sorry when she's well enough for me to go. She suffered so much pain in the early stages—that was before you saw her—and she was a little saint, may heaven bless her. But she really is on the road to recovery now. A pity her mother couldn't come.'

'My niece is an actress, you know,' Miss O'Malley said shortly.

'So I understand. Little Killary seems fonder of Miss Fitzgerald than of her mother. I suppose it's only natural.' As no comment seemed forthcoming she continued, 'Give her her due, Miss Fitzgerald has been a godsend and no nurse could have done better for the child at nights.'

The evening before they were to go off Killary said, 'I wish you were coming away with us, Joan.'

'I should think you're sick of the sight of me,' Joan answered with a smile. 'And I must go and see my granny.'

'You will come back, won't you?'

'But of course,' Joan said in surprise. 'Why ever not?'

'I would hate it if you didn't, wouldn't you, Daddy?'

Renvyle nodded.

'And when I next see you, I shall expect to see someone with very rosy cheeks and nice and plump too.' Joan bent down to kiss Killary, who threw her arms round her neck.

Renvyle went out to the car with her. 'I don't know what to say to you, dear love,' he began.

'Then don't. And I think it's probably a good thing we're all going to be separated for a bit. The only thing I shall miss terribly is not being able to talk to you, even on the telephone. You do realize we can't, don't you?'

He nodded gloomily. 'Will your grandmother scan your letters and query daily Dublin postmarks?'

She giggled. 'I'll try and prevent that,' she said.

'Promise me you'll have a complete rest,' he begged her.

'I will. Now that it's over, the worry and anxiety, I think I shall sleep like the dead. And I think I may be able to persuade Granny's old Katie to bring me some breakfast in bed.'

'God bless you and take care of you, sweetest heart,' he said, taking her in his arms.

'Beloved one,' she said, kissing him gently, 'I've been so happy helping you. Have fun in Dublin and don't forget me.'

She got into the car.

'I shall count the days till I see you again, and you know it.'

Joan blew him a kiss, put the car into gear and drove away.

Part III

CHAPTER ONE

FOR the first time in his life, or at any rate for as long as he could remember, Renvyle began to enjoy the company of strangers. He had been at Dalkey only a short time before he ran into Shaun O'Donovan, whose poems he had admired from boyhood and who asked him along to his house after dinner. There he met several other men, all of whose names were familiar to him, and he was delighted when he discovered that his own work was not unknown. O'Donovan's house was the meeting-place outside Dublin of the literary, artistic and musical world, and his Sunday afternoons were as famous as the late Sarah Purser's had been a couple of generations before. One was sure of meeting the most interesting people from the city, and there was generally a sprinkling of rich patrons of art and an occasional ambassador or minister. Talk ranged on every subject, from art to world affairs, religion, the colour bar in various countries, racing, travel . . . The only subjects that were strictly taboo in the house were politics and scandal. Micky met a good many people who until now had only been names to him, and he was delighted when he was asked back to their houses in Dublin.

'I want to introduce you to Lady Constance Rowan-Colville,' O'Donovan said one day. 'She's an admirer of yours.'

'Of mine?' Micky exclaimed. He turned to face a woman who was taller than he was by a couple of inches, and who was, he judged, some years older than himself.

'I don't know so much about your books. It's your pictures I'm crazy about. The more so as my forebears came from your part of the world. Now come over here and tell me about yourself.'

She drew him to where there was a chesterfield, and he felt he was being shepherded by some very compelling force. She talked without ceasing to him for half an hour, at the end of which, although he had answered in monosyllables, she seemed to think she knew his life story.

'And now that the troubles are over and mostly forgotten—' she looked round the room and continued in a stage whisper, 'I always have to look for any eavesdropper if I so much as mention the word "trouble"—I intend to come back to Ireland. I suppose it would be unwise to return and build on the property itself, but I'd like a little place somewhere in your part of the world. Clifden or Westport. I've never been back since I grew up. But now, my dear man, to get back to you. What are you working on at this minute?' She looked at him fiercely. 'Just because you have a sick child on your hands you mustn't let your talents slip from under your feet. And you say you've a relative helping to look after her. What sort of a relative?'

'My wife's aunt,' he muttered.

'Your wife, of course, I keep forgetting her. She's on the stage, I know. Something O'Malley. Very beautiful, Vivien Leigh type. Why isn't she with you and your child? No, don't tell me. Of course. She's acting. And seeing she's not wasting *her* talents on domesticity. Very wise. In some respects. Now, young man, I want you to lunch one day with me. Shall we say Jammets at one o'clock on Wednesday?'

Before Micky had time to gather his wits she had risen and sailed across the room, bearing down on another young man.

'Tell me about that overpowering female,' Renvyle asked Susan Fellows, a novelist who was having a great success with the publication of her recent novel.

'Lady Constance?' The woman seemed amused by his ignorance. 'She's—well, a bit difficult to explain.'

'Who is she? I've heard of her vaguely, I suppose.'

'She's Lord Rowan's only daughter.'

'The Earl of Rowan? Yes, I seem to recollect things about the family. Their property, Castle Rowan, was burnt in the troubles, wasn't it? What I call English–Irish aristocracy, as much at home in England as over here.'

Susan Fellows laughed. 'A good deal more so, nowadays. Protestants of course. But Constance Rowan-Colville likes to be thought Irish. She even assumes a brogue at times. She's very rich and if she takes an interest in a protégé she can do a lot for him. And when I say him, I mean *him*. She has no use for women.'

'She sounds forbidding. Must I keep a luncheon appointment that I hadn't the time to refuse?'

'I should if I were you. It may in time make all the difference to your bank balance.'

Micky was outraged. 'I have no intention of—' he began.

'I only mean she'll probably buy your pictures. And at a larger sum than they're worth. And finance a show for you,' she added, looking at him rather pityingly.

'I see. But you do agree she's rather alarming?'

Susan Fellows shrugged her shoulders. 'Yes. I suppose she could be. But don't be browbeaten by her. It's her stock-in-trade. I sometimes have the feeling that like that Chinese princess in the opera—*Turandot,* d'you know it?—she could be tamed by love.'

'God help the victim. What sort of age is she? She looks forty-ish.'

'Ish. Very ish. How old are you?'

Renvyle laughed. 'Much too young for her. Thirty something. I've really forgotten what. Very ish!'

'She likes 'em young.'

'You terrify me. However, forewarned is forearmed.'

When Micky arrived at the restaurant three days later he found Lady Constance already seated at the table. She seemed even larger than on their previous meeting. She was dressed rather rakishly and wore a large black sombrero hat, and although it was a mild day a mink cape covered her shoulders. He noticed her fingers were adorned with old-fashioned rings, handed down from generation to generation, he supposed.

'I dare say you'd have liked one or two other people, Michael Renvyle, but I wanted you to myself,' she began when he apologized for being late, an apology which she swept aside.

He felt more than ever like a fly in the web of some colossal blood-sucking spider. 'I've ordered oysters,' she said, 'and I suppose we can get through a bottle of Chablis. And then a pheasant. Followed by a *crème brûlée*. I like food. Do you?'

'I—I suppose so.'

'My poor dear! You look as if your knowledge of it consisted of a poached egg. Now I want you to tell me a great deal more of your life. Not the poached egg part—that would bore me inconceivably. I want to know why you paint birds?'

He tried to tell her, and curiously enough found that she was, after all, a sympathetic listener.

'I've followed your work for some years,' she told him. 'I suppose partly because I love the same sort of country as you depict. Since we were to all intents and purposes banished from Ireland I've had a little place in Scotland of my own, on the Isle of Mull, but I want to return to Ireland. My old father has none of my feelings for it, alas. And I live with him a great deal of the time. He's ninety, you know. I have your love of mountains,' she said, as she put a liberal helping of pheasant into her mouth. 'I should miss the stalking of course if I came back here, but I could keep on Achnachoil.'

Micky tried to conjure up the vision of his hostess lying flat on the ground wriggling on her stomach up some corrie.

'You ought to get abroad. Italy or Spain. Your treatment of mountains is excellent. I should like to see what you'd make of the Gredos. Ever been to Castile?'

Micky said he had never been to the Continent.

'Well, my dear boy, you must. I generally take some little something every winter. You can come out for as long as you like. This winter I'm going to Jamaica. Not perhaps your style. You don't paint people, do you?'

Micky told her that he had in fact done a successful book of studies of heads, mostly of peasants from Mayo and Sligo.

'I don't know the book.' She sounded quite annoyed. 'Who published it?'

Presently she said: 'You should, of course, have an exhibition of your own. I saw the one you shared with what's-his-name here in Dublin.'

Renvyle explained that it was a question of getting the requisite number of pictures together.

'D'you want financial help?' she asked. 'Most young people seem to.' As he began to hedge she said: 'Don't be ashamed of being poor. I'm disgustingly rich, it's I who should be ashamed. My mother was American, y'know. All my money is from canned meat, it helped my father's various properties, of course, but my brother was killed, and there's no heir, so I do my best to help lame dogs. It really hurts me to find young men who are geniuses in the field of art—whether it's music or painting or literature—who can't make their mark merely owing to financial worries. I've helped one or two people to the top and it makes me very happy. Have a liqueur!' She called the waiter. 'I myself like armagnac. You don't know it? My dear, you haven't lived.'

Before the luncheon was over Micky found himself promising to escort Lady Constance to the Abbey Theatre one evening the following week. She rang him up the day before, telling him to wear a black tie and they would be a party of six. Oddly enough Micky did not enjoy the evening as much as their tête-à-tête luncheon. At the theatre he sat next a rich débutante who was only interested in horses, and at Lady Constance's house in Fitzwilliam Square he sat between Lady Constance who was more taken up with old Sir Joseph Bullevant, a one-time judge, and on his other side Sandra O'Toole, the shy sculptress step-daughter of Sir Joseph.

'She does those amazing things in stone that look like nothing on earth,' Lady Constance whispered loudly in his ear, 'but she's expected to win the Prix de Rome.'

The other man was a young penniless musician who after supper was made to play Chopin endlessly to the gathering.

It was extraordinary, Micky thought, as he was on his way back to Dalkey, how uninterested Lady Constance seemed to be in the domestic side of his life. He had tried to tell her about

Killary, and her illness, but she had brushed the conversation aside after saying that children caught any illness going. She obviously was equally uninterested in the fact that he was married to Paddy O'Malley.

Miss O'Malley was, on the other hand, intensely interested to hear everything about Lady Constance that Micky could tell her.

'She was such a good-looking girl,' she told him, 'and went superbly to hounds, but after her brother was killed out hunting the story goes she never got on a horse again. Strange she never married.'

'Not if you've met her,' Micky assured Miss O'Malley. 'No man would have time to propose. One hardly gets a word in. She's an extraordinary woman.'

'What's she like to look at nowadays?'

'Very big and overpowering. I don't mean fat, just big. Dark sort of hair, I'd say. And she wears peculiar clothes. Oh, a very odd thing, yes, she smokes cigars.'

Both Micky and Miss O'Malley were delighted at the progress Killary made in regaining her strength and after a month away they found themselves discussing a date for returning to Ardbreen. Micky knew that the weeks in and near Dublin had not been wasted, he had enjoyed meeting many of the country's celebrated sons and daughters, but he began to yearn for Connemara and quiet, and above all for Joan. Her letters had been frequent and full of love for him, and he suddenly realized how little success would mean to him, should he ever attain it, without her beside him to share it. Inevitably he found himself comparing her to Lady Constance of whom he had been seeing a great deal, and he longed for the very ordinariness of Joan and all that went with her good middle-class upbringing, after an hour or two spent in Lady Constance's overpowering company.

The latter was obviously surprised when Micky told her he would be returning to Ardbreen.

'But I shall still be here,' she exclaimed, as if staggered by the thought that any friend or protégé of hers could dream of leaving a city which still boasted her presence. 'I'm not going abroad till after Christmas.'

'Killary is well enough to go back, and so it's really pointless remaining.'

'Pointless?' Astonishment, outrage were apparent in her voice. 'Does your child rule your life?'

'Certainly not. But it was solely on her account we came east. I told you she nearly died of meningitis.'

'Yes, I remember you said something apropos,' she said impatiently. 'What will you do when you go back? You can't paint during the winter. Not your sort of painting.'

'I can. I do. A lot of my work is done in my studio. From sketches I make out of doors. For books. The books you don't read,' he said.

'And have you friends?'

'One or two.'

'Amusing ones?'

'That's a matter of taste, isn't it?' he said. 'Don't forget I'm a boy brought up on a bog, not one of your cosmopolitan Dubliners. I easily tire of social life and—this may shock you—wit.'

'I really believe you do,' she said slowly. 'But don't make mistakes, Michael. Don't let success slip from your grasp from sheer laziness. One has to work if one's ambitious.'

'But that's it, you see. I'm not ambitious.' He paused. 'And I've seen what ambition did to my wife.'

Lady Constance glanced at him quietly. 'You never talk about her, so I've not liked to ask you—'

'I suppose you might say we've separated. She left me—after a row for which I may have been to blame—and I've not heard from her since. It's many months ago. Paddy is very ambitious. She's an extremely good actress, she's very beautiful, the loveliest thing I've ever beheld—'

'And you long for her to come back to you. Poor boy,' Lady Constance said in soothing tones.

Micky shook his head slowly. 'It's the last thing I want. No, I should say we're through with each other.'

Lady Constance felt she was treading on delicate ground. 'Are you,' she hesitated, 'contemplating a divorce?'

'We're Catholics,' he said shortly.

'Even so, such things can be arranged. With influence.'

'I have no influence, and in any case it would be pointless.'

'When I return to Europe next summer,' Lady Constance began, and Micky breathed with relief, 'I shall come and look you up at your precious Ardbreen. And you must look about for me and keep your eyes and ears skinned for any small property that's coming into the market. Of course if you feel you'd care to come out to me you've only got to send me a cable. People come and go, come and go. I'm never alone. I shall be there till March, and then I shall go straight to Italy. I always try to be in Rome for Easter.'

Micky's look of surprise brought a hasty rejoinder.

'Oh no, I'm not of your faith, but I adore Italy and Italians, and I have a great many friends out there. But I shall be back here by the beginning of May. I've not much use for London any more. And in any case it's only a matter of an hour or two in a plane if I want to see an opera. Or my father,' she added. 'He clings to the Belgrave Square grandeur, dear old boy.'

'He must find it very lonely,' Micky said, feeling suddenly sorry for the nonagenarian peer.

'He doesn't, you know. What with the House of Lords, his clubs, and Mrs Dishforth.'

'Mrs Dishforth?'

'His *bonne amie*. Of your faith or they'd have married years ago. She's a young thing of seventy-seven, and I may say doesn't look it. She was a Gaiety girl when even your parents were probably in their cradles.'

Micky was intrigued in spite of himself. He visualized Aunt Cathleen with both ears turned back.

'And Mrs Dishforth actually became—er—'

'I told you. Yes. Very discreetly, of course. Generally at Monte Carlo. But she has a charming *pied-à-terre* near Papa in South Eaton Place. Which is just as handy, more so, when you come to think of it. And they still play bezique together, six packs.'

She smiled as if conjuring a picture that gave her much filial joy.

'I've never met people like that,' Micky said simply.

'There's something very naïve about you, Michael, which I find extremely charming. Now don't forget. Come out to me if ever you feel like it. And also look for a bolt-hole for me. Galway, Mayo, Sligo—anywhere in the wild romantic west.'

CHAPTER TWO

RENVYLE knocked and then rang the bell at the cottage. He knew that Jill Fitzgerald was not coming back till Christmas and it was his intention to surprise Joan who was ignorant of his return. She opened the door.

'Mick!'

He went into the house, slammed the door and took her into his arms.

'Darling, darling, darling,' he murmured.

'I can't believe it,' she whispered. 'Why didn't you let me know?'

'I wanted to surprise you.'

'Oh, God! How wonderful to have you back.'

They clung together, and presently she asked: 'How's Killary?'

'Fine. Just like her old self. Let me look at you,' he said, pulling her down beside him on to the sofa.

'Darling, if only I'd known you were coming! I've got on a filthy old blouse, and my hair needs washing, and I thought you were someone from the village and didn't even powder my nose.' She was nearly crying.

'As if I could care!'

'You should!'

'You're perfect to me whatever you look like,' he said, and kissed her.

She took his face in her hands and kissed his mouth. 'And I believe you mean it, strange as it is,' she said. 'God bless you for it. You with all the beauty of that Paddy and yet you love me with my glasses and squint.'

'You don't squint!'

'I do. That's why I wear them.'

'I thought you were short-sighted.'

'I am, but I've a cast in one of my eyes. Haven't you ever noticed?'

He shook his head. 'You forget my eyes aren't that wonderful either,' he said.

'You manage to paint.'

'I'm long-sighted. I'd not noticed this famous squint. Give me another kiss. Have you missed me?'

When she could escape from his arms she said, 'Are you going to have some supper with me? I've only got eggs, but I can make us an omelette. And there's some cheese and a few apples and oranges. But in any case you'd like a drink, I'll fetch the whisky.'

He looked round the little room, to which he'd been so seldom. It was cosy but not a bit as he would have imagined Joan's room to be. An upright piano, the two easy chairs and the sofa were covered in some sort of green stuff and there was a cabinet filled with not particularly good china. A warm turf fire burned in the grate, there were chrysanthemums on the table and on the walls hung a couple of lithographs and a water-colour of his own of the Twelve Pins which he had given her. On the mantelpiece was a snapshot of Killary. He wondered subconsciously where she kept the one of himself, taken the same day.

'What are you thinking about?' she asked when she came back into the room.

'Nothing, really. I was thinking—perhaps—it isn't like you, this room.'

She laughed. 'Well, of course it isn't, silly. It belongs to people who are in India and thank God for it. I could put up with a lot worse to be near my love.'

He felt an absurd sense of relief. For some unexplained reason it would have been a disappointment if the room had been Joan's idea of taste.

'I want to hear about everything,' she said, perching herself on the arm of his chair. 'All those strange exciting people you were hobnobbing with.'

183

He tried to describe O'Donovan and others, and the Sunday parties at his house.

'And tell me more about Lady Constance what's-her-name.'

'Why her in particular?'

'Well, for one reason I used to see her down in Cork where she stayed with friends of hers. I don't mean I ever met her, but I used to see her.'

'Oh, well, she's very odd—very overpowering. But I believe she's kind. At heart. She's very forthright. Told me funny yarns about her father's love life!'

'No, really? And her own?'

'No. I shouldn't think she has one. Should you? I mean you've seen what she looks like!'

'Darling, she may be queer but I've heard quite a lot of people think she's beautiful.'

'Beautiful? Lady Constance? Don't be absurd!'

'She can be. I saw her in tableaux for Charity. She was some Irish medieval queen. And she looked magnificent. All that hair in long plaits down to her knees and she carried a shield. You needn't laugh! She was beautiful.'

'You'd laugh if you could see her in the clothes she wears in Dublin.'

'Tell me.'

She got up and poured him out another drink, and started to lay the table. Micky described Lady Constance's appearance with as much detail as he could remember, and Joan giggled, and then he said: 'She invited me to Jamaica or wherever she's gone to. And we've got to find her a house or a property or something hereabouts.'

'Oh.'

She went into the kitchen and presently called out:

'Are you going?'

'Not until I've had supper.'

'I mean are you going to Jamaica?'

'Don't be crazy! How could I? It'd cost me all the money I have in the bank and more.'

She came back into the room. 'Would you like to?'

'Go to Jamaica? No, I'm not interested in the West Indies.'

'If she'd invited you somewhere that you are interested in, would you?'

'I don't think so. Why?'

Suddenly her eyes filled with tears. 'She's probably in love with you, Mick. She can do lots for you with that money of hers. She's fabulously rich. She—'

He kissed her. 'Darling, whatever the reverse to wishful thinking is, you've certainly got it. I wouldn't give that,' he snapped his fingers, for her help, her riches, anything she likes to offer. And I don't suppose we'll ever see her again.'

'I thought you said you'd got to find her a house?'

'Well, let's forget about it. You may say she's beautiful, but to me she's a middle-aged hag.'

Joan shook her head. 'She's not, you know. I don't think she's fifty. And she's had several lovers.'

'How on earth do you know?'

'It was common knowledge. There was a jockey, and a violinist, and a prince of something—'

'And not Micky Renvyle, so don't worry. Where's this omelette? I'm getting hungry. Kiss me again and tell me you love me.'

'You don't need to be told and well you know it.'

Somehow the weeks spent in Dalkey and Dublin had an un-settling effect on Renvyle's work. He became dissatisfied, the more so when the book he had thought of writing was lost in particularly tragic circumstances.

Before Christmas he said one evening to Joan:

'I'm thinking of writing a novel.'

'Darling, how absolutely thrilling. What's it to be about?'

He said he wouldn't tell her, that he felt it might be unlucky.

'Why a novel after all these years?' she asked.

'I suppose I've never had an idea for fiction before. But I have—suddenly—and I want to try my hand.'

So everything was pushed aside and assiduously he set

himself to write for a great many hours daily, far more than had been normal in the past. It did not come easily to him, but he confessed that he was enjoying creating characters and situations. In the early spring, which was a particularly wet one, a plague of rats appeared for no reason in Ardbreen, getting into buildings, barns, and even into occasional houses and cottages. Renvyle had not been unduly annoyed or worried by this pest, and had thought very little about it until one night he was aware of a noise unlike anything he had known in the house before.

'My turn, I suppose,' he said to a neighbour. 'What a darn nuisance!'

He still took very little notice as the house was well built and he was pretty sure that entry into the place would be impossible. What he did not realize was that a door into the studio was constantly being left open, and one morning when he went into it he stood transfixed with horror, rage, mortification and despair. The manuscript of his novel was strewn over the place as if a whirlwind had entered the studio. The sheets were torn, eaten, nibbled, destroyed. He tried to pick them out and at random piece them together, and it was soon obvious to him that the task was beyond him. He was in a bitter mood when Joan rang him that night and asked brightly how the book was getting on.

'There is no book,' he answered tersely.

'What d'you mean?'

He told her what had happened.

'But that's frightful, how—how agonizing for you! Can you begin all over again?'

'Hell, no! I'm no Lawrence, and my book no Seven Pillars, but I feel bloody angry. The more so as I suppose it was my own fault. I should have taken heed and listened to other sufferers in the village. Not been so damn careless either. But who would dream . . . Oh, well, there goes your mink coat,' he laughed, but Joan deduced despair in the sound of it.

From that moment Micky seemed to lose interest in any work he began to undertake, and to lose confidence in himself.

'I'm a failure,' he said to Father Delaney, 'whichever way you look at it. Paddy was right. I'm nothing but third-rate. My books don't sell, I can no longer paint, I was a failure as a husband, and no great shakes as a father. I found Killary wandering around the other day in shoes that had no soles left on them.'

'And that won't help you,' the priest said, as Renvyle poured himself out a large whisky, and drank it neat. 'Since when have you been doing that?'

Micky shrugged his shoulders. 'Oh, not long. Don't worry. I'm not going to become a soaker, but it helps.'

'Not at this hour in the morning. And your hand is unsteady, Mick. Boyo, what's got into you?'

Renvyle sat down disconsolately and said, 'What I told you. I'm a failure and only beginning to realize it.'

'Pull yourself together. Plenty of great writers and poets—and painters—were penniless in their lifetime—'

'And what consolation is that to me, with a small daughter to bring up? Besides, I'm not penniless. As you know, I don't have to depend entirely on what I make. But I've lost the purpose of living—my work was something, meant something to me. I loved it. I believed I was getting somewhere. But it's gone from me.'

'Mick, you mustn't give way to despair. Despair, like pride, is one of the unforgivable sins.'

'I wonder why. They're so usual, most people suffer from one or both some time in their lives.'

The priest went home dispirited. He was going to do something of which part of him disapproved. He was going to enlist Joan Fitzgerald's help.

'You're a friend of Mick's,' he began when he found her. There was no beating about the bush. 'I'm worried about him.'

'You mean he's so depressed? Ever since those awful rats got his manuscript. I know. I'm worried too.'

'Can you help him, my daughter? He's drinking too much.' 'Oh *no*?'

Joan was distressed, for she had noticed something different in the manner of the man she loved and had not been able to put it down to anything other than the depression caused by worry over work.

'I went to see him in the morning. He had a large whisky. Neat. That's only going to add to his worries.'

'Of course. I'll see what I can do, but Father, it's not easy. You know I thought those weeks away when he met a lot of interesting people would have boosted him up, but it seems to have done the reverse. He seems to have lost confidence in himself. D'you think it's because he met a lot of people more successful than himself? Because if that's so it's awful. I mean it makes Mick out so weak and I don't think he is.'

'He's had more than his share of worry, poor fellow. We must pray for him.'

'Father, can I speak to you as a friend and not as a priest?' Her tone was urgent.

He bowed. 'Of course.'

'I love Mick. He loves me. We know we can never marry unless something was to happen to Paddy which is very unlikely. The only way I could help him, I believe, would be to go to him. In the way that both of us—both of us want.'

She stopped. The priest remained silent.

'I can't do that. Can I?'

It was a strange entreaty to come from a girl's lips to a priest's ear. For a moment Joan had forgotten the priest, and only knew the friend, the father-figure. The priest in Father Delaney fought against the temptation of the man, the friend. He was to be neither priest nor friend, nor judge. He must be counsellor. And a counsellor for God to a girl who loved God and who also loved a man, and he knew in his man's heart that her words held some truth. Slowly he shook his head.

'Joan, my child. Why do you tempt me? You know what is wrong as well as I do. Of course you cannot go to Mick. If that were the only help it would be poor indeed. And the very distress in your voice tells me you would rather hurt Mick than betray God. Isn't that so?'

'Yes,' she whispered. 'But how, how can I help him? You ask me to help, but how? How?'

'Have you forgotten how to pray?' His voice was gentle.

'I pray for him without ceasing.'

'I'm sure you do. But pray against the temptation of the devil, for the two of you. And remember that the devil's ways are many. At the moment he's putting the drink into Micky's mind. And he's putting ideas of romance—but an ugly romance which is a denial of its name and of real love—into yours. I think you can help him, my child. You were splendid when little Killary was ill, have you forgotten?'

'I shall never forget.'

'Then don't despair. I believe in you, and I have faith in you. Don't imagine you can't be of help, because it's a different kind of help that God has found for you,' he said, patting her shoulder, before taking his leave. 'God bless you,' he said as he let himself out of the door of the cottage. 'My own prayers will be for both of you unceasingly.'

CHAPTER THREE

DURING the weeks which followed Joan found her love frequently tested. Often Micky was irritable or morose, and yet if he did not see her he would fall into a mood of even greater despondency.

'Paddy got fed up with me after a few years. It's only taken you a few months,' he said bitterly one Saturday when Joan telephoned to say she could not come to Ardbreen the following day as arranged.

'Listen, Mick. I'm not letting anyone, even you, speak to me like that. Jill is in bed, very seedy, and I can't possibly leave her. It's bad bronchial trouble. So please try and understand.'

He made no reply.

'I don't think you realize that I give you every bit of my spare time,' she went on.

'Do you? Most evenings you're at home.'

'You're impossible when you're like this, my dear. Goodnight.'

Although she spoke steadily, Joan burst into tears when she replaced the telephone.

Neither mentioned the conversation when next they met. Joan noticed that Renvyle was indeed drinking more than was normal, but at the same time he was never drunk. She felt she was in no position to talk to him, she had no right, she told herself. One evening he complained of a bad head and she suggested tentatively that too much whisky might have caused it.

'Are you accusing me of drinking?' he asked angrily.

'No, darling. I'm trying to think of an excuse for your heads which some people do describe as hang-overs.'

'Don't prevaricate, Joan. You *are* accusing me.'

'Mick, what's happening to you?' She looked him squarely in the eyes.

'General fed-upness,' he said.

'Darling, many people go through bad patches in creative work.'

'What do you know about it?' he said almost rudely.

'I'm trying to help,' she sighed.

'I'm a failure,' he began.

'Don't be weak, Mick,' she cried. 'Begin again. Good heavens! You've written for years, your other books I mean. Surely you can do some more like them? Or paint as you used to?'

'I've shot my bolt. I've gone stale.'

Without thinking he poured out another drink. Joan put her hand on his.

'If not for me, then for Killary,' she begged.

He pushed the glass aside. 'You're right,' he replied. 'I must think of her.'

They were silent for a while.

'Oh, Joan love, if only we were together. To hell with marriage vows! I want you and it's eating into me. You ask what's the matter, that's the matter. Partly at any rate.'

Presently she said: 'What is it about me that you love and want? I'm not pretty.'

'You're you. You're peaceful. You're good, you're—'

'You say good. And if I lived with you as your mistress, yes, that's what I'd be—'

'We'd go away somewhere and pretend you were my wife.'

'And what would be the good of that to your soul and mine? The goodness in me would be destroyed. I'd soon be something you were used to and when you were through with me—and men get more tired of their fancy ladies than they do of their wives—you'd be disillusioned and the last state would be worse than the first. If I thought that by sleeping with you just once—'

'Don't talk like a fool, Joan, I want you with me for always. And you don't know what you're talking about, anyway. Fancy ladies! What an expression! Where on earth did you pick that one from?'

'Darling, I'm not going to live with you, and that's flat. Do you think I don't want to? I do. God forgive me, but I wish Paddy would move on to the next world, and there's sin for you. But as long as she's alive she's your wife, and bed with you is a pipe dream!'

'There can be few girls with quite such scruples nowadays,' Micky said.

'I expect there are a great many more than people think. Specially ones of my vintage. The young ones may be more sophisticated. But darling, you who know me as you do, how can you think I could go to Communion with sin on my conscience? Or confess to something which I knew I was not going to give up? For whatever else I am I'm not a hypocrite. If I were to come to you I'd have to deny Our Lord, and that I shall never do.'

He was silent for a little while, and then said, 'I still think you take it all a damn sight more seriously than a great number of people do. You should be a nun!'

'That's an idea.'

'What would you say if I was a Protestant?'

'It's silly, Mick, to put hypothetical questions. You're not.'

'I suppose one day some other fellow will turn up, some lucky bloke without a wife, and you'll marry him,' he said.

'That will never happen,' she answered very quietly. 'I shall never marry anyone but you, my love. Or sleep with anyone either, if that makes you feel better,' she laughed half-heartedly. 'But if you love me, please, please take a pull on yourself and try and write or paint or something.'

Micky reached for her hand and kissed her fingers.

'Dear, dear love,' he said. 'I'll try. And I'll only have a couple of drinks a day.'

And it seemed as if he really began to work again. The days were longer and the weather fine and he took *Deirdre* out and started to paint once more. Sometimes he would be away for days on end, visiting the islands and down to Mannin Bay and round to Roundstone and farther south to Lettermore. When Killary's holidays started she begged to be allowed to go with him and Micky found the child's company a strange help and was surprised at how useful she was in the boat's small galley.

'I can do almost any sort of egg dish,' she said proudly, 'and I fry bacon deliciously.'

And often the cooking was left to Killary, who seemed entirely happy to be at sea with her father.

'I wish Joan was here too,' she said one day.

'So do I. But there isn't room for her.'

'She could be in Mummie's bunk.'

'Only Mummie or you are supposed to be in that.'

'Oh. And she couldn't be in my tiny one as she wouldn't fit into it. Oh well, it's a pity.' Killary seemed content with the explanation, especially when Micky told her it was the captain's cabin for the captain and his family.

They moored off the shore in Cashel Bay one day and Renvyle said they would go ashore in the dinghy and have a good lunch at the hotel. They were half-way through the meal when Micky heard a near-by laugh and a voice that was somehow familiar.

'There's a very funny lady, Daddy,' said Killary, 'I mustn't point, it's rude. But she's smoking a cigar.'

'Holy smoke!' said Mick, turning round. 'It's Lady Constance. Come on and let's talk to her.'

He noticed she was alone. After paying his bill he got up and went over to her table.

'Lady Constance!' he said. She looked up.

'Michael!' she cried, springing to her feet. 'This is wonderful. I'd given up all hope. I've rung your number at least half a dozen times and never got an answer.'

'I'm in my boat, sailing and painting. This is my daughter, Killary.'

Killary put her hand out. 'How d'you do,' she said very politely, unable to take her eyes off the woman's hair.

'What are you gazing at?' Lady Constance asked.

'Your hair,' the child said, without a tremor. 'I've not seen a lady's hair done like that before. Is it very long?'

'Down to my knees.'

'I thought all ladies had short hair.'

'Don't you believe it. Hair is a woman's crowning glory and only a fool has it off.'

'Oh,' said Killary, awed at last.

'And what are you doing here in Cashel?' Micky asked.

'Trying to find a house. Sit down and have your coffee with me.'

'I've had it.'

'Then have some more. Waitress,' she beckoned imperiously. 'And your child! Hilary, what would you like?'

'Nothing, thank you. My name's Killary, not Hilary. I'm called Killary the same as Killary Harbour where Daddy and Mummie had a honeymoon.'

'I see. Well, Michael, what have you been doing?'

He told her, a little diffidently, of his inability to do very much until just lately.

'And tell her about the rats,' Killary said, who was listening with great attention.

'What rats?' asked Lady Constance. Renvyle told her about his still-born attempt to write a novel.

'My poor Mike, I call that a heart-rending story. Now, I want to see your yacht. Can we go out to her?'

Killary giggled, and while Lady Constance went to get a scarf and other garments the child pulled her father's arm. 'Will she be able to get into the dinghy?' she whispered.

'We'll hope so,' he said.

A few minutes later Lady Constance noticed the child eyeing her suspiciously.

'I'm used to craft of all kinds and sizes,' she said, 'from men-of-war to prams.' She scanned the water. *'That?'* and she pointed to *Deirdre*.

'Not up to Royal Yacht Squadron standard, I fear,' Renvyle said, winking at his daughter.

'She's called *Deirdre*,' said Killary.

'Deirdre ahoy!' Lady Constance's voice rang out like a valkyrie's, convulsing the child.

'You've got to get into this,' Micky said, pointing to the dinghy. To his surprise she leapt nimbly into the little boat.

'Now, I'd like to see your paintings,' she said when they had arrived on board. Micky pulled out sketch books and a few canvases which Lady Constance looked at in silence and then turning to Killary said: 'You should be very proud of your father. He's a genius.'

'What's that?'

'A very, very talented man. And don't ask me now what that means, my good child. Mike, these are really beautiful. What are you intending to do with them?'

'Well,' he hesitated. 'I want to get enough to have a small show.'

'How many more have you at your house?' she inquired regally.

'Not more than a dozen I'd want to show.'

'And you've these ten. You'd want another ten or twelve for an exhibition. You leave everything to me, my dear. I shall see to it all.'

'But I couldn't possibly let you,' he said a little stiffly.

'Rubbish! You needn't think I'm being kind. I'm doing it because I believe in you. I told you when I met you I'd followed your career with interest.'

Micky swallowed hard. He did not know what to say. Lady Constance began to put the pictures about the small cabin.

'What a bore there's nowhere we can see them better. Let's take 'em back to the hotel.'

'Suppose they upset and get wet?' Killary asked.

Lady Constance looked at her. 'You're quite intelligent, aren't you! You're right. It wasn't a very good idea. I shall come over to Ardbreen,' she said. 'When are you returning?'

'As the wind takes us,' Micky replied. 'This was our swan song. We're making for home if all goes well tomorrow. I'll ring you when we get back. It may take just the day, but if it blows we'll have to shelter.'

'Would you like some tea?' Killary asked.

'She does all the cooking,' Micky said with pride.

'How astonishing. Are you a good cook?'

'I do eggs and bacon scrumptiously, don't I, Daddy? And bangers.'

'Bangers? What are they?'

Killary giggled helplessly.

'Sausages,' she eventually gasped.

'Horrible things.' Lady Constance shivered.

'They're my favouritest thing,' the child said. 'Except for ice-cream.'

'Did you make this excellent cake?' Lady Constance demanded, when tea was ready.

'No, Joan made that.'

'Who's Joan? Your servant?'

Killary laughed and then looked horrified. 'Joan is Joan,' she said primly. 'Joan is very special. She's Daddy's and my favouritest friend.'

'I see.'

As Renvyle remained silent Lady Constance did not pursue the conversation.

'I've not found a house for myself. And I suppose it's useless to ask you if you've found one for me?'

Micky confessed he had not.

'Forgot all about it, I'll wager.' She sniffed. 'Killary, I want a house. Somewhere near where you live,' she spoke to the child graciously.

'Daddy has another house. A bigger one than where we live.'

'You see? This child is of more use than you. Why didn't you tell me?'

'Because it wouldn't do for you,' he said quickly. 'It was my father's. He was the local doctor. It only has a very small garden and—well, I don't think you'd care for it.'

'Meaning you don't want me on your doorstep!'

Micky mumbled incoherently that in any case it was let.

'All right, all right. Don't bother with a lot of excuses.'

A fair wind next day brought Micky and Killary back to Ardbreen in a matter of hours, and on the following day he rang Lady Constance.

'D'you really want to come over?' he asked.

'Don't be absurd. Of course I do.'

'How about lunch on Saturday?'

'With your poor child having to do the cooking?'

'No!' he shouted. 'She only copes in *Deirdre*. Will you come?'

'Why can't I come before Saturday?'

'Because I want to tidy the place up and get my stuff ready to show.'

'But it's a charming cottage,' she said without any trace of patronage, 'and of course Ardbreen is the most beautiful place I've ever seen.'

'Oh, come,' Micky started to chaff her, '*I* think so, but then I'm no traveller. You, who've been all over the world—'

'Think it a jewel. The top jewel on a crown of splendid jewels. I mean it. How tiresome you can't find me somewhere here to live.'

She professed herself delighted with the lunch that had been prepared, and was again enchanted with the remainder of Renvyle's paintings.

'Why not have a show in Dublin during horse-show week? I can arrange it all. And then we'll do something for London in the autumn.'

'Are you serious?' Micky asked.

'I was never more so in my life,' she answered.

Joan came over as usual the following day. While she and Killary were laying the lunch Killary said:

'We had a very funny lady yesterday. We met her in Cashel. And she thinks Daddy's a genius.'

'Are you telling Joan about Lady Constance?' Micky had come into the room. 'Extraordinary thing. Killary and I were lunching at the hotel and who should be there but Lady C. She insisted on boarding *Deirdre*—'

'She's very huge, Joan, but she leapt into the dinghy like a fairy. Daddy and I had 'magined we'd all sink when she got in. And she has hair in plaits all round her head and said it was a crown of glory.'

Joan stood still, watching Renvyle; the plates seemed fixtures in her hands. Her face was pale.

'I must say she made some remarkable propositions.'

'Such as?'

'She says she'll finance an exhibition in Dublin—in horse-show week. I ask you—and London in the autumn.'

'I wondered why you looked happier,' Joan said brightly.

'She thinks Daddy is a very, very something painter.'

'She was extraordinarily encouraging, I must admit,' Micky said.

'And so you had her over here again yesterday?' Joan's voice had a slight edge on it.

'She wanted to see what other pictures I had here.'

'Fair enough.'

'What's the matter, d—' He stopped in time. He had never called her 'darling' in front of Killary.

'Nothing. I'm delighted. I told you she'd probably be the solution to your troubles. You didn't believe me.'

'She wants to live here,' Killary announced.

'Oh no!'

'Keep your hair on,' Mick laughed. 'There's nothing up her street for miles. She acknowledges that.'

Joan did her best not to appear distraite or disgruntled for the rest of the meal, but she was troubled and felt angry with herself because of the fact. But she was unable to prevent herself from continuing to question Killary.

'Was this Lady Constance beautiful?' she asked the child as they washed up.

'Oh no, Joan.' Killary was certain on that point. 'She's funny.'

'Funny? You mean amusing?'

'I didn't mean that. She was the tallest person I've ever seen. And she had her hair all round her head, like I told you. And she smoked a cigar. And she has a funny voice.'

'How funny?'

'Like a man's, sort of. Low. But she called out *"Deirdre* ahoy"', oh it was funny, Joan.' Killary began to laugh. 'That wasn't like a man. That was like—Daddy!' she called.

'What?'

'You 'member when that lady called *"Deirdre* ahoy"'? What did it sound like?'

'A foghorn,' Renvyle called from the adjoining room.

Two days later Joan had the chance of seeing Lady Constance for herself, as she came to the library to buy some books. Entering the shop like a galleon in full sail, Joan at once recognized her.

'Can I get you anything?' she asked politely, and kept her countenance when asked for several of Renvyle's books, one of which had been out of print for years.

'Ridiculous,' Lady Constance said crossly, when told of this fact. 'Can't you do something about it? A local genius in your very midst and you let his books go out of print.'

'It's the publisher's fault, not ours,' Joan reminded her.

'Have *you* read his books?' Lady Constance fixed a piercing eye on Joan.

'Yes, I have.' And then, throwing prudence to the winds, Joan added: 'He's a very great friend of mine.'

'Indeed?' Lady Constance seemed slightly taken aback. She looked the girl up and down through lorgnettes and said: 'Is the name Joan?'

'Yes. It is.'

'The child told me about you. Apparently you're very special to her—and her father.'

Joan felt embarrassed. 'When Killary was very ill I helped to nurse her,' she said.

'Oh. I see. That accounts for it.'

After making some purchases she left the shop, giving Joan a patronizing nod.

'Hateful creature. And dangerous,' Joan told herself.

'Why dangerous?' Jill asked her sister after Joan had let slip unconsciously her feelings about Lady Constance. 'I should have thought anyone likely to help Micky Renvyle was the reverse.'

Joan coloured. 'I—I don't know why I said dangerous. It was stupid. I just didn't like her. She's a steam-roller.'

Jill smiled. 'What you really mean, dearie, is that she might become an influence over him.'

'Yes. I suppose that is what I feel,' Joan replied slowly. 'And the awful thing is that at last I'm beginning to think Mick is weak, and if Lady Constance is a very strong personality—'

'She may get him in her toils? That's what you mean, isn't it?'

Joan nodded, sighing.

'Is it likely a rich woman like her, an earl's daughter, is going to want a mediocre—'

'But that's what he's not,' Joan rounded fiercely on her sister. 'She even called him a genius to me. And she's going to organize exhibitions for him in Dublin and London.'

'But you should be glad, not carrying on like a jealous school-girl,' Jill exclaimed. 'She's hardly likely to fall in love with him!'

'How do I know that? She's had lovers galore, including a jockey.'

'Joan, don't talk so ridiculously. And remember, for Pete's sake, Micky Renvyle's a good decent Catholic and a married man, as you well know.'

Joan remained silent, bitterly ashamed of her outburst in front of Jill.

A few days later Renvyle walked into the library, accompanied by both Killary and Lady Constance. Out of the corner of her eye Joan was aware that Lady Constance did not appear quite so strangely dressed as usual. She wore well-cut tweeds and had a woollen cap on her head. Joan heard her address Renvyle as Mike and this in itself annoyed her. She saw that Micky was paying her quite a lot of attention and so far had made no move to come over to talk to her in the library section. Killary had found a child she knew and was taken up with her, and for the first time Joan felt herself out of the picture. Presently they made their way to her desk and Micky introduced them. Joan was gauche and Lady Constance took no trouble to put her at her ease, and presently they left the building without any plan for a future meeting. Joan thought he would make some excuse and reappear, but as the morning went by and he did not come in again she was filled with misgiving and became nervy and jumpy with everyone who spoke to her. In the evening she could bear it no longer and telephoned to him.

'I was silly this morning, I had a beastly head,' she began.

'I thought you weren't yourself. Are you better?'

She thought he sounded a little casual. 'Not much,' she said. There was a long pause.

'When am I going to see you?' she asked. 'Properly, I mean.'

'Well,' he hesitated. 'I *hope* our Sunday will be all right, but Lady Constance is very anxious to go out to Louisburgh where she hears there's a house, and she wants me to go and look at it.'

Joan's heart sank. 'Surely you can get her to go on Saturday or any other day?' Tears welled up in her eyes and she hoped he could not detect the break in her voice.

'Yes, I should think so,' he said. 'I'll tell her I can't manage it. I expect she'll want to know the reason.'

'What cheek!' Joan exclaimed.

'She's a frightful autocrat, bosses one out of house and home,' Micky said with a laugh.

'And you stand for it?'

'It may be my bread and butter, don't forget.'

'Surely you're not going to prostitute yourself for filthy lucre.' The words were out before Joan could stop herself. 'I'm sorry, darling, I didn't mean that.'

There was silence.

'Mick, are you there?' But Joan realized he had put down the receiver. 'God, what am I doing, what am I behaving like?' she asked herself. She came out of the telephone-booth and walked blindly into a passing figure. Looking up to apologize, she saw it was Father Delaney.

'You look distraught, my child. Is anything wrong?' he asked.

'No, yes. Oh, Father, I'm such a fool,' she cried.

'D'you want to tell me?' he asked her.

'You'd be ashamed of me,' she said. They walked along the road together and she poured out to him the story of her recent behaviour, hiding nothing.

'Don't you think this good lady's interest in Micky Renvyle may be the solution to a lot of your problems?'

'Indeed I do. And that's what's troubling me.'

'Come, come, Joan. Behave like a grown woman. You know that only misery lies ahead in this love you have for Mick. If Lady Constance can really further his career it would be a splendid thing. And if it means shows away—abroad, even perhaps America—then I can only think it is by God's providence. Micky has got great talent, I fully appreciate the fact, and it's a thousand pities it has not been recognized more fully.'

'I know all you're saying is true,' Joan said. 'I suppose it hurts because I who love him can do nothing for him and a stranger can. Or may be able to.'

'Don't forget it was you who helped to save Killary's life. Mick will never forget that.'

'I don't want any thanks or remembrance for that. All I'm asking is that she doesn't take him away from me. The bit I have, and you know how little and how much that is.'

CHAPTER FOUR

WHEN Renvyle rang Joan a few days later he never mentioned her recent outburst, but merely said that he and Killary were expecting her on Sunday as usual. She went out to Ardbreen determined to behave naturally and to show no jealousy however much justification there might be; she was gay with Killary and had Micky been more perspicacious he must have seen that Joan was putting on an act.

As the day wore on and Lady Constance's name was never mentioned, the tension eased, and when Micky saw her into her car in the evening and asked her if she had been happy she kissed him, saying, 'It was lovely,' and then spoilt it by adding: 'I'm sorry I'm tiresome sometimes. I never realized I was temperamental.'

He laughed shortly and said, 'Now you know why I go off the handle occasionally.'

But not for the same cause, thought Joan.

A week or two later she saw in the local newspaper that Lady Constance Rowan-Colville had taken a house near Louisburgh for the summer months. She tried to console herself with the knowledge that Louisburgh was a tidy run from Ardbreen, not the sort of drive anyone would do daily. If he was seeing a lot of Lady Constance, Micky certainly was keeping it from her.

And Renvyle *was* seeing quite a bit of Constance Rowan-Colville. She motored over to Ardbreen at least twice a week throughout the summer months, during the week when Killary was at school. So Killary also was unaware of the growing friendship between her father and Lady Constance.

'It's ridiculous you haven't got a car of your own,' Lady Constance grumbled.

'I never learnt to drive till fairly recently,' he said, 'and I can always borrow my father's old one if I want the use of it. Aunt Cathleen doesn't use it much.'

'I don't notice you do,' she remarked. 'It's invariably a question of the mountain coming to Mahomet, myself being the mountain, of course. I wish sometimes you'd bring yourself over to me. You know you could do some lovely work, the views are out of this world. You must know it, anyway.'

Micky replied unconvincingly that he would one day, and then, when pressed, admitted that the car had broken down indefinitely.

'And I suppose you'll tell me you can't afford to get a new one?'

He said that was the case.

'It's absurd,' she announced later. 'Here I am with two cars. What can I possibly do with two in Ireland? You can have one.'

Mick knew by now that she made decisions on what impulse moved her at the moment, and he refused her offer.

'Don't be a fool, Mick. Moreover, you're very selfish dragging an old woman all these miles when you could do the journey yourself with a car.'

It was the first time she had ever made any mention of her age. Without thinking what he was saying, Mick said, 'How old *are* you?'

'What should you think?'

'I'm bad at women's ages. I'd say forty-odd. Forty-five?' he hazarded, wondering if this would put an end to any exhibition.

'I'm fifty-seven,' she said.

'Gosh, are you? You don't look it.' He was genuinely amazed and began to feel that if he refused the offer of one of her cars it might hurt the poor old thing.

'I've always felt young,' she said gaily, 'and done amusin' things when I've felt like it.'

'Such as?'

With a roguish look in her eye and a pout on her lips she said: 'I shan't tell you, you old Papist. You'd be shocked.'

Micky roared with laughter, and suddenly remembered

Joan's story of jockeys, princes and the rest. He looked at her. 'Good for you!' he chuckled.

'Glad it amuses you,' she answered. 'I've had a good deal more fun and run for my money than you, my dear boy.'

'That wouldn't be difficult,' he answered quietly.

She collected him from Ardbreen a couple of days later, and drove him back to Cleahy, and in front of the entrance was a perfectly respectable Zephyr which Micky was told he could look on as his own.

'D'you really mean it?' he asked, colouring with pleasure.

'What a boy you still are,' Lady Constance said, putting her arm through his.

'By Jove! Killary will be tickled to death. And so will Joan,' the last slipping out unintentionally.

'Joan?'

'Joan Fitzgerald. You met her the other day. Works in the library at Ballymannin,' he brushed the words aside a little too quickly.

'Ah yes. Killary's friend.'

'And mine,' he said quietly.

'Are you in love with each other?' she asked, expecting denial.

'Since you ask me, yes.'

This affirmation came as a shock to Lady Constance. She could understand that there was a certain amount of glamour surrounding the local genius—married to an actress who had left him, and struggling along with a small child, and who in any case attracted her. But what on earth was there in that plain, bespectacled, tongue-tied wench to inspire love in Renvyle? She decided that something must be done about it.

'And are you having a divinely romantic *affaire*?' she asked sympathetically.

Micky shook his head. 'You forget I'm married.'

'What's that got to do with it? Your wife left you, didn't she?'

'True. But we're Catholics. The lot of us. And Joan has scruples.'

'Thank God I'm a heathen!' Lady Constance flung her arms

wide to the winds. 'Or a pagan. Yes, I'm a pagan. The Greeks had a word for everything. Mike, dear, forget about Joan. It sounds a very dismal business. Come in and have some of the delicious lunch Emelie has prepared, and I've brought up some exquisite hock from Dublin.'

She walked swiftly into the house.

'I say, it is nice,' he remarked, looking round.

'I've brought up a van-load of my own stuff,' she answered, vaguely looking about her. 'The Knole, and that sofa-table. And of course my piano. My dear, there was a frightful upright thing that hadn't a note left to strike. I can't live without my Bechstein for long.'

She went across and started to play a Spanish love song.

'I worship Albéniz,' she said, closing her eyes, humming an obbligato. 'But you want a drink.'

He was looking at a portrait which was hanging on the wall. It certainly bore some resemblance to Lady Constance, but must have been done a good many years ago.

'That picture,' he began.

'Oh, the Orpen,' she said. 'I love it. I take it about with me so that strangers realize what I used to look like. I always like it better than the Lavery which Papa has at Belgrave Square.'

A little foreign woman slid into the room at that moment and announced that luncheon was served.

'That's my faithful Emelie. I found her in a ditch in France. Near Perpignan.'

By now Renvyle had learnt to be astonished at nothing Lady Constance told him, and if she had said Emelie had dropped as manna from heaven he would have believed her. When the meal was over she took him by the arm, and puffing a cigar drew him into the garden.

'What about that?' she asked, pointing to the view that embraced Clare Island, Achill and Clew Bay.

'It's—it's sublime. I know,' he said.

'Well, what are you going to do about it?'

'I'd love to paint it. But I haven't time today.'

'Then stay the night. I can lend you a pair of my pyjamas.'

He managed to smother laughter and said it was impossible as he had made no arrangements for Killary. 'But if it's still fine I'll come back tomorrow if I may? And I'll bring my own pyjamas,' he laughed.

When he told Killary that she would have to stay with her aunt for a couple of nights as he was going to paint up near Clew Bay, he did not mention Lady Constance. Nor, that evening, was the child made aware of the new car. Next day, feeling extraordinarily light-hearted, Renvyle left the house early, and as he sped along the shore of Killary Harbour and through Leenane he wondered what Constance Rowan-Colville made of it, and later asked her.

'It's your special place, according to your child, as far as I remember. I'd like to go there with you.'

'I'll bring the boat in one day and pick you up and take you for a sail round the islands.'

During the day he worked hard and she left him severely alone. By the evening he had finished the water-colour which Lady Constance said was 'quite exquisite'.

'I shall give you fifty pounds for it,' she told him, 'unless in the exhibition you get a better price for it.'

'You'll do nothing of the sort,' he answered her, and putting it into her hands said: 'Here, take it, it's yours.'

'My sweet Mike,' she began, 'how am I to help you if you're going to give things away? I want you to sell, sell, sell!' Her great laugh boomed forth, 'Bigger and better sales.'

'But you're different, Lady Constance.'

She looked at him. 'Am I? And don't you think you might call me Constance?'

That evening after dinner, which he found exceptionally delicious as he had only eaten sandwiches during the day, Constance played Rachmaninoff, Debussy, and de Falla to him as he lay outside the drawing-room in a chaise-longue drinking coffee.

'Do you know this?' she said, and played to him 'The Lover and the Nightingale'.

'I'm ignorant about music,' he confessed, 'but I love it. I

never had enough money to go to concerts when I was studying in London, and when I was there with my wife we went
to a theatre if anything, or a film. Somehow I've never got
around to music. All I know is what I hear on the radio.'

Lady Constance got up.

'My poor dear, you've a new life ahead of you. *How delicious*!
And *I* shall introduce you to the gods. Wait!' She held her
hand up imperiously. He watched her go over to what he
supposed was a gramophone. 'Another of my imports,' she
said. 'My radiogram. Now, you're not to move or speak.'

Presently the strains of the 'Good Friday Music' came across
the air. Toscanini was conducting, a name conveying little to
Renvyle, but he watched with mild surprise Lady Constance
in her long green velvet garment crouching on the ground near
him, and noticed tears in her eyes. Not knowing the story of
Parsifal he was completely unaware that she was identifying
herself at that moment with Kundry and that he was the
'blameless fool'. He remembered Joan telling him that
Constance—yes, Constance from now on—was supposed to
be beautiful. And he had laughed. But it was true, she was
beautiful. At this particular moment she looked very beautiful
indeed, magnificently beautiful. He began to wish he could
paint her as she looked at this moment. Suddenly she looked
up and caught his glance. She held out her hand to him and he
took it, without paying much attention. The music was sublime, utterly stupendous he realized. He wondered if Joan
liked music. He must ask her. Again his gaze fell on the strange
elderly woman crouching beside him whose hand he held in
his own. Why was she being so kind to him, he wondered? It
was up to him to justify her belief in him, anyway; thanks to
her he had once again felt the urge to paint and to paint well.
To create. The strains of the music soared. How strange it all
was. It was doing something to him. In the twilight with the
first faint sign of the moon he wanted to paint it as it was.
Now. He started to rise, but Lady Constance pushed him
gently back.

'S'sh,' she whispered, and he felt a prisoner.

When the music was over, she slowly rose and made her way indoors. He got up and followed her. She had switched on a dimly lit electric light and everything seemed green to him.

'I've never heard anything like that,' he told her. 'Thank you.'

'We're going to have some wonderful times, darling,' she said gaily, and he did not notice the endearment. 'I'm going to introduce you to an entirely new world. I'll take a box at Covent Garden and you shall hear *Tristan* with me.'

'That thing we've just heard, is that an opera?' he asked.

'I'm surprised that you, a Roman Catholic, shouldn't know *Parsifal*. It's a religious opera.' And in matter-of-fact tones she began to instruct him in operatic stories until one o'clock in the morning, every now and then leaping up and putting on records until Micky's head was in a whirl of sound and he no longer knew what he was supposed to know or not know.

'You're giving me too much at once,' he cried finally.

Immediately she was contrite. 'So like me,' she said, 'when I'm full of enthusiasm for something I boil over with it. It's the same with love.'

Micky thought of the jockey, and the prince, he could not remember the third of the triumvirate.

He returned to Ardbreen the following day. Killary saw the car for the first time and expressed great satisfaction with it but no curiosity.

'The other was an awful old thing,' she said. 'Will Auntie Leen be able to drive this, should you think?' And Renvyle told her that this time the car belonged to him, which answer satisfied her.

That evening, late, Joan rang.

'Darling, I tried to get hold of you last night—twice. And couldn't get an answer. Were you fishing?'

'No.' He tried to speak naturally. 'I'd gone up to Constance at Louisburgh, to do some painting, and stayed the night.'

Constance now. Joan's heart was ice.

'Was it fun?' she asked.

'I did a good picture, I think. My God, there's a view and a half!'

'No better than Ardbreen, surely?'

'True. But I've done Ardbreen so many times.'

'What else did you do?'

'Well, nothing really. I was working all day, until practically nightfall. Then after dinner she played the piano and put on some gramophone records.'

Joan sniffed audibly. 'What an extraordinary way to spend the evening. Did she want you to dance with her?'

Micky felt his temper rising. 'Don't be a fat-head. Not that sort of music. Wonderful stuff. Opera. Wagner. Something called *Parsifal*. D'you know it?'

'No, I don't. I'm afraid I'm not one of your highbrows.'

'Well, keep your shirt on. I'd never heard any of it before either. Completely bowled me over, it did. I wish I had a gramophone and some of her records, I believe it would help me to paint.'

Joan laughed. 'Really! How absurd you are! How could it?'

'I don't know, but last night sitting outside with the moon rising and all this glorious music, I felt I could have painted something for the—the Prado!'

'And why didn't you, then?' she asked coldly.

'It was dark,' he answered lamely, 'and Constance didn't want one to disturb the peace.'

'Dear, dear, dear!'

There was a pause and both of them said at once, 'Are you still there?'

'Since when did you get on to Constance terms?' she asked.

'She asked me to. I couldn't very well refuse. Incidentally she's fifty-seven.'

'*Is* she?' Joan felt suddenly happier. 'And did the poor thing have to bring you back?'

'Actually no,' he hesitated, 'actually she's lent me one of her cars. An old Ford which apparently she doesn't use.'

'Oh. Well,' Joan began, drawing a long breath, 'you seem to be doing nicely. I shouldn't think there'd be any difficulty in getting a gramophone out of her. Well supplied with your precious opera records.'

'Well, I'm certainly not going to ask for them. And, darling, don't be silly. Don't go all jealous again. I've told you she's fifty-seven, tho',' he added stupidly, 'I must say she didn't look it last night.'

'Oh? Why?'

'I don't know. She just didn't.'

'What had she got on?'

'I don't know. Something green. Long and green. Velvet.'

'How ridiculous in the summer!'

'Well, it was quite chilly in the garden.'

'I thought you were listening to the gramophone and her piano-playing?'

'I was outside. And when she put on the gramophone she came outside too.'

'I see. Well, I'm getting chilly too. And as I don't possess anything long and green—or at all glamorous—I'll say good-night, Mick.'

'All right, my darling. You needn't worry, you know. She knows about us.'

'*What?*'

'I told her about us. I think she had guessed.'

Joan was outraged. 'You told this woman, this stranger you've only known a short time, about us? About our love? Our secret? Oh—' She couldn't go on.

'I thought you'd be glad,' Renvyle said helplessly. Really, women . . .

'Glad? Mick, you're impossible. I simply don't begin to understand you. For all you know she'll start spreading the whole story around the whole place.'

'I'm sure she won't,' he answered.

'And what on earth am I going to feel like when she comes into the library again?'

'She—well—' He was at a loss.

'No, really, Mick. I know men are pretty hopeless and helpless, but I never dreamed you could do such a thing as betray our love. And to that woman of all people.'

Another long pause ensued.

'Well, I'm sorry,' Micky said at last. 'As I'm in the dog-house I'd better say good-night. Are you still there?'

'Oddly enough, yes,' Joan replied.

'Good-night, then. Darling.'

'Good-night, Micky.'

CHAPTER FIVE

It was a difficult period for Micky Renvyle. Simpleton as he undoubtedly was, he was unaware that two women—neither of whom had a real claim to him—warred with each other for his friendship, his companionship, his love. In spite of her eccentricity he found the company of Lady Constance stimulating; and in Joan was all love, all desire, all spiritual need. Never were two women more dissimilar; neither, moreover, to the average man would have appeared to have physical attraction. And Renvyle had been married to a woman of great loveliness.

'I don't think Joan likes Lady Constance,' Killary said one day.

'What makes you think that?'

'She frowns when you speak about her. And she never wants to be here the same day.'

'Well,' Micky scratched his head, 'I don't think they'd have much in common. Do you like Lady Constance?'

Killary pondered the question and then said, 'She makes me laugh. I was rather frightened of her at first, but I believe she pretends.'

'You're an intelligent brat. But you love Joan, don't you?'

'Oh yes!' Killary at once sounded enthusiastic. 'I often wish she was Mummie. She's not pretty like Mummie was, but I like her better now that Mummie's forgotten us.'

'Don't you want Mummie back?'

'Not particularly. Do you?'

Renvyle took Killary to Louisburgh one Saturday and she was enchanted by the house and everything in it.

'You must be awfully rich,' she said, eyeing Constance

Rowan-Colville with awe. They were upstairs in the bedroom to which Constance had brought a four-poster bed which added splendour in the child's eyes.

'I am. And it's very useful,' the woman said, trying to size up the child.

'I should like to be rich when I'm a lady.'

'What would you do with your money?'

'Well. I should live in a castle. And wear lovely clothes. And I'd give lots and lots of my money to Father Delaney for all the poor little children who haven't clothes or enough to eat.'

'I call that very commendable.'

'And I'd like to be married to a person like Daddy because I love him more than anyone. Can I marry Daddy?'

'No. You can't do that, I'm afraid, and he'd be too old for you when you're grown up.'

'I suppose he would.' After a pause Killary continued, 'Have you someone like Daddy?'

'I've got an old father of ninety, if that's what you mean, who isn't at all like Daddy.'

'No, I don't mean that. Have you got,' she hesitated, 'I think they're called husbands.'

'No, I haven't.'

'Or children?'

'No.'

'Are you sorry?'

'I'm thankful I've no children. I don't like 'em as a rule, but you amuse me, I can't think why. As for husbands, I guess I've been too fussy. Come along, we must go and find Mike.'

'Why d'you call him Mike? Nobody else does.'

'For that reason.'

Downstairs Renvyle was pacing up and down.

'What on earth have you two been talking about?' he asked.

'Life,' said Lady Constance, 'and husbands. And children.'

'She doesn't really like them,' Killary vouchsafed.

Later in the day the subject of beauty cropped up.

'My Mummie is very beautiful,' Killary said, 'but she's gone away and has forgotten us.'

'That is a sad state of affairs,' Lady Constance allowed, as she poured out tea.

'Well, it doesn't really matter very much. We have Aunty Leen. And of course Joan. And now we seem to have you.'

'Thank you,' said Lady Constance, giving the child a large slice of cake.

'We went to Lady Constance yesterday,' Killary told Joan the following day, looking at her with great intensity.

'Oh? Was it nice?'

'She's very rich. She said she was.'

'How disgusting of her.'

'Why? Why disgustin' of her?'

'To boast.'

'She didn't boast, Joan. I asked her and she said yes, she was, and it was useful.'

Joan sighed. It was clever of the woman if she was going to reach the father through the child.

'D'you like her, Killary?' she asked.

'Quite,' Killary answered, and then seeing something unusual in Joan's expression she flung herself at her and exclaimed, 'But not the same as you. *I love you, Joan*. I wish you were my Mummie.'

Joan held the child to her and kissed the back of her neck tenderly.

'Oh, my darling, so do I.'

One evening Renvyle came in after a day in *Deirdre* and saw a letter in Paddy's writing, lying on the mat. It was a long time since any communication had passed between them. He picked it up and slowly opened it.

'Dear Micky,' it ran, 'Do you think you could bring yourself to consider a divorce for the two of us? Don't fly off the handle at once. But this life of ours is hopeless. And frankly I'd like my freedom and I dare say you would too. I expect your religious scruples are still a hell of a lot stronger than mine which have gone by the board, I know divorce in Ireland is impossible and that it will mean coming to England and a lot of trouble—or maybe you could even cope with Reno! I've left you long enough for it to be whatever it is when one does leave someone in the lurch. But I can supply adulterous adventures if you'd rather, though would prefer not for obvious reasons. Please don't say no right away. Yours, Paddy.'

And here was a pretty kettle of fish, thought Micky. Although for some time now he had sincerely wished he was free in order to be able to marry Joan, he had never seriously considered the possibility of divorce. How could he, as a Catholic, and living in Ireland?

He strolled down to the shore. Surely if he went to Joan with freedom on a plate, as it were, she would consider a registry office marriage in England? He knew any religious ceremony was out of the question. Suddenly he came face to face with the little Calvary that stood at the promontory overlooking the ocean and islands. The face of the dead Christ—weather-beaten by centuries—still influenced Micky as it had since his childhood. He looked away, unable to bring his eyes to those of the figure on the cross.

Next day he rang Joan and asked her to come over after work.

'Darling, this is an unexpected bonus,' she said, kissing him. 'What's it in aid of?'

'I want to talk to you. D'you feel like going for a drive?'

'Of course.'

'Well, go slowly. And keep your mind on the wheel as well as what I'm going to talk about.'

'Where shall we go?' she asked.

'Oh, anywhere,' he answered impatiently.

They drove in silence to Tully Cross where she took the shore turn and he realized she was making for Leenane.

'I've had a letter from Paddy.' He felt the car swerve slightly. 'She wants a divorce.'

Joan slowed up and stopped.

'So?'

'I don't know what to do. How to answer her.'

'It's quite simple, darling. She knows perfectly well we don't have divorce. Annulments sometimes, yes. Divorce only for non-practising Catholics, and anyway not in Ireland. I don't know anything about Paddy, but you're still a Catholic, thank God.'

He was silent as she started the car again. As they drove along the shore of Lough Fee, Micky said, 'If I were free, if I consented to a divorce in England, would you marry me? I know it would be a registry office, and we'd not be married in the eyes of the Church, but legally we'd be man and wife.'

'Are you serious?' she asked, driving very slowly.

'Very serious.'

Joan shook her head, and there were tears in her eyes as she answered, 'Of course I couldn't marry you. It wouldn't be marriage. We'd be excommunicated. Darling, you can't be in your right mind.'

They drove on again in silence until they reached the road which led directly to Leenane.

'I've always thought this the most beautiful place in the world, and it's where I first met you properly,' Joan said.

'And you're ready to chuck a chance of permanent happiness for a medieval belief?'

She blanched. 'What an appalling thing to say, Mick! Deny what you've said immediately. Permanent happiness can only be found in heaven. And Catholic belief and the teaching of the Church aren't medieval, they're for all time and eternity. And if I thought you really felt otherwise I'd never see you again.'

'You don't mean that?'

'I do. Don't you even now realize I love you through God? Because we belong together to the Church? Because I thought we stood for the same ideals, and the same belief?' She was crying now.

'I suppose men are different,' Renvyle said slowly.

'Not all men,' she sobbed.

'Well, my dear, I'm not a priest. And I'm not abnormal either. If I can get freedom I shall. I've not spoken to Father Delaney, I've not spoken to anyone but you because you were the only person except myself to be affected by a divorce. Or so I hoped,' he finished bitterly.

A few days later he went to Cleahy, and whilst lunching with Lady Constance, said lightly:

'My wife wants a divorce.'

'Splendid!' she replied. 'On what grounds can you go ahead?'

'Desertion. But you realize as a Catholic I can't re-marry, or if I do I face excommunication. And it means going to England—or anywhere out of Ireland.'

'And what will you do with your freedom? Marry your Jane? Jean? Joan?'

'That remains to be seen. At present—I—I can't say.'

'Does your religion mean very much to you, Mike?' Lady Constance asked.

'It used to.'

'Does a woman's body mean more?'

He looked up, startled. 'I'd rather not discuss that.'

He spent the next few days in mental and spiritual torment. Now that the test had presented itself he no longer felt sure he could go through with it.

He sought advice from the priest.

'You and Paddy are both Catholics, you should not have to ask such a question,' Father Delaney told him, 'but speaking for yourself only, you must know and realize that if you do acquiesce to her wish you put yourself beyond the pale should you re-marry. I hope you do no such thing, it will come doubly hard on the poor girl you love.'

'You mean Joan?'

'I mean Joan, yes. She will see you acknowledged free in the world's eyes, but as a good Catholic, which she is, it can mean nothing to her but further temptation from the devil. If you love her, my son, don't do this thing.'

When Micky next saw Joan he never mentioned Paddy or her wish for divorce, and as time went by she felt he had given up the idea. All thoughts of it were repugnant to her and she took care never to bring up the subject. In the meantime plans had gone forward speedily, engineered by Lady Constance, for his show in Dublin in the summer, followed by one in London in the autumn.

'What an influential person you seem to be,' he teased her one day.

'I am. There's very little I can't accomplish once I get my mind to it,' she replied.

'What an alarming thought.'

'It needn't be. And while we're on the subject of your show, I propose you make my house in Fitzwilliam Square your head-quarters.'

'That's terribly good of you,' he replied.

'It's merely sensible. And the same thing applies for the London show.'

'But that's your father's house.'

'I have my own suite, but in any case Papa would be delighted.'

CHAPTER SIX

LONDON under the auspices of Lady Constance Rowan-Colville
was a very different affair from the life Micky Renvyle had
occasionally led with Paddy, or that of his student days at the
Slade. At first he had felt so completely lost in his new surroundings that there were days when he hoped that the nightmare
existence would cease suddenly, and that he would wake to
reality in Ireland. The visit to Lady Constance's house in Fitzwilliam Square had in no way prepared him for the solemn
grandeur of Lord Rowan's establishment in Belgrave Square.
In Dublin in spite of two or three nice Irish servants, all of
them women, life had been come-as-you-please and Bohemian
as only Dubliners know how to make it. Parties were gay and
informal, laughter and wit abounded and Micky was soon
made to feel as much at home as in Ardbreen, moreover he
was achieving no small success, as the show which Lady
Constance had sponsored had fulfilled his highest aspirations
and he sold many of his pictures well.

The sombre Edwardian—almost Victorian—atmosphere of
the house in Belgrave Square came like a cold douche after
days of lingering in sub-tropical warmth. It was not that the
old earl was casual, impolite or hostile in any way. He was in
fact over-polite, and did his best to listen to every word that fell
from Micky's lips, but he was extremely deaf and insisted on
an old-fashioned ear-trumpet if he allowed any aid at all, which
was seldom, and many were the meals taken in the vast dining-
room, the table laid with a white damask cloth and a footman
behind every chair, with only Lord Rowan, his daughter and
Micky present, each of them several yards from each other.
Constance and her father would reminisce—sometimes for half
an hour at a time—about people and places totally unknown

to Renvyle, who would sit ill at ease trying to take an interest in past exploits of a fading near-dead aristocracy, feeling that the waiting men-servants were despising him as one more hanger-on of his lordship's daughter.

Breakfasts were torture alone in the breakfast-room—only a shade smaller than the dining-room—at nine o'clock, by which time all appetite had left him, hungry as a hunter as he'd been at seven. Two footmen stood stiffly in attendance, doing their best to ply him with kedgeree, kidneys, haddock, eggs, but quite unable to contend with any conversation which Micky had tried out the first morning. Lady Constance breakfasted in her room, appearing downstairs at ten, and from then on things improved, and the purpose of the London visit would be embarked upon. Sometimes Renvyle felt she was the painter and he a groom-in-waiting as questions fired at one or other of them were invariably answered by her, and when the great day itself took place Mick was quite astonished to find himself as a centre of attraction, being interviewed alone and photographed for society periodicals.

Hundreds of invitations had been sent out for the Private View and when the day wore on and Constance disappeared for a couple of hours and there was time to breathe, Renvyle realized at last that he knew not one soul in the room and no one knew or recognized him, and that he was at liberty to wander as one of the invited and listen to criticism adverse and kind.

When he read the reviews he was humbly delighted by the praise his pictures received and was more than astonished as the days went by to find that people were buying them. But life at Belgrave Square still depressed him, it felt like living in dust-sheets, so he wrote Joan. The parties Constance gave were mostly peopled by faded aristocracy of her parents' generation and middle-aged friends of her own who were far more at home balancing cups of iced coffee or tea (which was all they were offered in the way of drink) than they would have been with highballs, cocktails and whiskies. He was eager to meet Mrs Dishforth and was surprised to find a pretty, plump little woman who reminded him of a pigeon. She still bore traces of extreme prettiness and he found himself longing suddenly to write a novel around the romance of her and Lord Rowan. When he said as much to Lady Constance he was surprised by the look of horrified consternation in her eyes.

'I hope you'll do nothing of the sort,' she said in an outraged voice, and seeing his surprise, she said: 'That sort of thing isn't done, my dear boy. Just isn't done.'

'I thought it was, every day,' he replied.

'Not about people of Papa's generation. It would be a very ill-bred thing to do, having been a guest under his roof.'

'Good heavens! Constance, I didn't say I was going to, I merely said I'd like to. I'm no novelist anyway, as you know. And why did you tell me about Mrs Dishforth if it's so secret?'

'Because it's not a secret. Everyone knows of the *affaire*. It's centuries old.'

Micky gave it up.

Gradually he began to meet the more interesting of Constance's friends, and when Lord Rowan departed for his usual winter sojourn on the Riviera things began to look up, as he wrote to Joan. He was determined to put an end to what he considered foolish jealousy on Joan's part and wrote constantly, telling her of picture sales, sending her reviews, telling her about parties and theatres and visits to the opera, and described amusingly enough the stuffy old people he continually met, relics from the days of Henry James or even Thackeray.

At home in Connemara Joan led a miserable existence living only for the days she got Micky's letters, and with a fear which grew daily that things would never be the same, and that something would happen that would part them more surely than the barrier of Renvyle's marriage had hitherto done.

Micky did not write and tell Joan that he had decided to go ahead with Paddy's request and divorce her. He discussed it frequently with Lady Constance, who encouraged him with all the subtlety she possessed.

'It's ridiculous to be tied when you both wish for freedom,' she counselled, 'and if your Joan's worth her salt she'll capitulate when you're no longer tied to your wife. Or else her love doesn't amount to much.'

'I wish I could be so sure,' he answered.

'I don't understand these pure virginal damsels,' Lady Constance expostulated. 'To me they're plainly frigid. When *I've* been in love I can assure you everything is thrown to the winds. Bonnets over windmills and a great many more garments than bonnets,' and she laughed with pleasure.

'Joan is very devout. A far better Catholic than I am, I'm afraid.'

'Of course I don't begin to understand all your claptrap. I thought you could have a hell of a good time and rush off to Confession and get it off your chest?'

'I believe a lot of people are under that impression. It's not true, y'know. You can only receive absolution if you really promise not to sin again.'

She looked at him slyly. 'So what? Easily said.'

Micky was shocked. 'Few of us are real hypocrites. Most of us have the fear of God in our hearts. For my part I could commit sin, but I couldn't go to Confession, unless I really meant to put an end to it.'

'D'you really mean that?'

'I do. That's why all this business with Joan is difficult.'

'You mean you're ready to forgo your heaven?'

'God forgive me, but my heaven is in Joan's arms.'

They had been lunching alone in Belgrave Square, and Constance rose from the table.

'We must see what we can do about it all,' she said slowly.

If Lady Constance's friends were old and dull, she had other ideas for Micky Renvyle which he found entrancing. The ballet alternated with opera at Covent Garden and with her usual generosity she took a box for the 'little' season and introduced Micky to both. Supper usually followed at Boulestin or the Savoy and they were occasionally joined by some interesting personage. A regular first-nighter in the past, Constance found no difficulty in getting on to theatre lists again and the two of them were frequently photographed together in the foyers of theatres or at private views of picture shows.

'I must get back for Christmas, you know,' he told her one day.

'Bring the child over,' she replied.

He knew Killary would be miserable in the huge house with all its unfriendly English servants and told Constance he was against London for children.

'Besides,' he said, somewhat unconvincingly, 'I must see Joan.'

Constance's eyes narrowed and she wondered whether there was a subtle difference between 'I must' and 'I want'. 'Well, if you must, you must,' she said, 'but don't go till after the ball.'

'What ball?'

Apparently there was to be some ball for charity for which Lady Constance as usual had taken a great many tickets and had undertaken to bring a party. Even Micky, who had become used to the various changes in Constance Rowan-Colville's appearance, was astonished by her looks when he came into the saloon the night of the ball. She towered above everyone, clad in stiff white satin, and her mother's pearls in ropes hung from her neck. On her head, mounted on the coronet of her own raven hair, was the diamond Rowan coronet. She looked more regal than any queen, 'like Boadicea' someone whispered in his ear. He was surprised to learn later in the evening that she was an excellent dancer, as light as a feather.

'I suppose you think I ought to sit round like all the dowagers,' she snapped at him.

'Not at all, Constance,' he assured her.

'I feel much more like a débutante,' she replied gaily. 'Ah, those were the days, when *I* was a deb.'

'Were you kissed in hansom cabs?' he asked.

'Certainly not,' she answered him coldly. 'Papa always sent the Rolls for me.'

'What a shame! I mean it must have been rather an anti-climax to many a romantic evening.'

'My dear, I always made good use of conservatories and punts.' She sighed. 'But I suppose you'd think I'm a ridiculous old woman if I told you the wonderful affairs I've had.'

'I never—could never—think of you as an old woman, Constance,' Micky said, and meant it.

'Well, that's something.'

'To me you're ageless.'

'I'm not sure that I like that. You could visualize a creature like Rider Haggard's "She", which I read in my youth. Long before your day,' she sighed.

'What was it about?'

'A woman of fabulous beauty, old as God, and who suddenly withered—in flames if I remember rightly—into the oldest of old hags.'

'What a horrible story. But you're certainly very beautiful. Tonight you tower above everyone in the room.'

'I always do. I'm six feet and more.'

'You know I didn't mean that. I meant no one holds a candle to you.'

When they arrived back at Belgrave Square, Lady Constance dismissed the footman who was still waiting up, and ordered sandwiches to be sent to her sitting-room, with champagne.

'Come up to my sanctum, you've never been. I allow very few people there,' she said, as if she was conferring a knighthood on Renvyle. They ascended in the lift and Constance called to Marie her maid that she could go off to bed. It was, as Micky expected, a surprising room. Antique furniture, velvet furnishings, bric-à-brac galore; Burmese gods, Sèvres vases, an ormolu clock, a drawing by Sargent of her as a child of about ten. Scores of photographs of people mostly in embossed satin frames; minor royalties were well to the fore, as well as a celebrated actress, a famous bull-fighter, the jockey (at least Micky supposed the little man on a horse with jockey cap was he), Russian dancers and a rather questionable member of a one-time Labour Government. Apart from the actress and one or two royal ladies the victims of the camera—and possibly of Lady Constance, he thought—were male.

'Looking at my dear ones?' she said, coming back into the room popping the champagne cork as she spoke.

'Are they all?' he inquired.

'Ah! That would be telling,' she said roguishly.

Presently he asked her, 'Why don't you write your life?'

'I couldn't tell it truthfully, too many people would be offended. And I'm damned if I'd sign my name to half-truths. But I've had a very interesting life. Very wonderful at times. But I'm laying up for myself a lonely old age.'

'Why did you never marry?'

He knew it was an impertinent question and wondered if he would get his ears boxed.

'I was spoilt. Too choosy. I disliked the eligible *partis* Papa rounded up for me. I was engaged for a very brief moment in the first war, to a charming boy who of course got himself killed the moment he arrived at the front. Then I started to fall in love with unsuitable persons. They were married, or not our sort. One day perhaps I'll tell you about some of my affairs.'

'It seems a waste.'

'Of all my wealth, you mean? No children to leave it to? A cats' home? I assure you I have everything mapped out methodically, but even so I change my will annually.'

'I wasn't thinking of your money.'

'What then?'

He got up to go. 'I don't think I'll tell you.'

She refilled his glass. 'Let's have some music. Thank God the house is big enough to play the piano or the gramophone in the small hours without disturbing anyone.'

She went to the radiogram and put on the *Tristan* Prelude, and went back to the sofa. Patting the place beside her, she said: 'Come back here, Mike.'

It was an order and he obeyed. It was dangerous music, as well she knew.

'Are you coming abroad with me presently?' she whispered as the Prelude ran into the *Liebestod*.

Renvyle looked up, startled. 'I—I don't know. I mean I've not thought about it.'

'Then think about it.'

She took his hand and pressed it to her heart.

'This music always slays one,' she said.

Renvyle swallowed. He had drunk too much champagne and he was ready to agree about the music too, and when the climax of the opera came and Isolde was about to die, and Lady Constance pressed her lips to his, he knew there was only one thing to do and he must do it. Taking her in his arms, he returned her embrace fiercely. 'And now what?' his rather befuddled brain cried, as he presently tried to extricate himself.

'What's the matter? You don't have to go,' were the smothered words he heard.

'It's late. I must leave you.'

Carefully concealing a hiccup he managed to get up on to his legs, swaying slightly.

'Silly boy.'

The record had begun again, she had fixed it to continue endlessly, and she herself was Isolde, but an Isolde of the second act and, without the arms of her lover Tristan, a trifle lost. She looked up under veiled eyelids and said quietly:

'One night you'll stay. Kiss me again before you return to your chaste bed.'

On unsteady legs he knelt beside her and she rumpled his hair.

'Take those awful spectacles off,' she said. He did so.

'What a shame to hide them. You've got divine eyes.'

Micky began to feel very foolish as the champagne stupor was starting to wear off and he wondered what he had said and done. Without his glasses all he was aware of was a sort of Gorgon's head, and the scent of gardenias, which he realized he had crushed, wafting strongly to his nostrils.

'I'd give you a great deal more than that silly Joan of yours,' Constance said. A sobering thought; and Micky came to his senses. Joan. My God! What had he been doing?

'Unfortunately it's Joan I want,' he said very ungallantly.

'I know,' she replied. 'I'm just telling you I've forgotten more about passion than your Joan could ever learn, even if she had the mind to.'

Micky was sorely tempted to tell her that he was in no need of passion, or of a woman, but of one woman, Joan.

'Good night, my dear,' he said, and kissed her hand. 'Thank you for a very great deal. You've been a wonderful friend to me, and I can never repay you.'

Slowly she got up from the sofa, and looked at herself in the mirror.

'What a mess!' she said. 'Off to bed, then, little boy. You're really very sweet, and all I want is that you should be a successful painter. If you achieve that I shall be fully repaid.' She blew him a kiss and he left the room. As the door closed she said, almost to herself, 'You'll repay me, and before very long, my dear, and you'll forget there was ever such a girl as Joan.'

CHAPTER SEVEN

I

MICKY returned to Ardbreen for Christmas. He still said nothing to anyone about the impending divorce. He discovered he must be domiciled for a time in England in order to legalize his status and to prove Paddy's refusal to live with him. Paddy was acting in London and one day he went to a matinée of hers. He was astonished to realize by the end of the afternoon that he felt nothing at all for the woman on the stage who was his wife. He had neither love, desire, hate or even dislike. Paddy O'Malley might have been an unknown actress as far as he was concerned. He left the theatre feeling reassured and relieved.

During the Christmas holidays he told Joan and Killary that he would be returning to London to work. Joan tried to hide her distraught feelings.

'I thought you couldn't work there?'

'I find I can if I'm on my own.'

'Aren't you going to be with Lady Constance?'

'Good heavens no!' he said airily. 'She will be abroad. No, I've taken a little studio flat for a few months.'

The holidays went by peaceably enough. His old longing for Joan mounted steadily, and on the rare occasions when he was able to hold her to his heart and kiss her lips he found himself cursing the evening he had attempted to make rather drunken love to Lady Constance, whose mouth had known so many kisses from so many lips.

'Oh, darling, I love you,' he cried the first time he held her in his arms on his return. 'What awful creatures men are!'

'Why?' she laughed.

'I like to know you belong to no one but me.' And then:

'Not that you belong to me as I could wish. Have you kissed many other chaps?'

She looked surprised. 'Well, darling, I can't pretend I was never kissed before I met you. But not many. So you needn't worry.'

Renvyle was surprised on his return to England to find he could work quite well. The studio flat he had taken was on the river near Chiswick and there was an old-world country air about the place that appealed to him and made him forget it was London. He started to write again, short stories, and to his surprise his publisher was pleased enough with them to consider publishing them in book form. It was Renvyle's first attempt at fiction, apart from the ill-fated novel, and he was fascinated when he discovered he could work in this métier.

At last the day came when his divorce was to be heard. As it was undefended there was very little publicity attached in spite of the fact that Paddy O'Malley was by now well-known. A few lines in the London evening papers said that her husband had been granted a decree due to her desertion, and Micky hoped this was all the publicity the divorce would create, never thinking that the Irish press at home would have mention of the business. He was therefore unprepared for the hostility awaiting him from several quarters on his return to Ardbreen. The fact that Paddy was the guilty person in so far as she had left him and genuinely refused to return, seemed to have no bearing on the case. What did he, a Catholic, mean by doing such a thing? he was asked. In vain he tried to explain he had merely done what his wife had asked of him.

'Two wrongs don't make a right,' Miss O'Malley said, with tight lips, 'and you've put the girl in the way of greater temptation.'

'In heaven's name, what d'you mean?' Micky asked, exasperated.

'She may even marry again, and come to that so may you—and you'll both be burning in hell. It's terrible for me,' and she started to sniffle.

'Don't talk such nonsense,' Micky said crossly. 'Neither of us is contemplating marriage as far as I know.'

'What d'you want your freedom for, then?'

'Paddy asked for it, so I gave in to her wishes,' he said wearily. 'I should be sorry indeed to believe in a religion or a God that thrust us into a burning hell for so little.'

Miss O'Malley crossed herself. 'The trouble with all you young people today is that you all think you know better than the Church itself. I don't know what's come over the world. I suppose you think you can argue with His Holiness himself?'

Even Father Delaney seemed cool, or so Micky fancied. The divorce was not mentioned but gone was the old pat-on-the-shoulder, 'Micky-boyo'. The Jamesons, who obviously knew about it all, were too bright and talked about hotel guests and notabilities, which was not their wont, and Micky found himself dreading the first meeting with Joan. He noticed she looked pale and thin, with rims under her eyes as though she hadn't slept. She said nothing, and it was Micky himself who brought up the subject.

'I appear to be in Coventry,' he said lightly.

'Did you expect it would be looked on with approbation? I think the chief reason they've got it against you is that you've kept everyone in the dark. Even me. You never told me. Darling, why didn't you?'

'What would have been the point? As I've told Aunt Cathleen—now no longer my aunt, I suppose—Paddy asked for a divorce, as I told you, and eventually I agreed.'

'It does seem a shame, I know, that people should be blaming you.'

'And how will it affect us, belovèd? Or shall I say how are you going to let it?'

'I told you that ages ago. It makes no difference.'

He said no more.

'You'll have to watch your step as far as I'm concerned, moreover,' Joan reminded him. 'Have you forgotten king's proctors, or are they now called queen's? As you brought the case you've got to be like Caesar's wife, and no picnics alone and lovely kisses in the dark, or some snooper will queer your pitch.'

'Surely they don't follow one over here?'

'Of course they would. Oh well, my sweetheart, that's all right. You know I'm happy to be with you *unemotionally* if we can so describe what I'm trying to say. It's best for us both. Now tell me about the book.'

Curiously enough Joan made no inquiries about Lady Constance. The weeks went by, and occasionally Micky received a postcard from Constance Rowan-Colville from various Mediterranean resorts, and a letter from Paris. He had written and told her about his divorce and of the reaction at home. 'They're all living centuries behind the times, dear boy,' she wrote, 'don't take any notice. The Irish, like the Spaniards, are notoriously priest-ridden. The Italians are much more sophisticated. I don't think I'll come to Louisburgh, I might compromise you,' (which amused him slightly). 'Belgrave Square will always find me. I don't know when I shall be there but letters are forwarded. One day you and I must go to Greece in a yacht. Am going in the autumn with an ex-lover and his tiresomely pleasant wife. Why not join the party? Think what pictures you could paint!'

Somehow where Lady Constance was concerned it was a case of out of sight, out of mind, with Micky. Unconsciously he was ashamed of the physical attraction she had had for him on the night of the ball, and if he thought about her at all he would guy her and laugh about her, and even talk about her to Killary, reminding her of the first time they had seen her in the hotel at Cashel. He felt a cad at the same time, when he recollected that the success he had had of late was solely due to Constance.

When the decree was made absolute Micky once more tried to persuade Joan to change her mind and marry him. She started to cry.

'Darling, darling, why must you torture me as you do? I've told you and I tell you now for the *last time* that as long as Paddy is alive I can never be your wife.'

He was silent.

'If you want me to—to sleep with you,' she hesitated, thinking how bare and brazen the words sounded, 'I will. It won't give me happiness I may as well tell you, because for me it will be a sin, and I can't bear for sin to wed us. So you must say.'

'Thank you,' he said quietly. 'I wouldn't dream of having you under those terms.'

She blanched at the words he used.

'O God!' he stormed. 'Whatever I say or do is wrong. However, I'll not ask for your love again until Paddy gets herself run over by a tram or something. And then it'll probably be too late.'

Her eyes filled with tears. 'You know you have my love always. I'm sorry you don't understand that.'

Later he said, 'We've reached an impasse. There doesn't seem much point in going on.'

'Your love for me can be very little if you really mean that. If I can see you, caring as I do, I should have thought—'

'I told you before, my dear, you don't know enough about men. There comes a moment when one faces the fact that it must be all or nothing.'

'D'you really mean that? Because if you do I must chuck my job and go away. I couldn't stand living near you and not seeing you.' She had grown very pale.

'Why must we hurt those we love? God! Why, why, why?' he cried, and kissed her eyes, her throat, her mouth. They clung together for a little and then he said:

'There's no future. No end, no beginning.'

II

In spite of letters from Lady Constance which came spasmodically throughout the months that followed suggesting visits and trips, she found no forthcoming response from Micky

Renvyle. He made excuses every time. 'I'm happy painting, and though it may be inexplicable to you, I enjoy the company of my little girl in her summer holidays. Not for me, I think, the roses and raptures you say you can provide.' He never alluded to his freedom, or to Joan, nor was Constance's name ever mentioned to Joan.

It was towards the end of the holidays during a day's trip to Clare Island that Renvyle, Killary and Joan were caught in one of the worst storms that Micky could remember. They had anchored in the harbour and had found a path which led up Knocknaveen which Joan said would be fun to explore. They had been gone about an hour when Killary pointed out the advancing black clouds.

'I don't think it's going to bother us,' Renvyle said, and because he was as a rule an infallible judge of weather they continued to walk. The wind changed, and before very long torrential rain descended. None of them had waterproof clothing and before they reached *Deirdre* all were soaked, and Killary's teeth were chattering.

'Surely we can go in somewhere and ask for a rub down for the child, if not for us?' Joan asked.

'Better get back as quickly as we can. The sea's getting up. She'll be all right when we get aboard. Ducky, you must take all your things off and wrap up in my long sweater. Joan, you'd better boil up kettles in the galley for both of you, and strip.'

'And what about you?'

'I'll have to chance it.'

'We'll all catch our deaths,' Killary said through chattering teeth. Joan did her best to warm the child with a hot drink, and dried her as far as she was able.

'I do look funny,' Killary said as she tumbled about in an Aran jersey belonging to her father.

When they reached Ardbreen some hours later Joan had a bath in the cottage and borrowed some old clothes of Paddy's and said she thought she had better get back. The storm had abated and a lovely evening was heralded. Mountains and islands stood out like jewels, beneath the rainbow which was always Ardbreen's apology after a storm.

'Are you feeling all right?' Micky asked Killary, whose earlier pallor had changed to a burning red little face. She nodded, and said she was sleepy.

'Get her to bed quickly,' Joan advised.

The following day the child seemed unwell, and Micky told her to stay in bed, and rang up Miss O'Malley for advice.

'I don't like the looks of her,' the older woman said later, 'I'm sure she has a temperature. I think we should send for the doctor.'

On his second visit, the following day, the doctor told Micky that the child had pneumonia, and that it would need very careful nursing.

'I'll never forgive myself,' Renvyle stormed as he paced the room. 'Killary herself warned us about the bad weather coming up, and pig-headed fool that I was, I took no notice.'

Doctor Malone said he would send in a nurse, and as he was leaving he said to Micky:

'Miss Fitzgerald—Joan—was in the same expedition with you, wasn't she?'

Startled at first, Micky said, 'Yes. I've been meaning to ring her. How did you know?'

'For the same reason that you telephoned me. The poor young woman is in bed with a shocking cold. I can't think what you were all about not to take warm things with you, you know how treacherous the weather is.'

'It looked to be such a wonderful day. But you're right and I ought to be shot,' Micky replied.

Killary was very ill, and her convalescence was slow. She seemed listless for a long time, and developed a lingering cough which worried her father.

'I'm not happy about her,' Miss O'Malley told Micky one day. 'Has Dr Malone been lately?'

'He saw her a week ago.'

'If I were you I'd get him to look in again. You mustn't forget that she had that awful meningitis which must have left her with less stamina than other children have. And pneumonia can lead to,' she hesitated, 'well, to complications.'

When Dr Malone came he admitted to Renvyle that Killary had 'gone back' and said that he would like the child to be X-rayed.

'She may have a patch on one lung,' he told Micky, who was then beside himself with anxiety.

'It's no use blaming yourself now,' the doctor said. 'The trouble's done. But let's hope I'm proved wrong.'

Even the prospect of a trip into Galway did not excite Killary, who seemed to tire at any exertion, as Micky told Joan.

The result of the X-ray not only confirmed the doctor's fears but presented a problem to Micky Renvyle that at first confounded him.

'You must get the little girl away from Ireland,' he was told. 'She must go to a dry climate for at least a year.'

'But—where?' he asked, his mind ceasing to function.

'She should go to Switzerland,' he was told.

'Switzerland? For a year? I couldn't let her go without me, and I could never afford it.'

'You could raise the money somehow, couldn't you?' Dr Malone asked.

'I—I—I must try to, I suppose,' he stammered. 'How soon should she go? How urgent is it?'

'She should go as soon as you can manage,' Dr Malone said. 'And I hope and think we can save her.'

'*Save her?* D'you mean she's going to die? My Killary?'

'No, I didn't say that. But if you don't take steps she'll definitely be a bad tubercular case.'

'I see. Very well. I'll do what I can. Raise the necessary from somewhere.'

Micky spent the rest of the day in a dazed stupor. He felt he could not ask for adequate help from his publishers as he had nothing new to offer Edwards. He supposed he would have to obtain a loan from the bank, but were his securities worth anything? His pictures sold from time to time quite well, but life in a sanatorium and Swiss doctors for a year . . . He was sitting at his desk, pen in hand, wondering how to word a letter to his bank manager when the telephone rang. What was he going to say to Joan? But it was not Joan.

'Mike?'

'Good lord! Constance?'

'Hullo, my dear! Yes, it's me, I'm up at Louisburgh. When will you come over?'

'Constance, I'd love to see you, but at the moment I can't think straight. Killary has T.B. The doctor told me today, and moreover says it's essential she goes to Switzerland for at least a year. It's a nightmare. I can't think.'

'I shall drive over tomorrow, my dear. And Mike? You're not to worry. Everything will be all right. I shall arrive at lunchtime and I'd like two hard-boiled eggs.'

He put down the receiver. Constance. He felt as if an enormous weight had been lifted from his mind. He knew she would suggest something that no one else had thought about. Obstacles were somehow flattened and rolled away when Constance Rowan-Colville took a hand. At the worst he wouldn't mind asking her to lend him the money, she was rich and generous and although he had never borrowed a penny in his life from anyone, he knew he would rather take from Constance than from anyone else, he would feel less of a borrower.

'Now, what's it all about?' were her first words when she stepped out of the car the next day. As she drank the Guinness which she surprisingly asked for, Micky told her the whole story.

'I know a wonderful place,' she said at once. 'It's above Davos and run by an old friend of mine, Carl Schmeddheim. We'll send her there, and there's an enchanting small hotel near by where you can go and stay when you want to visit her. Schmeddheim won't want you hanging round all the time, you know.'

'Is it terribly expensive?' he had to ask.

'Carl is under an obligation to me. But if you're hard up, Mike, I'll stand the racket and you can repay me when you can.'

'Constance, my dear, I couldn't—' he began.

'Oh, fiddlesticks! What's the point of having wealth if one can't help one's friends? Now, Mike, we must be organized. You must get your doctor to give me the full details of—what's your child's extraordinary name again?'

'Killary.'

'Killary's illness. He must give it to me in typescript and I'll send it off immediately to Schmeddheim. Poor child. And you, my dear, what of your own life?'

Micky showed her some of his recent work. Water-colours in various districts of Connemara, and charcoal sketches, mostly heads of peasants.

'Brilliant, darling, brilliant. You must draw me.'

He laughed.

'I'm serious,' she said.

When Killary came downstairs for her lunch Constance was shocked by the child's appearance. For once, however, she kept her feelings to herself and was careful to hide her feelings from Renvyle.

'I've been ill, Lady Constance,' Killary told her with an air of importance, 'so I have to rest an awful lot.'

'It's made you grow. You're bigger than when I last saw you.'

'I know. I've growed out of lots of my clothes. They've had to be let down. And in fact I've had to have some new ones. These trousers, f'rinstance.' She paraded slowly, very pleased to show off the new corduroys.

'Most becoming,' said Lady Constance. Presently she said, 'Would you like to go and stay in a lovely place with lots of snow?'

'Like Switzerland?' Killary asked eagerly.

'In Switzerland, in fact.'

'Oh, *yes*. It was on the calendar last Christmas. I'd love to go there. But I don't expect we ever will. I'd like to go to Robinson Crusoe's island too. And the Never Never Land where Peter Pan was.'

'I don't think I can manage invitations for the last two, but I believe I could arrange a long holiday in Switzerland for you.'

'And Daddy?'

'And Daddy. Possibly not all the time for him. You see,' she continued cleverly, seeing the child's face drop, 'he might want to go to other places to write and paint, places that would be of no interest to you. And you would stay in the lovely village and get strong again and soon be able to toboggan and ski and do all sorts of amusin' things.'

Killary very soon became absorbed with the plan and when she went to bed that evening she said for the hundredth time:

'We can go, can't we?'

The following day was a Sunday, and Joan was due to come for the day. Hardly had she stepped into the house when Killary ran to her with the news.

'We're going to Switzerland, Daddy and me. Would you like to come too?'

'I would. When shall we go?' replied Joan, imagining the child was inventing the story.

Micky came out of the studio.

'Is she telling you about Switzerland?'

'Yes.' Then, seeing the serious look on his face, she said, 'Are you really going? I thought she was making it up.'

He beckoned her into the studio. 'She's got T.B.,' he said flatly, 'and Malone and the Galway man say her only chance is a year in Switzerland.'

'Darling,' Joan whispered, 'how horrifying! When did you know?'

'Two days ago. I was off my head with worry.'

'Why didn't you let me know?'

'I knew I'd be seeing you today.'

'How on earth are you going to afford it?' she asked in concern.

Helping her to a drink and pouring one out himself, he said: 'A miracle occurred. I was literally at my wits' end, not knowing who on earth to turn to or ask advice of, and Constance suddenly rang up. Out of the blue. From Louisburgh. Of course I told her, and she came over yesterday. She's arranging everything. What a marvel that woman is!'

'She is indeed,' Joan said slowly. 'And isn't it extraordinary how she crops up when you're on your beam-ends. Lucky Constance,' she sighed.

'Lucky?'

'To be able to help you when you need help. What I'd give to be able to!'

'Darling.' He kissed her. 'Apparently she has some old boy friend who runs a sanatorium and she says there's a pub handy for me to stay in.'

'Will you have to go?' she said, trying to keep the anguish from her voice.

'Certainly I shall take her and stay a while.'

'Yes. I see. Of course.' The prospect was bleak. 'But apart from her knowing about the place, will it be very expensive? She's so rich I should be afraid of going to somewhere she suggested.'

'She angelically said I wasn't to worry. That she'd cope with the finance and I can repay her when I'm able to. She wouldn't listen to my pleadings that I couldn't do such a thing.'

Joan slid her arm through his, and leant her head against his shoulder. 'Oh my darling, how wonderful. For you. And for Killary. And for Lady Constance. Oh, how I envy her.'

Killary was in great spirits throughout the meal that followed, and both Micky and Joan admitted that they had not seen her so happy and full of life since her illness. Much later in the afternoon while they were playing cards with the child, they heard a car draw up and the bell at the door rang.

'I dare say it's Malone,' Micky said, getting up, 'tho' he doesn't as a rule come in on a Sunday afternoon and he usually comes right in without ringing.'

He went to the front door and opened it to admit Constance.

'I went to see your Doctor Malone yesterday,' she announced in booming tones. 'Everything is settled. I rang Schmeddheim—a marvellous line, he might have been in the next village—and explained in detail the position and the case. Malone is also writing to confirm the diagnosis, and now you have but to put

240

your house in order and get plane reservations. He'll expect you at the end of the week.'

She stalked into the room, looking, as Joan was forced to acknowledge, extremely handsome.

'Hullo, Killary.' She shook the child's hand. 'All is now set for your trip to Switzerland.'

'Really and truly?' The child's eyes glistened with excitement.

'Honour bright, cross my something-or-other, I believe boy scouts say,' Lady Constance replied. Then she saw Joan. 'Oh, you're here!'

Her voice held patronage, contempt, amusement.

'Can she come too?' Killary asked.

'I hardly imagine so,' Lady Constance answered.

'I've got to work in the library, darling, you know that,' Joan said quietly.

Conversation became desultory, stilted and decidedly difficult. The two women reminded Renvyle of a couple of dogs eyeing each other before a fight and coward-like he left the room on the pretext of finding refreshment for Constance. When he left the room silence fell.

'How good of you to take all this trouble for Killary,' Joan said finally.

'Not at all, the child looked ghastly when I saw her two days ago and Mike, poor boy, was beside himself with worry. What's the use of money if you only hoard it or spend it on yourself? She's rather a nice child.'

'She's a darling,' Joan quietly replied.

'And of course as her father is something rather special for me,' here Constance peered at Joan through the mirror on the wall at which she was powdering her nose, 'I couldn't do anything else.'

'I see.'

'I wonder if you do?' She wheeled round. At that moment Micky came back into the room carrying a tray. 'I was just saying to Miss—Miss—I am so sorry, but I've forgotten your name?'

'Fitzgerald,' Joan snapped.

'Of course! I was saying to her I wondered if she realized how special you are to Ardbreen, Connemara, in fact one might say Ireland?' She popped a lipstick into her pocket.

'You flatter me,' he deprecated. 'I'm of no value at all. To anyone.' He did not see Joan's eyes as he made the remark.

'Silly creature,' Lady Constance said and put her arm through his. Joan felt like screaming as she watched the pair standing in front of the fire, Constance assuming an air of proprietorship. 'You ego needs bolstering up, my dear. You're far too inclined to belittle yourself. Don't you agree?' She smiled patronizingly at Joan, as if to enlist her support. 'And I shall tell you what I mean to do. When Killary is happily established I shall take a little villa somewhere,—Ascona, Lugano—somewhere from where it's possible to get to the child easily. And you shall stay with me and paint. And write if it amuses you— but I know painting is your love and you'll go mad with joy at the beauty of Switzerland as spring gradually dawns. Won't that be fun, Killary?'

'I'd like to kill her on the spot,' Joan's mind was running.

'Oh yes,' said Killary excitedly.

When Lady Constance left and Micky returned from seeing her into her car, he found Joan alone. She was standing with her back to the room looking into the dying embers of the fire which nobody had made up. He put his arm round her shoulder but there was no ensuing response. He said nothing and presently she looked at him with no expression on her face and said:

'I might as well pack up, mightn't I?'

'What d'you mean?'

'Constance, your wonderful Lady Constance, Lady Bountiful, will beat me in the end, so why not let's get it over now.'

Pouring himself out a neat whisky, he said slowly, 'Constance is probably the means of saving my child's life. You were the means once. Can't you—you of all people—realize my gratitude?'

'Oh yes, of course.' She sounded bitter and weary. 'I don't

grudge her the means of saving Killary. But don't you realize she means to have *you*?'

'And don't *you* realize *I* love *you*?'

'I can't give you what she can. Money, position,' she did not notice the look of distaste that spread across his face, 'the means to establish yourself in the forefront of the field of art. And I won't give you what she'd give her soul to give you, and probably ultimately will.'

After a few minutes he said, 'You put an extraordinarily high value on physical love, darling, which indeed I've wanted desperately from you. But, in the eyes of our Maker, do you think the sin of giving yourself to me in love is so much worse than your hideous jealousy of a woman old enough to be my mother? Your tongue has lashed out at me like a serpent's. I feel powerless to argue with you.'

Presently she said, 'Isn't it ghastly how two people who love each other can tear each other to pieces, slaying with words of cruelty? Why, why, why? I love you, and you love me, and yet the time has come when we both say such terrible things to each other. I can't bear much more of it,' she broke down. 'I suppose it's our punishment. For falling in love in the first place.'

She fumbled for a handkerchief, and Micky gave her his.

'I'm sorry, my darling,' she said when her sobs had subsided. 'I said hateful things and didn't mean them. The only thing that matters really is for Killary to be cured.'

He held her close and in silence for a long time.

'D'you know what I think I shall do when you both go away?' she said after a while. 'I shall go into Retreat. I haven't been for years and I believe it would help. The last time we motored along the road to Leenane I noticed that convent again with its beautiful name. The Convent of Mercy. I wonder if one could go there.'

CHAPTER EIGHT

It was through Father Delaney that Joan was able to make arrangements to go to the convent at Leenane for her Retreat.

'It's strange that for all the time I've lived up here I've never been inside the place,' she told him. 'Have you ever known anywhere that has such tranquillity surrounding it?'

He smiled. 'It looks quiet enough, but don't forget that it's also a school. In term time I'll wager the children's voices make up for the sisters' quiet.'

'I've not been to Retreat since I was at the convent. At school, I mean.'

'You'll love Reverend Mother, she's a great soul. And both she and Father Devlin will help you, I'm sure.'

Joan looked alarmed. 'They don't know about me? I mean you haven't told them . . .'

'Of course not, child. But you'll find peace there, I know, and you'll be able to give back to God what you've neglected to give of late. I know, my daughter,' he continued kindly, seeing a sudden look of sorrow in her face, 'I know it's not easy always. Worldly affections play too great a part in our lives.'

As Joan made her way to Leenane on the appointed day she was filled with a joy that at first seemed foreign to her. She drove the car very slowly as she approached Killary Harbour, her eyes searching the well-loved beauties of the Maamturks and Garraun on either side of the road. There had been a recent fall of snow, but a thaw had set in and she thought she had never seen the mountains look more beautiful, nor the blue of Killary Harbour so startling in its colour. She passed the hotel, and came to the village where she put the car into a garage. Then with only a small suitcase she climbed the road to the convent. Before entering the gates which hid the building from prying eyes she turned and looked the length of the eight-mile harbour. Its solitude and grandeur with the mountains descending to its very shores made her catch her breath in wonder. She knew that she would find peace here if not happiness.

Joan was shown to a small bare room with just the essential furnishings by a smiling young-looking nun who told her that Reverend Mother would see her as soon as she had unpacked her few belongings. When Joan presently came face to face with Mother Mary Teresa she thought she had never seen a face of such serene beauty. Joan was told that there were only three other people making a Retreat but that some people found it easier when there were so few.

'You will come to our Holy Masses, but of course you will sit in the part of the chapel that is used by our congregation. The sisters will be behind the grille in their own quarters. Father Devlin will be taking the Retreat, he's a dear man, and if you wish to make your Confession to him he will be ready and pleased to receive you.'

In the days that followed, Joan subconsciously admitted to herself that a sense of sublime peace had entered her soul. The visitors were allowed to walk outside the convent, and she occasionally wandered about the hills and along the road, but she spent many hours alone in the little white chapel, where with all its simplicity the peace of God was to be found in abundance. Her only regret was that visitors and nuns did not mingle, and only Reverend Mother and Mother Mary Angelica, who was in charge of the visitors, were available to talk to. She learnt about the daily life that went on at the convent from Mother Mary Angelica who told her that it was quite a thriving school, that the children from nearby villages attended as well as boarders from afar, and that they were taught by the sisters who, however, did not mingle out of school hours with the laity. She also learnt that part of the convent had a wing in which the enclosed nuns remained and who were not even seen by the children.

'It must be a lovely life in some ways,' Joan said, 'but is it lonely? I mean, do you ever feel utterly cut off?'

The nun looked surprised. 'Lonely? How could we? Surrounded by our Lord's love and with the work He has chosen for us to do? I myself am one of the teaching sisters and mix with the children, and I can assure you there is very little time to be lonely.' She smiled at Joan. 'And those of us who are enclosed would not be otherwise.'

Mother Mary Teresa, 'Reverend Mother', was a foreigner but spoke perfect English; Joan could not discover her exact nationality. It was not easy to assess the age of nuns, Joan knew well, but she judged Mother Mary Teresa to be between sixty and sixty-five. Joan had several conversations with her in her private sanctum which smelt of lilies and yet there were none to be seen.

'And are you feeling better, my child?' she asked Joan the evening before she was due to leave. Joan hesitated, feeling curiously embarrassed. 'I know you were unhappy when you came to us. I've been praying that you would find peace with us and regain what you lost.'

'In some ways I've never been happier than I've been here,' she answered slowly. 'I work in a library, it's my job. I must return to it. But so much of me would like to remain.'

Mother Mary Teresa smiled.

'That could be an easy way out, couldn't it? We're all here for a purpose, difficult as it is for some of us to realize. The very peace of this place, and the general atmosphere of a Retreat well made, sometimes give false values to everyday life. I mean it is easy to go from here and long to return and thus bid farewell to worldly troubles and worries, whether they be personal or world-wide. But the enclosed life, the life of the *religieuse*, was not meant as a safety curtain, as a way of throwing off responsibilities. It is a hard life, at least for some people.'

'Do you think, would you consider it to be a cowardly action, to become a nun if one found too great unhappiness in the world?' Joan asked.

'That would depend on what the worldly misery was caused by,' Mother Mary Teresa answered. 'I would never persuade anyone to take the veil for what might be only temporary sadness. And I know, my dear, that worldly loss of home or loved one can be almost too great to bear at times. Women have become nuns, it's true, who have lost what they considered to be their All in the world. But I say to people, to sad lonely people specially, is it such a great love that you are offering to Our Lord Jesus that you only do so because you have lost such-and-such and so-and-so? A second-best love in fact?'

Joan nodded. 'I see what you mean.'

'In the world today there is a great deal of talk about glamour. Oh! You need not look so surprised,' she smiled at the look on Joan's face, 'I know what goes on in the world today, although I live behind a convent's wall in Leenane. There are people, young girls very often, who at some moment appear to find glamour or think they do in being a nun. *I* think it is because they go to cinemas and see beautiful actresses dressed in becoming habits. I do not believe that all the women who say— sometimes casually—that they would like to be nuns realize what they're saying. If an unhappy woman wishes to do so— let us say owing to a miserable love affair—is it likely she will welcome Our Lord as she should as her bridegroom, in the place of some fellow who has deserted her or whom she has thrown over in a fit of temper?'

'Yet,' Joan said slowly, 'surely in some such cases it would work?'

'Work? You make it sound very down to earth.'

Joan blushed, she knew she was expressing herself badly. 'Mother,' she said, 'I'm so unhappy. It's been wonderful here, I've been able to forget. And—as Father Delaney at home said —to give back to God what I've not always given of late.'

'Tell me about it, dear child, if it will help you.'

'I love a man who's divorced, and he keeps begging me to marry him. I can't and I won't. And I've been able to bear it— badly, it's true—but I have. Till now, and someone else has appeared and I think she'll—she'll do her best to trap him.'

'My dear, it's your own immortal soul that you must first think of, not his.'

'But you see,' Joan cried, 'he's a Catholic too. I can't bear it if he does something that'll imperil his soul.'

'Poor child, I can understand your wretchedness. I will pray for him. And for you. But surely you have had advice from good priests in your Confessions?'

'Oh yes, of course. But I worry for him, and it's not for me to—well—bargain for his soul, can I put it? in my own Confessions. And while I've been here I've been at peace. Happy. Extraordinarily so. I dread going back to work. To getting letters which will make me unhappy, and jealous. To the life in which so much will remind me of him.'

'Can you not break with this man altogether?'

'We come from the same place. More or less. He's abroad now and will be for a year, with his little girl who has been very ill.'

'Then surely that is the will of God? This necessary parting is part of His plan for you. I do not think you should contemplate the life of a religious, my child, under the circumstances.' She looked at Joan and smiled. 'Don't think I'm being hard, or not understanding your unhappiness. It may be that in time you will be ready to give Our Lord the love He demands of us but I do not think that the time has yet come. You would not wish to commit the sacrilege, for sacrilege it would be, of taking His Love on what is commonly called the rebound? And there's another thing, another aspect. Is it Leenane itself that possibly gives you such peace? It might well be. If you became a nun you could be sent anywhere. You couldn't stipulate for Leenane,' she laughed a little, and Joan smiled.

'I expect I'm one of many dreary lovelorn females that you have to contend with, Mother, I don't know how you have the patience.'

'It's one of the virtues we try to learn,' the other said, laughing again.

'Can I come again? And can I come and see you sometimes?'

Mother Mary Teresa nodded. 'You can. We have one or two rooms that we keep for visitors, should they wish to come when the term is in progress. You would find it very different then. The children lend an air of gaiety to the place. We love them. You mustn't go away with a false idea of us, you know. Most of us are very ordinary, very human. All too human.' She patted Joan's shoulder.

'I was brought up in a convent, I know,' Joan replied. 'All the same I have found something here which I did not realize existed, which I've found nowhere else.'

'Perhaps you did not search for it before?'

'It could be that, Mother.' She knelt as she said good-bye, and looked up at Mother Mary Teresa. 'Please give me your blessing,' she begged.

As Joan drove away from Leenane the following day she knew that she would return to the Convent of Mercy.

CHAPTER NINE

AND so the days at Ballymannin ran into weeks, and the weeks ran into months. At first Joan frequently received letters from Micky and was happy to learn of the progress Killary was making and to know also that he was happy. He wrote eulogistically of the beauty of the country, which he thought was far grander than he had expected, and said that he was painting and had managed to find a chalet with a room which it was possible to turn temporarily into a studio. He was able to see Killary, and the doctor had assured him that they had caught the disease in time and that after a year in Switzerland the child should be able to return to Ireland in a fit state of health.

Joan wrote of the happenings in Ardbreen and Ballymannin, and of the occasional visits she continued to make to the Convent of Mercy.

'But I feel my letters are hopelessly dull, my darling, for who do I see of interest to you really?' ran one of her letters. 'Every walk, every drive I take seems to breathe you and I miss you daily more and more. I've joined the local branch of Red Cross in the hope that I might be of some use but how or where I can't imagine!'

In another letter she wrote sadly, 'Our dear Father Delaney has left us. He was suddenly taken with a thrombosis and is in hospital at Galway till he's fit enough to be moved somewhere permanent, I believe. They say he must—can—never work again. In the meantime we have a horrible little priest (God forgive me!) who might have stepped straight from the days of the Inquisition. He slays us all from the pulpit, and what he'll be like in the confessional I dread to think! Am almost tempted to confess murder just to see, but I rather believe he's hottest on minor sins. One of his sermons was against greed and he fixed his eyes on a small boy who eventually ran screaming from church!'

A postcard frcm Venice in May disturbed her slightly, coming as it did after several weeks during which she had received no letters from Micky. Moreover he put no address, and merely stated that Venice was unbelievable. A few weeks later a letter came from a villa on Lake Como where he admitted he was staying with Lady Constance.

'Darling,' he wrote, 'this is utterly perfect. Constance has rented for the summer this house above the lake and I can stay as long as I care to. I paint all day, and listen to nightingales. Fireflies flitter like fairies at night, and I wish you were here to watch them with me. Constance now has a superb Bentley which I can drive and we go up to Davos every ten days or so to see Killary who has improved miraculously and is very happy. She has learnt to speak German quite well, clever brat! I couldn't cope at all with it but am trying to learn Italian as I should like to live out here part of the year. It's the most romantic country imaginable, and I can't help feeling your scruples would crumble and totter if you were here. Darling one, won't you come? I'm serious. I love you as much as ever but neither of us is getting younger.'

This letter distressed her and for hours she could not keep her mind on the work she was doing. She had visions of Renvyle and Lady Constance in gondolas, on cypress-clad mountains, in lake-side restaurants. She could imagine the two of them arriving for Killary like a couple of parents at half-term, and she could see Killary growing fond of Constance Rowan-Colville as she had been fond of her; getting used to her, expecting her, claiming her as part of a trio as once she herself had been. Killary's possible acceptance of a situation that Joan could only guess had arisen, hurt as much as anything. Knowing the naïve remarks the child had often made in the past she agonized at the thought of Constance's probable pleasure if Killary were to repeat some of her past ideas and wishes.

That summer Joan took her holiday in July and as usual went

to her grandmother's. At first all went well and there were the usual tennis parties, dances and regattas, but the old lady had been unwell for some time and tried to persuade Joan to give up her job in Ballymannin and come south to live with her. She wrote to Micky asking him what she should do and it was not until the day she was due to return to Galway that his reply came.

'I think on the whole you'd be wise to do what your grandmother suggests, my dear,' he wrote. (*My dear* . . . why not *darling* her mind ran) 'Your job at Ballymannin holds no future for you, and since you refuse to marry me perhaps it would be as well if we were farther apart. My plans for returning to Ireland are dreadfully vague. I've been having great good luck with my pictures, and I feel I should strike while the iron's hot or whatever the expression is. Constance with her usual influence arranged for a show at the Villa d'Este of what I'd been doing out here, and has introduced me to a man in Milan who may be very useful. I may be rich yet! Let me know what you decide, for you know I shall always have your well-being close to my heart. As ever, Mike.'

Mike. *Mike.* Constance's name for him. Joan read the letter through three times and then went to the bathroom where she was sick.

'You're not looking well, my love,' old Mrs Fitzgerald said to her when Joan went to say good-bye to her grandmother.

'It's all right, Granny, I've a horrible migraine. But I've thought everything over. I shall give in my notice when I get back and then I shall come and live with you again.' She bent and kissed the old lady's forehead.

'Darling, how lovely that will be. But what will Jill say?'

'She'll be delighted. I don't think she ever liked Connemara as much as Cork. She always says it's wild and unfriendly.'

'But you, my dear? You love it so?'

Joan did her best to keep her voice steady, as she replied, 'It's time I left. There's nothing for me up there any longer.' She looked away and her grandmother wisely refrained from questioning her.

Before she left Ballymannin, Joan went to bid farewell to Mother Mary Teresa at the Convent of Mercy.

'Reverend Mother is expecting you,' a nun whose face was new to her said as she opened the door.

After kissing Joan on the forehead, Mother Mary Teresa said:

'I'm glad, my dear, you're going away. In spirit you will remain with our little community, I know, but I'm delighted that you're going to look after your grandmother. It's a worthwhile thing to do in any case, and I believe you'll be happier. And, you know, in spite of what a lot of people erroneously believe, God wants us to be happy.'

'How lovely her smile is,' Joan thought, and said, 'I don't think this will be good-bye to the convent. To Leenane. I feel I shall return. Some very compelling chains pull me towards it.'

'Not chains, I hope,' Reverend Mother replied.

'No, perhaps not chains. Invisible hands, invisible threads.'

'You know there will always be room for you, Joan.'

'And I loved it when the children were here, that last time I stayed, you know,' Joan said, unaware of the beseeching sound in her voice which the nun recognized.

'You're fond of children, aren't you?'

'I think I must be. I was devoted to one.' She stopped for a moment and her voice shook slightly as she went on, 'So I dare say I'd be fond of any child once I knew it. I never had much to do with children till I knew Killary.'

'Killary?' asked Mother Mary Teresa in surprise. 'What a strange name.'

'Her parents called her Killary after this place.' Then after a pause she said, 'It's her father . . .'

'I guessed so, my dear. Try and forget the past.'

'I must. By his letters I know it's over. But I shall always love him, Mother.'

'Love never harmed anyone yet. But alas, so many people abuse the word. And now, my dear, I know you want to go into the chapel and I have things I must do. But come in again before you go, to say good-bye to me. A temporary good-bye we'll call it.'

Joan could not bring herself to visit Ardbreen and she packed the few things she had collected, along with her clothes and personal belongings, with a heart of lead. Jill, who had never really been in her sister's confidence, and who had watched in silence the friendship with Renvyle turn to what she assumed to be a hopeless love affair, was thankful that they were leaving Connemara.

The winter passed, and turned to spring, and after a Christmas card and some chocolates from Switzerland no further letters arrived from Micky Renvyle. In May Joan felt the need of going into Retreat again and suggested to Jill that she should go with her.

'As Aunt Madge is coming to be with Granny we could leave her safely and I long for the peace of Leenane,' she said.

'Haven't you found it—peace—here?' her sister asked.

'Of course. But I want a different peace. The spiritual peace I find at the Convent of Mercy.'

They drove north and Jill was delighted to realize that Joan appeared to have thrown off her past moods of depression and seemed eager to recognize well-loved landmarks as they approached Connemara. She was surprised when shortly before Kylemore Joan drove straight on.

'Aren't you going to take the Leenane road?' she asked. 'Or have you forgotten the way?'

'I've forgotten nothing. I just wanted to come this way.'

Jill said nothing and presently realized that her sister was driving straight through to Ardbreen. This was either madness or bravado, she felt, but again said nothing. The car stopped at the top of the hill.

'Will you look at it?' Joan whispered. 'There's no beauty to equal it.' And Jill saw the islands and the sea and the mountains, and agreed.

Slowly the car was driven downhill through the village and stopped outside Renvyle's cottage. In the window was a board, on which were the words 'To Let'.

On their way down to the South after a week spent in spiritual quiet and happiness, Joan said, 'I feel I ought to go and say hello to my late boss.' She drove the car to Ballymannin and stopped at the library, and when later she came out of the building she walked right into Cathleen O'Malley.

'Joan! My dear.'

Joan had purposely refrained from visiting Aunt Cathleen, she had been afraid of the wound that must surely reopen.

'Come next door and have some coffee and tell me all your news,' Miss O'Malley begged, but Joan made excuses on the plea of the long journey ahead. Then Miss O'Malley said, hesitatingly: 'When did you last hear from either Killary or—Micky?'

'Not since Christmas,' Joan replied.

'Then you don't know?'

'Know what?'

'My dear, I'm afraid this will come as a great grief to you.'

'Killary? She's not—'

No, no, no. She's recovered. She's home with me. What a pity you didn't come to see me. It's Micky.'

'What's happened to him?'

'He's married that Constance Rowan-Colville.'

'Oh!'

Joan swayed for a second. All colour had left her face and for a moment Cathleen O'Malley wondered if the girl was going to faint.

'When did it happen?' she asked after a long pause. 'I mean when did he marry her?'

'In March, I think. Believe it or not, by the British Consul somewhere or other. Killary had a letter from her father last week from New York.'

'And Killary. What does she feel about it?'

In spite of her agony of heart Joan felt great concern for the child she loved.

'Children are very odd,' Miss O'Malley answered. 'She just seemed to take it in her stride. I imagine she saw a great deal of the woman abroad and I suppose got thoroughly used to her.

But I couldn't help being amused when she suddenly said that perhaps after all she'd now have a brother or sister!'

'Poor Killary! She's doomed to disappointment on that score.'

'So I should hope. The woman's sixty if she's a day. Micky must have been mad. But the best and nicest of men are putty in a clever woman's clutches, though it beats me what she wanted to marry Micky Renvyle for.'

Every word the woman uttered was a nail piercing Joan's heart. Constance Renvyle. Joan Renvyle . . . Mr and Lady Constance Renvyle.

Suddenly she could bear it no longer. Hastily bidding Miss O'Malley good-bye, she fled to the car.

'What a time you've been,' Jill said. 'Heavens! What's the matter? You look as if you'd seen a ghost or something.'

'I've just heard Micky has married again, if you must know. To Lady Constance. Lady Constance Rowan-Colville.'

Slowly she put the car into gear and drove away.

CHAPTER TEN

I

FOR weeks Joan lived in mental torment. There was no one with whom she could share her misery, even to Jill she could not speak openly. She longed for the help and friendship she had known from Father Delaney, but not only was the priest ill but she did not know where he now was. If only Micky had written to her, telling her of his marriage, she felt it would have helped, but the cruelty of his silence and the way in which she had heard the news crucified her spirit. She admitted she had no moral rights over him, but surely the love which they had known in the past entitled her to some decency from him? Then, apart from her own misery, there was the anguish she felt for the sin he had committed. She spent weeks torn between the anxiety she felt on behalf of Renvyle's soul and the quite hideous human jealousy that tortured her night after night when visions of Constance in Mick's arms prevented her from sleeping. She recollected her jealousy of his past life with Paddy, but this she knew was fifty times worse for it was something she could have prevented; at the peril of committing mortal sin; and there she was again, having come full circle. Confession did not help, as no priest could overlook the sin of jealousy.

After many months had passed she was surprised and distressed to receive a letter in Micky's handwriting. In it he wrote how worried he had been to have back—undelivered—a letter he had written to her about his marriage. He realized that by now she must surely have learnt of it through other channels and been justifiably hurt. He went on to assure her that his marriage to Constance had been prompted by extreme gratitude and pity (*pity?* Joan wondered indignantly) for a very lonely woman. She was not to believe that in his new life he expected to find the love and wonder which he would have known with her, but as she had decreed that that was not to be, he had realized he could make one person happy and therefore he had decided to marry Constance. He hoped that she would find happiness and peace with someone worthy of her one day, and she was to believe he would remember their love always and the greater part of him was still in her keeping.

Joan locked herself in her room and cried after she had read the letter, which she proceeded to read again throughout the day. She supposed it was something that he did not pretend to be in love with Constance. But no sooner had she set her mind at rest with this little relief than she at once realized that only a cad would have admitted love in the circumstances, and that perhaps he was merely doing his best to be as gentle as possible. She wondered how he could imagine she could be happy with anyone else as he had hopefully (she supposed) suggested.

A few days after Joan received the letter, old Mrs Fitzgerald fell ill, and for some weeks Joan had enough to do with helping two nurses, to think too much about her own wretchedness. The old lady sank eventually into a coma and died peacefully, leaving Joan and her sister with the problem of facing life afresh once again. When things had begun to settle and the solicitors had taken charge, Joan told her sister she wanted to go to Leenane.

'But if I do, what will you do?' she asked.

'Aunt Madge said I could go to her whenever I'd like to,' Jill replied. 'I should certainly go if you want to. You mean to the convent?'

Joan nodded. 'Reverend Mother told me I could always go. I wrote and told her about Granny, and had such a kind letter back.'

'You know,' Jill said presently, 'it wouldn't surprise me if you remained there.'

'How d'you mean?'

'Became one of them. Joined the Community.'

Joan looked at her sister in surprise. 'I only wish I could,' she said. 'But once when Reverend Mother and I were talking about it—hypothetically—she said one must have a vocation, that women with broken hearts couldn't imagine it was the answer to their worries,' she smiled sadly.

'Couldn't you be one of the teaching nuns? After all, you took your degree at Bristol, and you might be able to teach something.'

'I wonder if that would be possible? There again Reverend Mother said I could never be certain of getting to Leenane. One could be sent anywhere.'

'You did discuss it then?'

Joan realized she had given herself away. 'Well—yes. But not very seriously.'

II

Joan had not been many weeks at Leenane when she approached Mother Mary Teresa with the plea that she might be allowed to remain. She told the nun of her degree and qualifications and put it to her that she could help with the children. It so happened that one of the teaching sisters was away sick, and so Joan was allowed to take certain classes. She was astonished at the ease with which she found she was able to tackle her task, and was radiant with pleasure when Mother Mary Teresa sent for her after two weeks and told her how well she had acquitted herself. She went on to tell Joan that a visit from the Reverend Mother General of the Order was imminent, and that if Joan really had a serious desire to become a postulant she had better talk to the Reverend Mother.

'What do you suppose she'd think? What will she say? I mean I'm much older than most people.'

'People become *religieuses* at various stages, dear child,' was Mother Mary Teresa's reply. 'I shall give her some details of your background. She'll want to have a long talk to you. And you do know, don't you, that if you decide to join the Community you'll have to go to the Mother House for your novitiate and it may be a long time before you return to Leenane?'

'I've realized all that,' Joan replied. 'And I remember very well indeed the talk I had with you about people wanting to become nuns because they were unhappy, and how you said one must not offer God a second-best love.' She paused and then continued hesitatingly, 'I believe the reason I want to join the Community is twofold. You see—' she hesitated.

'Go on, dear child.'

'Although I admit I find unbelievable peace and quiet of mind here, I would like to atone for the sin I committed in loving Mick.' His name slipped from her unconsciously. 'For although we never did anything wrong—I never would, I refused, and that's why it finished'—she unconsciously excused herself from actual sin—'I always knew it was wrong to be in love with a married man. I think my great unhappiness is a punishment, and I would like to give the rest of my life to Our Lord. As a thank-offering for the happiness I did have and to atone for the wrong I did. Of course I won't pretend it would be any sort of punishment for me, for it's what I want to do and it would bring me great joy. And I think I could do quite a good job in teaching children. The little I've done for you here is not difficult and I suppose I could polish up and de-rust myself, so to speak, if the Order would consider me.'

She looked beseechingly at Mother Mary Teresa.

'I think you're sincere, and I will speak for you when Reverend Mother comes. And you will have plenty of time to think things over.'

Joan went to the little chapel and knelt before the statue of the Little Flower. 'Dear little saint,' she prayed, 'you who know so well the shortcomings of human souls, intercede for me in heaven that I may be allowed to come back here and help them with the children. I know I'm not fit to become a bride of Christ, but I long to belong to Him and never leave His side. Please help me.'

Later she walked along the road, and looked down Killary Harbour, at the mountains meeting the water's edge, and watched the sun set behind the island which always made the expanse of water appear like a lake. She thought of the picnics she and Mick and Killary had enjoyed here, the sails they had had in *Deirdre*, the walks and climbs she and Micky had done in the near-by hills. She remembered the very first time she had met Micky, not four miles up the road, when her car had broken down and together they had tramped to Leenane for help. As long ago as that she had fallen under the spell of the road to Leenane, and the magic wonder of Killary Harbour. And she remembered too how she had driven past the group of little white buildings on one side of the road, and had noticed the tiny cemetery on the other with its far-reaching outlook up the fjord, and how then she had seen the words carved on the entrance gates of the white building—'Convent of Mercy'. She turned when she reached the bend in the road and walked back, praying: 'Oh, live up to your name, Convent of Mercy, and grant that one day I shall be living permanently behind your walls.'

Part IV

CHAPTER ONE

MOTHER MARY TERESA had been dead two years when Joan Fitzgerald—now Mother Mary Imelda—at last returned to the Convent of Mercy. Although the years had seemed many, she had always felt that her future lay in that far corner of Connemara where her worldly heart was buried. She had enjoyed her novitiate which perhaps came more easily to her than to many a girl straight from home, and later in a convent of the Order in the South of England, where she was sent before she had taken her final vows, she already knew that a life of far greater fulfilment than she had ever known before or guessed existed was to be hers. It came almost as a surprise when she was told to return to Leenane, and her prayers of gratitude were fervent indeed. It was sad to return to the convent and find no Mother Mary Teresa, but she already knew that she had bidden farewell to human ties of affection, and took comfort in the realization that the dead nun was with God.

She had been at Leenane for nearly a year when Reverend Mother sent for the sisters and told them of the disaster at their other house in Co. Sligo, where fire had broken out and destroyed the building, and added that many of the girls were coming to the Convent of Mercy in Leenane. A great deal of work had to be done at once in order to get things ready, for the children were arriving the following day, thirty of them. Joan did not see the girls on arrival as she was in chapel, and at supper they all looked very much the same as each other in their brown uniforms and white collars. The following evening she was told to take the new girls in their sewing class, and was given the list with their names. As they trooped into the room, curtseying and saying, 'Good evening, Mother', she hastily scanned the list and hoped she would not take long in remembering which face went with which name. Suddenly, like a knife in her heart, her eyes fell on one name: Killary Renvyle. She clutched the desk and for a moment looked wildly about her as the girls pulled chairs about and got their sewing together, unaware of the consternation that had been caused. Presently she said:

'I will read each new girl's name out from this list which I have been given, and I would like the girl in question to reply "Present", and to stand up.'

Joan began to read their names. When she came to Killary Renvyle's, she looked up. The child had grown, and she realized she must be about fifteen. She wore her hair in two long plaits, and as she answered the roll-call Joan realized a look of slight perplexity came over the child's face. She hurried on to the next name. During the sewing lesson Joan read to the girls, and from time to time took a surreptitious look at Killary, who she noticed wore spectacles as she sewed and looked extraordinarily like her father.

When the lesson was over, and the girls were leaving the room, Joan hesitated for a moment and then said: 'I would like Killary Renvyle to remain behind.'

When the room had emptied and they were alone, she said, 'Killary. Don't you remember me?'

The girl looked at her in amazement.

'Are you—*Joan*?'

Joan nodded, and Killary flung herself into the nun's arms and burst into tears.

'Oh, darling.' Joan clung to her for a moment and then quickly pushed her away.

'I'm not Joan any longer, you know. You have to call me Mother—'

'I always wanted to—'

'And you know I mustn't call you darling or kiss you any longer. Oh, Killary, Killary . . .'

She sat down and they looked at each other in stupefaction.

'Why, why on earth have you become a nun?' Killary asked.

'I wanted to. It's a long story and this isn't the time or place to tell it. Killary, it's lovely to see you. You've grown so.'

The girl laughed. 'Well, heavens! So I should hope! It's *years* since you saw me. Oh, goodness, how I missed you. It's wonderful you're here. But I wish you hadn't become a nun. Did you really have to? We shan't be able to have much fun!'

Joan smiled. 'Not the fun we used to have. And please, *please* remember not to call me Joan!'

Killary giggled. 'That would be a brick! I should think they'd expel me. What's your name now?'

'Mary Imelda. Mother Mary Imelda.'

'Why?'

'It was given me.'

'Just fancy you and me being here. Leenane. I haven't been back for ages. Not since Daddy sold the cottage and Aunt Cathleen moved to Dublin.'

Joan swallowed. 'How is—Daddy?'

'He's all right.'

'And your—stepmother?' She had to know if he was happy.

Killary looked surprised. 'Lady Constance? She's dead, didn't you know? It was awful, she was killed in an airplane crash, and Daddy might have been too but his taxi was held up and he missed the plane. It was quite a long time ago, about two years ago. Mummie's dead too, but Daddy's never told me how.'

The room started to go round and Joan's head began to reel. Just then a bell went and she was able to say:

'Killary, you must go now. We'll talk another time. God bless you.'

Killary looked at her. 'Are you all right—Mother?'

Joan bowed her head in assent, but when the child had gone out of the room, her tears fell, and for the first time for many years sobs shook her body.

There now began for Joan the most difficult of all phases of her life. She had, so she sincerely thought, bidden farewell to past memories, earthly affections, human worry. The shock of finding Killary again had been great, but far greater was the realization that had she waited there was every possibility that she might have at last become Micky Renvyle's wife. Hour after hour she prayed that forgotten memories be taken from her, yet the torment continued and her sleep—so untroubled of late years—once more filled the night with dreams of Micky. She longed to ask Killary for further news of her father, yet held back for fear that the desire was prompted by a worldly affection that was wrong. At last she took counsel of Mother Mary Clare, who had succeeded Mother Mary Teresa as Reverend Mother Superior. She told the nun that she had known Killary very well as a child, had in fact nursed her through meningitis, and knew her family. Could she be given permission to inquire about the child's relations and to learn how they had fared since they had gone out of her life? She was granted permission, and Joan found Killary later in the garden and told her to walk with her.

'It's all very well,' Killary grumbled. 'I just can't get over your being a nun. I can't talk to you as I used to.'

'Please, Killary, try to. I want to know about M— your father. Has he done well? With his books and pictures?'

'Gracious, yes,' the child said. 'Didn't you know? He's really quite famous. And we're awfully rich because Lady Constance left him masses of money.'

There was a slight pause, and Joan said, 'It must have been a terrible shock for your father when she was killed.'

'Why d'you keep calling him my father? Aren't you allowed to say Micky or Mick? Anyway, it was awful, but I don't think he was actually awfully unhappy. He didn't cry when I saw him, or anything like that. She was jolly kind to us. Used to give me gorgeous presents and she admitted she didn't really like children. We got on very well. She gave me a wonderful bike. And a super camera. And this watch. But she wasn't restful, you know? We were always rushing about all over the place. That's why I first went to boarding-school.'

'Was Micky happy with her?' At last Joan forgot she was Mother Mary Imelda, the years fell away. For a few brief moments she could be Joan.

'Up to a point, yes. I think so. You see, she did help him tremendously with his work. Made him sort of ambitious and got him where he is. At least he always says that. But I don't think he was in love with her.'

'Killary, how grown up you are.'

'But J—Mother, I am nearly grown up. I suppose I oughtn't to say this to you now as you're a nun, but Daddy was in love with you.'

Joan stopped. Her face was white. 'Killary, we have both of us to forget that. I had Reverend Mother's permission to talk to you today because I told her I knew you as a child. And I wanted of course to know . . .'

'About Daddy.'

'Yes,' whispered Mother Mary Imelda. 'But never, never again must you or I talk of such matters. Do you understand?'

Killary nodded.

'If you try to tempt me to look backwards I shall have to leave Leenane. And you wouldn't want to be the cause for that, I'm sure.'

At once Killary was chastened. 'I promise, I promise.'

'And where do you live now? Where will you spend the holidays?' Joan asked.

'We have Lady Constance's house in Dublin, and a flat on the Italian Riviera. Daddy travels a good bit too. And if he's away in the hols I go to Aunt Cathleen who lives just outside Dublin.'

'And you said your mother died?'

'Yes. But there's a bit of a mystery there. I've never got to the bottom of it. I know she died in America. I think in Hollywood. About three years ago, before Lady Constance anyway.'

They walked on in silence and presently the girl said, 'Are you happy being a nun? D'you really like it?'

Joan—Mary Imelda smiled. 'Yes, Killary. I love my life here and I'm very happy.'

As the term proceeded, the shock which Joan had first felt grew less and she derived quiet happiness on seeing Killary about the place. There were times when she wondered if it was wrong to have a 'pet' among the children at the convent, but she was careful to show no favouritism and hoped that no one guessed the fact. It was too much to expect that Killary herself should keep their secret and it soon got round the place that Killary Renvyle had known Mother Mary Imelda before she was a nun. When Joan realized this she was worried and sent for the girl.

'I suppose I can't be cross with you for telling the whole place you used to know me,' she began, 'but I beg of you never to breathe a word about—'

'You and Daddy? *Of course not.*' Killary was most indignant. 'What d'you think I am? He told me once why you wouldn't marry him. And I've been thinking it over and suppose that's why you became a nun.'

Joan did not answer her.

'I promise I'll never mention anything about any of it ever, ever again, but oh! *darling* Joan, Mother Mary Imelda, if only you'd waited. Both of 'em dead and you'd have got Daddy in the end.'

Joan looked at Killary for a moment or two before she answered her.

'I suppose it's hopeless to expect a child of your age to keep to the promise she made. I asked you never to bring this subject up again.'

'You sort of began it,' Killary muttered.

'The subject is now closed. I hope for ever. I believe you're fond of me—'

'I love you, I've always loved—'

'Very well, then. If that's so you won't try to hurt me very much by reminding me of things that I'd rather forget. Surely, Killary dear, you're old enough to realize a nun must not have thoughts and ideas the like of which you've been doing your best to put back into my head.'

'I'm sorry. Truly I am,' the child whispered.

CHAPTER TWO

I

IT was the end of term. Many of the children were being taken to Galway by the school bus, and others were to be collected by parents and relations. When Joan had inquired of Killary what plans had been made for her, she was told she too would be going to Galway and on by train to Dublin. It was therefore a surprise when there came a timid knock on the door of her room and, opening it, she saw Killary.

'Goodness, child! You know you're not allowed in this part of the convent,' she exclaimed.

'I know. I don't think anyone saw me. I crept very quietly, but I thought you ought to be warned.' Her face was white, but there was a gleam in her eyes.

'Of what?' Joan asked.

'Daddy's coming to fetch me. After all. And I thought you'd rather know in case it was a shock for you.'

Joan put her hand to her forehead and closed her eyes temporarily.

'Thank you, Killary. It was kind of you.'

'It'll be just as much of a surprise for him because he doesn't know about you.'

'D'you mean you've not told him?' Joan was amazed.

'No.' Killary hesitated. 'You see, most of this term he's been abroad and I've not written to him an awful lot. I expect he's only coming to fetch me because I'm at Leenane and he always loved it. I was going to tell him about you when I saw him.'

'I see,' Joan replied. 'You had better run along now, or there'll be trouble. And Killary,' she said as the child was about to leave the room, 'should I not be around when your father comes, there'll be no need to come and find me. Now go back to the school.'

271

When the door closed and Joan was once more alone, she sank on to the narrow bed and tried to think. Her mind was numb, as if anaesthetized by pain-killing drugs. Slowly realization dawned on her that she was two people. She was Mother Mary Imelda, who was truly engrossed in her work and life at the Convent of Mercy, and who had no wish to be reincarnated into the life of uncertainty and sorrow that her other self had known; and that other self, or was it a mere ghost after all, was Joan Fitzgerald who, rising to the surface like a drowning person clinging to a straw, was in fact clinging to a hope, a wish to see once again the face of the belovèd before sinking for ever into the sea of happy oblivion. Now was the time, she realized, that she longed for Mother Mary Teresa, whose sound advice had always been so helpful. She felt she could not go to the good father and suddenly tell the whole story to him, for there would be no point. Her life as a woman was over, she was a nun now, and if she found herself face to face with some·child's father whom she had known in the past, what did it matter? It was something that must be left to Providence—to God, she quickly substituted. Perhaps it was to be the final test?

II

As Micky Renvyle drove his car along the road to Leenane his mind was a very melting-pot of memories.

Uppermost was the extraordinary fact that after so many years Killary should have been sent to school at the Convent of Mercy due to circumstances beyond his control. Much as he had loved Killary Harbour and Leenane, in fact because of his love for the place, it was the last school he would have chosen for the child. His memories of both places were too poignant. He had driven as far as Tully Cross when he knew he could not face going on to Ardbreen, his joys and miseries had been too great there, and he turned to the sea road past Mullaghglass and Gowlaun, past the stretch of sand where he and Paddy had bathed the day he had asked her to marry him, on past Lough Fee to the turn where the main road from Letterfrack and Kylemore joined, and the Maamturks together with the Twelve Pins showed their full splendour, and he wondered why his heart had bade him leave such beauty, and he remembered it was here at the junction of the roads that he had first met Joan.

Joan . . . He stopped the car and lit a cigarette. Paddy, Joan, Constance. Three women in his life, but Joan, whom he had never possessed, had been the woman he'd loved the most and would always love. If only he could find her . . . there was nothing to stand in their way. It was ridiculous how they had lost each other, but he could not have expected her to write after the way he had treated her. Of course he had behaved abominably to her, he admitted it all along the line. He and Paddy should never have married at the early age they had, he ruminated. But at least marriage had given him his precious Killary. Paddy . . . he felt nothing for her. Even the account in the newspaper of her death had left him unmoved. 'Well-known actress found dead from overdose' . . . It had been an accident, but even so he had not told Killary. There was something a little sordid about the affair. Killary . . . Killary Harbour, Leenane, his honeymoon with Paddy . . . they had been happy then, all right. And later. For the first few years, damn it. Was it because of happiness with Paddy and their ultimate rift that he could not bear to return to Ardbreen, he wondered? Or was it again because it held precious memories of Joan?

He looked around him; every inch of the road was familiar to him. He thought now of Constance and the times he had driven round Killary Harbour and on through the road that led to Louisburgh to see her in that comic house she had taken. Poor old Constance. It had been madness to marry her, but he owed his luck, his fortune, his success to her and it had been a small price to pay. He had grown genuinely fond of her, and there had certainly been moments when her beauty had tantalized and bewitched him into imagining himself in love with her. Love. Love . . . Love was Joan. And would be till the end of time. She had his heart. And his soul. He supposed his soul had been pretty well damned but perhaps not for ever. Paddy was dead. Constance was dead. If he could find Joan, his good pure unsullied Joan, would her prayers and love restore it from everlasting perdition?

It was Joan, belovèd Joan, who had so strangely remarked that no one could walk this road without believing in God. He forgot her exact words, but the purport of them came back to him now. There was majesty in the scenery which surrounded him, yet he had been to many lands in the past few years which held more grandeur than his precious Twelve Pins and the Maamturks. What, he wondered, was so special about this road which led to Leenane? He threw away the stub of his cigarette and got out of the car. A strong smell of peat filled the air, something one rarely found anywhere near Dublin. Only a few sheep were grazing near by and somewhere a curlew called. He was a fool not to have come back months ago, years ago. Not to Leenane but back to Ardbreen. Why had he been such a moral coward? A few ghosts from the past, little enough to pay for a return to his mountains and the islands. He tried to picture the beauty of Constance's world: Mediterranean shores, Alpine snows, the wonders of Italian lakes . . . islands in the Caribbean . . . the jewelled cities of Spain and the Orient . . . Constance had shown him a world he had not realized, but he knew that he had only to reach Killary Harbour and then watch in silence the mountains meet the blueness of its water and to feel alone in isolated splendour, to know that here in Connemara where he had been born, where he had lived and loved and begotten his child, were perfection, peace, and a return to his God. That, he suddenly realized, was the secret of the road to Leenane. It held a mystical grace, something that people sought in places like Montserrat where the Holy Grail was said to have been kept, but unlike Montserrat and the many holy mountains and islands in Ireland, the road to Leenane was untrodden by pilgrims and kept its secret inviolate for him—and Joan.

He looked at his watch and realized he must hurry or Killary would wonder what had happened. He drove slowly, none the less, along the road above the water's edge, on past the hotel—with the ghosts of himself and Paddy as his bride—through the village, and stopped at the convent. There were several cars and various children were being collected by relatives. He went to the building, the door was open, but a young nun standing by asked his name and showed him into the reception-room where she asked him to wait, and told him she would find Killary and send her to him. It was a bare room, simply furnished with white walls, a large crucifix, a few pictures of the Holy Family and some chairs. A table in the middle of the room had a plant and some Catholic newspapers. No one but Renvyle was in the room. Presently the young nun returned and asked him to follow her as Reverend Mother wished to speak to him. He followed her and Mother Mary Clare rose to meet him when he entered the parlour.

'It is because of the fire in our other house, and the reason that Killary is here by chance, that I thought you would care to have a few words with me,' she said. 'I know you were away abroad, and Killary's aunt has been taking the responsibility, and we have been in communication with her, as you doubtless know. But now that you are here, perhaps you would care to see a little of the convent? Killary only told us yesterday that you were coming for her, we had expected to put her in the Dublin train with many of the other children.'

Micky told Mother Mary Clare that he thought there wasn't a great deal of time, but that perhaps he could see the chapel. He was told that the house in Co. Sligo was too extensively damaged to return to yet awhile, and did he mind his child remaining at Leenane?

'Indeed, no. She has probably told you we used to live near, at Ardbreen. And that she was named after Killary Harbour.'

'Yes, I'm sure she told us.'

'Her mother is dead,' he said a little lamely, wondering how much this rather austere-looking Mother Superior knew about his life.

'So I understood.'

She walked towards the door and then said, 'Ah, yes. We have a Sister who knew Killary as a child. Mother Mary Imelda. I cannot remember if she knows you?'

Renvyle shook his head.

'I don't think so. I dare say it will be one of the nuns who taught her when we lived at Ardbreen.'

They had reached the door and Reverend Mother pointed towards the chapel. At that moment Killary came running down the passage and flung herself into her father's arms. After much kissing and excitement, at which Mother Mary Clare looked on good-naturedly, she said, 'Your father would like to see the chapel, Killary, before you leave.'

'It's heavenly, you'll love it,' Killary said. 'Come on. And oh! Daddy! I've got something to tell you that you'll never, never, never believe. I didn't write it because I wanted to see the surprise on your face. But I'll tell you when we're in the car.'

'Why not now?' he asked, laughing.

'Well,' she hesitated, and then said, 'it concerns a certain person and I think I'd better tell you later. Anyway, here we are.'

Together they entered the chapel. After crossing himself he looked around and was aware of a nun kneeling in prayer, which was not unexpected. In whispers Killary and he tiptoed round, and then knelt and prayed by the altar to the Blessed Virgin. As they came down the centre aisle, the nun who had been in prayer looked up. Mother Mary Imelda and Micky Renvyle looked into each other's eyes.

'It's not possible,' Micky whispered, his hand heavy on Killary's shoulder. She looked up at her father's face and then at the nun's and suddenly felt frightened.

'That was what I had to tell you,' she said falteringly. 'She's called Mother Mary Imelda now. She's not Joan any longer.'

The shock was almost more than Renvyle could stand. In a flash he realized only too well that with Joan as a bride of Christ barriers were far more insurmountable than they had ever been when he had been married to Paddy. It was, indeed, the end of the story. The wheel had turned full circle. In her nun's garb she appeared to have changed little, the sudden pallor of her cheeks, the agony in the eyes—half hidden by the glasses which he noticed she still wore—bore no trace of the passing years. He felt—he knew—that had he been a stranger and seen her face suddenly lifted from prayer, he would have noticed a serenity about her that had not been there before.

And Joan? What did she see, what did she notice about the man she had loved with her heart and soul who now stood before her, unseen for so many years? He looked older, were her first thoughts, and his hair had thinned and was grey round the temples. He still stooped, although no more than he had in the past. Her woman's instinct, suddenly reborn, noticed that his clothes were better, of richer material.

'Joan,' he whispered, agony in his voice. She shook her head slowly.

'Mary Imelda. Mother Mary Imelda.'

He could hardly hear her voice. She spoke so quietly. He suddenly turned to Killary.

'Why the—why on earth didn't you tell me?' he said.

'I—I told you,' she whispered apologetically.

'Don't be cross with her,' Joan said. 'Remember she's very young still. It's only you and I who have grown old. Grown up.'

She arose from her knees and went forward and stood beside him. They walked slowly from the building.

'I remember telling you years ago you'd better become a nun,' he said bitterly.

'I've known great unhappiness because of you, my dear,' she replied, 'but my life is now dedicated to God. I suppose you will find it difficult to understand when I tell you I'm not only at peace now but happy. I teach the children. And I probably have more to be grateful to God for than some of my sisters.'

'In what way?'

'For one thing I'm here, in Leenane, which has meant so much to me for a great many years. Then—perhaps I shouldn't think like this—I have my very dear Killary to teach and to remind me of things that I should forget. And thirdly I have memories—which I dare not look back on too often—of happiness and love that are worth the misery I suffered mentally in the price I've paid for them.'

There was silence for a while and Killary, feeling she had behaved unwisely, had gone on ahead leaving her father and Joan alone.

'You've made your final vows, I suppose?' Micky asked presently.

'I have. And here, if God wills, I shall remain.' Joan's voice sounded flat.

'Joan—Mother—' he fumbled for words—'would you rather I removed Killary?'

She turned quickly to him and he saw Joan's eyes behind Mother Mary Imelda's glasses.

'Oh no! Please, please leave me Killary.' The words left her lips before she knew how much of her woman's heart had prompted them.

They reached the gate which led to the road, and for the last time Micky Renvyle and Joan—Mother Mary Imelda—looked across to the waters of Killary Harbour together.

'And you're really happy?' he asked, unable to say more.

She nodded slowly.

'Yes, Micky. I am. But,' she said after a minute's pause, 'don't—please—come again.'

'May I take your hand?'

She seemed surprised and smiled.

'I don't think there's any rule that you mustn't. You're saying good-bye?'

He nodded, and taking her hand raised it to his lips.

'Good-bye, Joan my darling. Forgive me and pray for me. I loved you.'

'Go, go, go, go!'